The "Lose Weight" Scam

A Novel by

John Alexander Haskett

Also by John A. Haskett

Mike Shant Mystery series:
>> Policy Terminated
>> The Conversion
>> Happy Endings Off The Vegas Strip

Highly controversial political satire novel:
>> The Day B.C. Quit Canada. Co-author.

Financial:
>> How to Make Money Beating Horse Races

Consumer:
>> Mexico – Your Complete Guidebook

The "Lose Weight" Scam

A Novel by

John Alexander Haskett

The "Lose Weight" Scam
Copyright © 2020 by John Alexander Haskett

Published by:
Durango Publishing Corp.®
Suite 36 – 747 Princess Ave.
Victoria, B.C., Canada V8T 1K5
www.DurangoPublishing.com
Email: Support@DurangoPublishing.com

DEDICATION

To my sons Michael and Roger, who both have developed into men I'm proud to have as friends.

About the Author

John Alexander Haskett has been a freelance writer for many years. He has written hundreds of magazine articles, financial documents, promotion copy, and five novels. As a publisher, he has published newsletters, magazines, manuals, and numerous commissioned surveys. He has now entered the fascinating realm of book publishing, and has published 4 novels in the Mike Shant mystery series, 2 novels in the satire/political areas (The Day BC Quit Canada, co-authored with son Michael, and The God Franchise) and several other books on horse racing betting and freelance writing.

His line of mystery novels, starring Mike Shant, are gaining fans fast! To receive automatic updates about new and upcoming novels, send an email to Books@DurangoPublishing.com. You can also visit his Amazon author page to keep track of his latest novels.

Sneak Preview:
As A Special Bonus, Following The
Final Chapter Of The "Lose Weight" Scam
Is The Start Of The Newest Mike Shant Mystery
Novel.

Get A Sneak Preview Of What New
Adventures Mike And His Friends
Are Up To In
"Happy Endings Off the Vegas Strip".

CHAPTER 1

"Give it to us in tens."

"Naw, there'll be too many. Sam, make it all twenties," said Lennie.

"I don't like twenties. Who wants to look at a picture of the White House where that jerkoff bullshitter lives? Make mine tens, Sam." The Toro drew himself up to his full five feet four inches and casually edged Lennie back from the waitress station at the bar.

"God damn it, Toro. I don't want my pants pocket jammed up with a bunch of worthless ten dollar bills. You can't buy anything nowadays with a ten. One drink? A deck of smokes? You couldn't even get a fast blow job in the back alley for ten bucks. Sam, I'm telling you for the last time. Make mine twenties."

Sam stood at the bar, holding the small plastic garbage bag full of currency in his left hand. In his right smoldered the cheap cigar he was never without.

"Listen, you guys. Make up your goddamned minds. Assuming you still have them. Does this joint look like a Bank of America branch? Believe it or not, this is a bar. We sell drinks here, not make illegal currency exchanges."

7

"Hey, Sam, this ain't an illegal currency deal. We're just saving ourselves a little effort in going to a bank. And hey, we're probably some of your best customers. You should be happy to do us a small favor. In fact, once you stop farting around and change those bills we'll probably buy a drink. For each of us. Maybe even for you, Sam. So please get off the pot and take those perfectly good but small United States bills and replace them with the appropriate number of ten dollar bills. Have I made myself clear?" The Toro backed up and struck a bullfighter's pose.

"Aw shit", Lennie said. "Do as the Toro says, Sam, or we'll be here screwing around till noon tomorrow. And give me a bourbon on the rocks. Have whatever you'd like. But a single only. Keep the doubles for when a tourist hits a jackpot and springs for it."

Sam shook his head, exhaled a cloud of dense smoke that a small child could have safely walked on, and dropped the money bag on the bar. "Do you know how much is in here, or do I have to count it as well as acting like your personal Swiss banker?"

"I know exactly what's in there," the Toro said. "There's $960. And divided by six," he giggled, "that means 160 smart folks have made use of our professional services."

"Jesus Christ, Pedro. Do you have to blab everything? I thought we agreed to keep this scam, er, deal, confidential." Lennie threw his hands in the air, then looked around quickly to see if any spy had crept up on them. No one had.

"Okay, you guys. I'll give you 95 tens, but if I find out later your count is short..."

"95! What do you mean 95? $960 divided by ten equals 96, Sam. Do you want to borrow my calculator to check out that complicated arithmetic problem?" Whenever it looked like he was being ripped off Toro got ferocious.

"I don't need your crappy calculator, Toro. I can actually do the math in my head. The last ten is for me. That's my banker's fee. And you're getting off cheap. Walk into any other Vegas bar and ask to change a garbage bag full of what is probably hot or phony aces and fins and they'd call for a padded wagon. So take it or leave it."

"We'll take it, Sam. Just try to get this transaction completed before Super Bowl 123, okay? And don't forget my drink on the way back from your cash register. I assume it's included in your so-called banker's fee?" Lennie smiled what he thought of as his we're-all-buddies smile. It looked more like a barracuda sizing up a fat tuna.

"Assume what you like, Lennie. My fee has nothing to do with your drinking habits. Your bourbon will be three bucks, same as always. And what about you, Toro? Do you want a drink?"

"I'm so dry after all this negotiating I need something. And your air conditioning is lousy. It's 106 outside, and damn near that in here. Give me the usual, Sam. And this time please try to use a clean glass. The last one had lipstick on it from a shade that hasn't been seen since Sinatra stopped wearing bobby sox."

Sam rolled his eyes, exhaled another dense smoke screen, and turned toward the cash register, then stopped. "Where exactly did you guys get $960 in small bills? Are you running some kind of fraud again, Lennie?"

"I resent that. What do you mean 'again'? The closest I've ever gotten to a crooked deal is watching you bartenders water the booze once the tourists have got a glow on."

Sam shook his head and walked over to the register. He inserted his key, lifted out the top drawer, and pulled out several packets of bills which he began counting out.

"Why can't we at least tell Sam about our new venture?" whispered the Toro. "He wouldn't tell

9

anyone else, and maybe he'd give us a little more respect."

"Listen, Pedro, and read my lips. We tell no one about our little business venture. No one. Is that clear? We've discussed this a hundred times, Toro, and the end result is still the same. This deal is sweet and easy. It won't be if anyone else gets involved. So we don't let anyone else get involved? Comprendo?"

"Okay, Lennie, you don't have to be so overbearing about it. I won't tell anyone."

"Sam, what the fuck are you giving these guys all that cash for? Are they holding us up?"

"No, Dom, there's no holdup. At least I can't see one. I'm just changing some bills for these two sports who, as you probably know, are among our best customers." The last was said with what Sam used for a smile.

"I didn't get to be bar manager by letting every grifter off Fremont Street get into my wallet, Sam. What exactly are these two guys doing?"

"Not much, Dom. One, they wanted to change some small bills for larger ones. Two, they also sprung for a couple of drinks. Three, that's what I'm doing."

"Sprung for drinks? Where's mine?" Next to godliness, which he knew nothing about and cared less, Dominick ranked getting anything free very high.

"No, I didn't say they'd sprung for drinks for the poor peons who work here. I meant they'd actually ordered and were in the process of paying for drinks for themselves. But that's a step up from what most of our customers try to do to us."

"Well, what about all that money? We're not a bank, you know." Dominick often wished he did work in a bank. He was sure he'd figure out some way to take a few samples home.

"Just making change, Dom. They brought in $950 in small bills and wanted larger ones. I made the change with the house float from my register. Rest assured everything will balance."

"It better! If we came up almost a grand short, the boys who run this store would have our balls for breakfast. Hey!" He turned to Lennie. "Where did you guys get $950 in small bills? Did you knock over a 7-11?"

"It's really nice to patronize a bar where the manager accuses you of being a thief," Lennie said, mostly to Sam. Pedro was busy checking Sam's count. "It sure makes you feel like a valued customer. And as to where we got the money, are you with the IRS or something? If so, flash your badge, then I'll tell you to go fornicate with your aged mother. Otherwise, Dom old man, I don't think it's any of your business."

"No need to get up on your high horse, Lennie. I just asked where you got the bread. Is it a secret?"

"Yes."

Dom was taken aback by this somewhat condensed answer.

"Why? Is it something illegal? Or fattening? Or immoral?" Dom secretly felt he could give any current comedian a run for his money. Few people would have agreed with that, and they would have had serious mental impairments.

Lennie busied himself sampling the drink Sam put in front of him. "Ah, that's fine stuff. August was a great month."

"August, hell," said Sam. "That batch was distilled at least two months ago. This isn't your typical Vegas dive. We have class."

"Great. Where do you keep it?" asked the Toro, now satisfied that Sam hadn't shorted him with the pile of tens.

"Never mind that. What I want to know is where you characters got all that money." Dom turned to Lennie. "You're the brains of this outfit. What have you got going, Lennie?"

"We've actually started a correspondence school for bar managers," Lennie grinned. "We teach them how to act towards their classy paying customers. You know, how to bow, and say things like 'Yes, your highness, we do carry that brand of watered bourbon. Can I get you a pail full?' All that kind of good stuff."

"You really are a riot, Lennie. Too bad the booking agent from the Tonight Show ain't here. He'd sign you on the spot. But goddammit, just tell me where you got all that money."

"Can't do it, Dom. The Toro and me took a vow of silence when we became priests, you know." Dominick started to interrupt but Lennie plowed on. "But I can tell you this. If your crowded schedule permits, pop by tomorrow and see us cash in an even bigger bunch of chickenshit. That's if your mob bosses haven't rubbed you out by then for some infraction of the rules."

Dom's face whitened. He didn't even like jokes about his bosses.

"Hell, Lennie, I thought we was friends. Are you serious about having more money tomorrow?"

"As serious as humanly possible, Dominick old buddy. You want to buy some stock in the Lennie and Pedro corporation? You might get rich."

"Rich? More likely thrown into jail."

"Who's going to get thrown into jail? All you guys?" Marie was just starting her shift. She was one of the stellar attractions of the bar at the Golden Future Casino, although she was perhaps a little bit over her best hill. But she still could get second, even third, looks from customers, especially those who had been enjoying the products ably dispensed by Sam or even Dom.

"Hey, sweetheart, you light up this joint like a roman candle on the fourth. When are we going to shack up?"

"Lennie, you're a dope. There you make a nice compliment, then spoil it by even suggesting that I might let you get next to my young virginal body."

"Virginal? I thought the days of miracles had passed," said Dominick.

"And you're another waste of a penis," Marie said. "You wouldn't recognize a virgin if Mary herself sat on your face."

"Hey, Marie, you've put on a few ounces, haven't you? You ought to get onto some diet. Not a fad one, though," Pedro giggled.

"What do you mean, a few ounces? If I was any more trim I'd be invisible if I turned sideways. I don't need any diet, fad or otherwise."

"And neither do you, Toro. Button your lip." Lennie smiled to modify the insult but his eyes didn't join the party with his mouth.

"Okay, okay, I was just kidding." Pedro looked at Marie but was obviously answering Lennie.

"You got a customer over there in the back, Marie. You don't get to him soon he's going to think we're a member of the temperance club."

"Yeah, yeah, I'm going. I know you guys just want to get a look at me from the back."

There was a respectful moment of silence while they all did look at her rear. It was well worth the attention.

"C'mon, Lennie, tell me what you guys are working on. Maybe I could help you out."

"Sure, Dom. You could have your bosses lend us a couple of shooters in case we needed to knock off some competition. Thanks, but no. The Toro and me can take care of business. But we do appreciate you and Sam agreeing to change our currency into larger denominations. You can be sure we'll keep that helpfulness in mind when we're considering a downtown Vegas bar for our first company convention."

"Yeah, we'll get all our fatties together and really rock this joint," Pedro grinned. "You could charge us for drinks by the pound, or better yet, by the ton."

"Pedro, you just love hearing yourself talk, don't you?" Lennie reached over and gave him an affectionate pat on the shoulder which almost knocked him off his seat. "Don't burden good old Dom with our corporate problems. He has enough to think about, wondering how he can water the booze without touching the seal."

"I'll have you know I've never watered the booze here. And I object to your insinuations."

"Those weren't insinuations, Dom. They were statements of fact."

"The only reason I'm not really pissed off with you, Lennie, is that I know you don't mean that stuff. When you die you'll probably name me in your will."

"Sure. I'll name you as tightwad of the year."

Marie bustled back and elbowed Dom out of her area. "Hey, Sam. Give me a couple of pussies of brandy."

"What are pussies? Some kind of new drink? Pedro looked seriously interested.

"You've heard of snifters, Toro? Well, here in the Golden Future we can't afford those, so we offer pussies instead. Same effect." Marie smiled at the little man.

Pedro frowned thoughtfully, then suddenly laughed. "Oh, I get it. Snifters, that's what you do with pussies. Pretty funny, Marie."

"Lennie, this is the last time I'm going to ask you. Where did you get all that money?"

"You promise it's the last time, Dom? Because this is the last time I'm going to tell you. It ain't, as they say in New York, any of your business."

"All what money?" asked Marie. Like most females, next to herself money was her favorite subject. "How much?"

"Mucho, baby. Enough for you and me to run off to Reno together. How soon can you get packed?"

"Pedro, with you I wouldn't even have to pack my diaphragm. We could just sit in the motel room and hold hands. I hear it on good authority that you don't like girls."

"Don't like broads! Whoever said that was a damned liar. I was screwing broads when, when, when Dom wasn't watering the booze." The comparison didn't make any sense to the rest, who all looked at Pedro as if he had had too many pussies of brandy.

"Well, whatever. But I want to hear about that money." Marie zeroed back in on topic number one.

"Nothing to it, doll. We changed a few small bills here, and right away Dom thinks it's some kind of major international conspiracy that his honored employers might want to get involved in. But there's nothing to it."

"And that crack about your weight was just a joke, Marie," Pedro said. "It's just that we had been talking about diets, and when you came in, well, you know..." He petered off as Marie looked at him sternly, reminding him of Miss Spencer in the fourth grade, except that Miss Spencer never had the kind of boobs that Marie did, and as to her behind, well, in thinking back Pedro decided that Miss Spencer hadn't had much going for her after all.

"And what's all this about diets?" Marie persisted. "Does it have anything to do with all that money everyone's talking about, but of which I haven't even had a smell?"

"No." Lennie was emphatic. "Nothing."

"Well, I think it does," Dom said. "These guys have been beating around the bush for the past hour. First Pedro will mention something about diets, then Lennie will tell him to shut up. What's the real story here?"

"The only story here," Lennie drawled in a pretty good imitation of John Wayne, "is that there is no story here. Period. We just happen to have a bunch of small bills. Never got around to taking them to a bank, and as we're leading customers in this joint"--he threw a sardonic look at Dom--"I thought it would be acceptable to kill two birds with one stone, so to speak. I mean, me and the Toro could come in for a drink or two and at the same time solve our banking problem. Nothing to do with diets, or the Great Wall of China, or even Dom's liking for little girls."

"What the fuck do you mean my liking for little girls? I insist that they're at least 12."

"Yeah, right, another pervert," Marie said. "Is no one normal anymore?"

Pedro jumped off his stool, and stuck out his pigeon chest. "I am, Marie. I am. Why not give me a trial night. If I don't work out you can give me my semen back and we'll just forget the whole thing."

"You people are really disgusting. It's like working in a sewer here."

"Never mind that. What about those diets?" Dom was not to be put off.

"Old son, if there was anything about diets here you'd be the first one to know," Lennie said. "But as I've said 352 times, there isn't. Why don't we talk about something interesting. Like broads, for instance. Marie, what can you tell us about what the normal hot babe really wants in a stud?"

"What she doesn't want, fellows, is one of you. I can see now why there's so many lezies around. After spending my shift around you guys I'm seriously considering switching to girls only too."

"Aw, bullshit, Marie. You'd miss the ecstatic thrill you get when a guy really puts it to you. How's some other broad going to equal that?" Pedro sat down again, now that he had won the argument.

"Ecstatic thrill? Where you been living? The last time one of you gave a female an ecstatic thrill was when you said 'Good-bye'. All that you have to offer can be replaced quite easily by a one inch carrot. And that's giving you the benefit of a sloppy measurement."

16

"And to think you're such a great looking broad. Marie, you break my heart when you talk like that. Why not meet me after work and I'll give you a free psychoanalysis of your problem."

"Pedro, your idea of a psychoanalysis session is to tell the woman, 'Lie down. I've got a problem.' That's not really how it's supposed to work."

"This is all very educational, Marie, but table number six has been trying to get your attention for the last half hour. If you could take a break from your clever dialog with these jokers maybe you could see your way clear to doing a little work?"

Marie headed out toward table six, muttering under her breath something which sounded remarkably like "Fuck you, Dom".

"Now we can get back to the important subject," Dom said. "What are you guys up to?"

"Zip. Nada. Zero. Nothing. How many ways can I say it, Dom? Pedro and I wouldn't know a scam if one walked up and bit us on the ass. Asses, to be grammatically correct."

Dom held up a finger. "Aha! Who even mentioned a scam? It's obvious that you've got scam on the brain, Lennie, and that means you are pulling one. Tell me about it. I promise that I won't tell anyone else. Scout's honor."

"Scout's honor!" Lennie smothered a laugh. "They wouldn't let you join, Dom. You have to be clean cut and law abiding to make that group. You're disqualified on both counts." Lennie finished his drink, and got up off the stool. "This has been interesting, men, but it's time for the Toro and me to check out some other drinking establishments on good old Fremont Street. We don't want other saloonkeepers to think we're giving the Golden Future all our business. Toro, let's you and me take a walk down beautiful Fremont Street. There's something we have to do." Lennie casually grabbed Pedro's collar and lifted him off his stool. "We'll see you guys later."

17

"Giving us the business is just about right," muttered Dom.

"Yeah, chow," Pedro said. His grasp of foreign languages was somewhat limited.

Out in the searing desert heat Lennie shook Pedro. "You jerk! You're going to queer this deal if you don't stop mouthing off about diets. Can't you get it through that invisible brain of yours that too many cooks definitely will spoil this broth we've got cooking?"

Pedro looked like a kid caught with his hand in the cookie jar. Acting remorseful had cleared him of many scrapes in the past.

"Okay, Lennie. Mum's the word. I promise. I won't even think about diets, let alone talk about them. You have my word."

Inside the Golden Future bar Dom was gazing vacantly at Marie's rear as she hustled drinks. She really was a top bar waitress. "I wonder what those jokers really have going," he mumbled to himself. "Something's up, no doubt of that. That squirt Pedro hasn't had $950 at one time ever in his miserable life. Lennie has, but not recently. Maybe I should tell Dickie about this. Might be able to make some points with that prick.

"Sam, come over here for a minute, will you." Sam looked up from the Racing Form he was reading, grimaced, then sighed and plodded over to where Dom was leaning on the bar. "What is it now, Dom?"

"Sam, I want you to tell me everything about that money exchange with those two jokers. What did they say? Exactly?"

"Dom, they said zip. I don't even know where that talk about diets and scams started. I don't think Lennie said anything. The Toro may have said something, but if so it wasn't much. All they really wanted was to change those bills. I was just jacking them around, trying to see where they had got the money, when you came over. Hell, they probably just hit a keno ticket or a slot and asked for the payoff in small bills, just so they could bug us. Like they've been doing for the last hour or so, incidentally." He looked up as someone rapped on the bar down at the end. "And incidentally I'd better start serving some booze or our take today will look unhealthier than an old hooker's moneymaker."

"Yeah, go ahead. And give me a Coors light, will you? I want to think about what those jokers are up to."

CHAPTER 2

"Give me a vodka on the rocks, Sam. And a lime."

"Sure, Mike. House stuff okay?"

"Yeah. Despite all the bullshit ads you see, one vodka is the same as the next. Paying a premium price is for the tourists who believe that crap."

Sam poured a very healthy shot into a glass of ice, added a lime slice, topped it with water, and moved back to Shant.

"Here, Mike, first one of the day is on Dom. Although he doesn't know it. And I got something for you. One of the package delivery guys dropped it off here a couple of hours ago. Want it now?"

"Yes. I was expecting something. From L.A., right?"

"I don't know. I just signed for it, didn't really look at it." He reached behind the main cash register, pulled out a manila envelope, and looked down at it. "Yeah, from that sewer on the coast, L.A." He handed it to Shant.

"Sewer is right. The gang-wetback-slime ball capital of the country. No, the world. I can hardly wait until the big one and western Nevada becomes oceanfront property. It would probably be months before anyone even noticed that the golden state had disappeared. No one would miss it, aside from teachers of English as a second language who would obviously have lost 99 percent of their prospective students. Let's see what goodies are in this. Trust it's not some mad mail bomber who wants to eliminate poor freelance writers."

"Oh, is that what you do for a living? You spend enough time in the race book to qualify as a jockey agent," Sam said. "What exactly does a freelance writer do?"

"Basically, as little as possible, Sam. Get me another vodka while I read this crap, will you? This glass obviously has a hole in it."

Sam moved to the back bar. Shant ripped the end off the envelope, and took out a sheaf of blue-lined papers clipped together with a large plastic penguin clip who advised one and all that "Hi there! I have important papers for you. Read them carefully. And have a nice day!"

"Jesus Christ!", Shant muttered to himself. "You can't get away from it. Now even paper clips are telling you to have a nice day. Switch that d for an l and it might make some sense." He riffled through the sheets, then pulled out the last page. It had a lot of copy on it, including some with dollar figures. He read that sheet carefully.

"Hey, sport. Buy a guy a drink?"

Shant smiled even before he looked up. Only one person could belong to that voice.

"If it isn't Percy Alexander Percy in the flesh. How are you doing, you old bastard?"

"Mr. Shant, I've asked you many times before not to mention my ancestry in public. And the answer to your question, assuming you are going to buy me a drink, is fine. How are you?"

"Now you're here, Pap, better than ever. Yes, I'll be glad to buy you a drink. Hey, Sam, give old Pap here a drink, would you. On my tab."

21

Sam dropped off Shant's vodka, and turned back to make Pap's drink, which he knew from long experience was tequila on the rocks.

"What's happening, Mike? Any news on that Vegas assignment?"

"You sure timed it right, Pap. I just this minute got the word from L.A. Western World magazine has given me the okay on my idea to do a three part series on Las Vegas's overnight success stories. I pitched it on the basis of a switch from the usual mob crap about this town. Vegas until very recently been the fastest growing city in the country. Some of that growth is mob and gambling connected, of course, but a lot isn't. That was my query and they went for it. Incidentally, as I told you on the phone, the series will require a fair amount of photography. Do you happen to know any reasonably talented freelance photographer who might be interested in picking up a fairly easy and fairly fast three big ones?"

Percy struck a dignified pose, looked down his roman nose, and cleared his throat.

"By three biggies, my good man, am I correct in assuming you are referring to thousands, as opposed to piddling hundreds?"

"Exactimente."

"That being the case, Mr. Shant, sir, I suggest you look directly in front of you. There stands who is probably the best freelance photographer in the entire state of Nevada. You can even throw in Cal and Arizona, as far as that goes."

"You mean you'd like to participate in this journalistic endeavor, Mr. Percy?"

"Exactly what I mean, Miguel. When do we start, and when do I get paid?"

"Tomorrow and later. Later is the best I can do on the bread, Pap. This'll be the first time I've worked with this magazine. I know they're financially okay because I pulled a Dun and Brad credit report on them before I queried them. But when they pay their bills I don't know. If you need some cash I could probably advance you some."

"I always need money, young employer sir. But if you really are going to pay for this drink which Sam has just deposited behind you, then the pressure for folding green is off, at least for the next ten minutes. How many pix are you going to want?"

"Lots, Pap. Each article in this series will run about five thousand words, and I'll likely quick profile six or seven hotshots in each part. Depending on what the magazine's art director decides, I'd expect them to run a minimum couple of photos for each overnight success, so that makes maybe 15 to 20 published pix with each segment. Say 50 to 60 total. Knowing art directors as I wish I didn't, that also means he or she'll want to see at least 10 times that many shots. So you're looking at 600 shots. You still using the small 35 mm rolls?"

Pap nodded, too busy with his tequila to answer.

"So then maybe 25 rolls or so, Pap. Most of them will be candids, I imagine. The whole point of the series is young, new, or reborn whiz bangers. That approach lends itself best to candid, action, non-posed pix. Right?"

"Absolutely, oh knowledgeable one. And my 35 delivers far better quality than phone jobs. Given that quantity of supplies I may have to tap the Shant bank for a couple of Cs. Handle that?"

"Like my horse in the fifth at Golden Gate tomorrow is going to handle the turf course, Pap. He's never run on it, so the punters at the track will overlook him. But his granddaddy was a dandy turf runner, and I'm hoping he's got enough of the right genes to pull off a sneaker. I expect his closing odds will be about ten or twelve to one."

"Sounds good. Want to share his name with your humble snapshot servant?"

"Only if you swear an oath, and slash your left wrist to make the oath binding, that you will not,

not, I repeat, give this gem to anyone. I repeat, Pap, anyone. Not like last week, when I gave you the sure winner at Santa Anita, and you graciously gave it to enough of your acquaintances that the odds got knocked down from the morning line of 9 to 1 to a pretty dismal 5 to 2. And as I've told you lo these many years, Pap, you can't win in the long haul if you bet horses at 5 to 2 odds."

"Yes, it seems to me that you have mentioned that bit of wisdom before. Like maybe nine hundred times, old buddy. But I do promise. This time we'll keep it strictly to ourselves, and get rich on it. Assuming it wins, of course. Who is it?"

"Okay. I'll accept your word, although there are probably a score of bartenders--and broads, for that matter--who wouldn't. The horse," Shant cupped his hands around his mouth in a parody of someone passing on a hot tip, "is Mexican MananaMama. In the fifth."

"Got it. Say, isn't that a long name for a race horse? I thought there were limits to how long a horse's name could be."

"There are. A maximum of 18 letters and spaces. The triple M gets in right at the wire. If you spelled Mama with two ms it would be S.O.L."

"You learn something every day. Let me buy you a drink in return for your magnificent and munificent gesture in making me rich. That's if you will advance the bucks, of course."

"Of course. First, I want to hit the Race Book and get this bet down before I get involved in something and forget it. Want to come?"

"That's what I say to my lady friends. But okay. Maybe I'll get to see the great DiBonio, even get his autograph. You know I'm a great collector of famous people's autographs?"

"Yeah. Especially if they're on some negotiable instrument. Let's go." Shant nodded to Sam, indicating that they'd be back in a while and to keep their drinks alive.

The Race Book was in the west corner of the casino, and although open to the casino area it was partially cloistered due to the rows of writing desks which now were inhabited almost totally by grey or white haired men bent over their Racing Forms. At the far end of the room was the ticket counter where race tickets were purchased and, less frequently, cashed. All around the room, at a height of 16 feet, was a bank of television monitors, showing race tracks from across the country. Some screens showed races in progress, others showed odds and probable exotic bet payoffs, and still others showed serious interviewers talking to usually less serious trainers or owners or jockeys. The sound of the current major track was turned up. As its race was completed and the payoffs shown, another track took the limelight.

Two waitresses in very skimpy costumes solicited complimentary cocktail orders, although many of the patrons seemed content to drink a free soft drink or even bottled water. Handicapping was an activity that relied on considerable alcohol-free mental effort, the interpretation of complicated past performance lines, and the attempt to determine just how much skullduggery owners, trainers, and jockeys might be up to in the race being figured.

"Some investment broker once told me that if the same effort was applied to stocks as to horse race handicapping," Pap said, "the guy doing it would be rich. Believe that?"

"Within limits," Shant said. "There can be a lot of effort in handicapping. But a lot of it today is just busy work. Most handicappers get the bug about some aspect of racing, maybe speed, maybe pace, or trouble in the last race, or even a hot jock who's winning far more than his usual percentage, and they ignore everything else. Nothing is 'the' answer in horse handicapping, just as nothing is the single answer on Wall Street. If handicapping is done

25

correctly it can be complicated and mentally stimulating. But it's often just rote memory work."

"Hey, thanks, professor. I'm sorry I asked the question. Shall we dispense with the bullshit and get our bets down?"

"Trust you, Pappy, to cut to the chase. Yeah, let's do just that."

The two men walked up to a ticket writer who was gazing vacantly at one of the waitresses. Most of the tracks had completed their daily races, and just a few western tracks were still alive. The usual 10 ticket writers had dwindled to four.

"Haven't seen you in a long time, Mike. At least 12 hours." He chuckled. "What'll it be?"

"Tomorrow, fifth at Golden Gate. Mexican MananaMama. Do you have an early listing of her number?"

"Yeah, just a sec." He leaned over to the next window and grabbed a folded sheet. "Fifth at the Gate? Here it is. That Mexican has post position three. No early scratches or entries, so that'll be her number. How much and how?"

"Give me a thou on the nose, and put her with all the rest in $50 quinellas."

"Ten horses shown, so that'll be a grand plus $450 for the Qs. $1450 total."

Shant pulled out a sterling silver money clip, given to him years ago when he had spent a couple of years in Guadalajara by a feminine admirer, and peeled off a five hundred and ten hundreds.

The ticket seller punched out the transaction, and gave Shant a fifty and two tickets, one for the win bet, one for the nine quinella combinations. If his horse came in first he would cash the win bet. If she won or came second he'd win one of the quinella combinations. If a horse with odds at least 6 or so to 1 came in first or second with Mexican MananaMama, he'd show a profit on his $450 Q investment.

Shant checked the tickets, pocketed them, and moved sideways so Percy could get a bet down.

"Hey, Percy, how are you? It's good to see you. Where you been keeping yourself?" The ticket writer liked Percy, who often gave the ticket writer a healthy tip if his bet won. "And say, is Percy your first or last name? I've never been sure of that."

"It's both, Dan. My old man had a weird sense of humor, so he named me Percy to go along with his surname of Percy. So it's Percy Percy. That makes it easy to remember."

"Hey, that's neat." The writer gave away his baby boomer origins. "I wish I had it that easy. My name's Daniel--that's easy--McSorgelsontown. I forget how to spell it half the time myself. I think my old man made it up on one of his drunken orgies."

"Have you been getting much action on Golden Gate today, Dan?"

"Not really, Mike. About normal, I'd say. And this is the first bet I've written on your horse." He flipped open the Racing Form for tomorrow, checked out the morning line and consensus of the track handicappers' comments. "Doesn't sound too good, Mike. No one picks him in the top three, and morning line odds show 12 to 1."

"Yes, maybe I've made a poor choice." Shant had no intention of promoting his horse. The fewer bets down on it the higher the odds, and if it won the higher the payoff. Casino ticket writers were notorious for passing on tips to friends and big tippers when they saw a lot of action on a specific horse. Shant hoped to avoid that with his Mexican pick. "I just liked the name. It reminded me of some good times I've had south of the border. Maybe it'll be a big contribution to happy memories."

He nudged Percy, who immediately realized what Shant was doing. He had planned to get down on the same horse, but saw that two healthy bets would probably cause Dan to mention the action to other betters.

"Who do you like in the first at the Gate, Dan?"

"It's a maiden claiming, Percy, and that means it's basically a crapshoot. But Debonayre came second last out, and that's usually a good sign. If I had to bet, I'd go on him."

"Okay, Daniel, give me $20 on Debonayre's nose. You've got a drink coming if he wins."

"Good enough, Percy." He punched out the ticket and the two men strolled away.

"Nice thinking, Pap. You can get down on the triple M later on with a different seller. That way Dan won't see two big bets and start talking."

"That's what I figured, Mike. Why go to all the trouble of spotting a good bet, then have the wise guys knock down the odds? See, I do listen when you give out with your handicapping lessons."

"Way to go, Pap. I'll have you winning big time before we're through. Any other action you want to get down in here? No? Okay, let's head back...oh, oh. There's that prick DiBonio. And he's coming over. Shit. I hoped to miss his smarmy face."

"Hey, boys, how's it going? Getting down on the winners, Mike?"

"Time will tell, DiBonio. How're things with you and the Cosa Nostra?"

"You're a great kidder, Shant. Should be up on stage somewhere. I wouldn't know a Cosa Nostra if one came up and bit me on the joint. But with me things are good. The Race Book is going great guns. In fact, we're thinking of expanding it, knocking that keno crap out and adding that area. It would give us another 20 or 25 desk spots. Probably up our handle five grand a day, more than that keno crap takes in all week. Keno! About as exciting as watching grass grow."

"I have to agree with you there, DiBonio. Keno and bingo, even roulette, require absolutely no ability. Just hope that your number comes up. But that's the trend. So-called gamblers today don't want to think, and they don't want to wait. They want instant gratification. That's why there are so many broads around now in casinos. Even they can understand when a slot pays off or their numbers come up in keno or letters in bingo. No brains required. I heard some old broad talking in the bar. She said she picked horses because of the color of their silks. Jesus Christ!"

"Yeah, they made a big mistake when they stopped keeping broads barefoot in the winter and pregnant in the summer." Pap shared Shant's views on the proper place of females, although quite frequently he liked to explore their assets.

"Someone said you were being considered for casino manager. Is that true?" Shant couldn't refrain from baiting DiBonio. The man was so unsure of his abilities--with good reason--that he hungered for any hint of second party respect.

"Where did you hear that? They're thinking of replacing Martino, you know. He's good but getting over the hill. Hell, he must be seventy. Probably one of the best on Fremont Street, maybe even on the Strip too, a few years ago." He lowered his voice. "But past it. I heard the same rumors, Mike. Do you think they're serious? I mean, I've done a fantastic job of turning the Race Book around. When I came here it wasn't doing nothing like it is today. They had a bunch of loose tables for customers, and no bar service. You had to go out into the table area and flag down a waitress. Now, I have two of them concentrating almost totally on the Book. And comfortable chairs, especially padded for all those old farts and their skinny asses." His opinion of the customers who paid his salary wasn't too high.

"So I've done a great job here, and I could do the same in the casino. Hell, all I need is a couple of weeks and I'd have things turned around, crappy no-interest games like keno out in the alley. I'd replace almost everything with poker slots. That's what everyone wants nowadays, poker slots. They just want to sit down with a roll of coins, feed the machine, and wait for a payoff. You notice them? They don't even talk any more, almost don't even drink. Just sit in a daze and pump in coins. Christ, how boring! But that's what the customers want, and that's what I'd give them. Poker slots from wall to wall. What do you guys think of that?"

"I have to agree with you, DiBonio, that most casino customers would be perfectly happy if you put them in a warehouse with no drinks, no carpets on the floor, and even no waitresses in skimpy costumes. We live in an era of stupidity. Among other things that means poker slots, as you said."

"Well, if they replace all the table games and race books with slots, I for one will depart Las Vegas," Percy said. "It used to be you could go into a bar, especially away from the Strip or Fremont Street, and actually have a conversation with someone. Now, even in the strictly neighborhood bars, the bar is jammed with poker slots. No one talks to anyone. Even the bartender is liable to be playing one. I think the world is coming to an end, and it's starting right here in Vegas. In a couple more generations humans won't even have voices, because there'll be no need to talk. They'll just point, like monkeys. Evolution? We're going backwards."

Shant laughed. "You're right, Pap. Even at the track, people will just point to the horse--or the color of the silks--they like. There will be absolutely no need for speech. Today language is disappearing. When was the last time you heard someone say Thanks or Excuse me?"

Percy struck a tragic pose. "As the world turns, and ends, what can we do?" He paused, like a good comedian. "Have a drink, that's what. Let's get back to it, Mike. Nice talking with you, DiBonio." Percy believed in keeping all options open.

"Yes, let's. Good luck with the new job, DiBonio. Quite an improvement over booking street bets, wouldn't it be?" DiBonio didn't like to have people mention his previous employment as a common street bookie, handling small time bets for small time bettors. It was that experience which actually had opened the door for him to the job as casino race book manager. At the time the book was started no one else had any real experience booking horse bets, so he won it by default. "If the job comes through I expect you'll be throwing a party for all your old friends." The irony of the last sentence escaped the Race Book manager.

"Absolutely. And you two guys will be on the guest list. You can count on that." DiBonio had so few friends--none, actually--that he had to settle for people like Shant and Percy who even talked to him. Most people in the casino, employees and customers alike, just ignored him.

Shant and Percy walked back to the bar where Sam was deep in conversation with a tall, skinny man of middle age. As the two approached he was saying, "Absolutely, Sam. I can guarantee it. These stocks will likely double as soon as they're listed, and from there the sky is not even the limit, just the starting point. This is pure gold. Pure, pure gold, Sam."

Sam never bet in the casino, and considered all betting on games or horses sucker plays. But put him next to some new company with an initial stock issue and he tugged at the reins.

"You really think so, Adolph? It looks that good?"

"Sam, think about it. This outfit up in British Columbia has had a couple of stores retailing this stuff for five or six years. And they're profitable. Really profitable. Their sales increases for the main store, for the most recent three year period, were up an average of 41 percent. 41 percent! That's astronomical! Fabulous! And now they're going to start franchising the idea. First up there in Canada, then next here in the States. They can't lose. And neither can the early investors. Remember, Sam,

31

those who got in early on the McDonald's franchise saw their investments increase over 160 times. For each ten grand they put in, they were able to haul out one point six mil. Man, a couple of units invested and you say goodbye to Vegas. Or maybe buy yourself a couple of casinos. Sam, it's a sure thing."

"And what do they sell, Adolph?"

"The product," Adolph slowed his speech for a minute, "is solar and safety films. The coming thing, Sam. As the company says, 'the product of the 21st century'. That stuff can do wonderful things. You just slap it on any window, and it stops ultraviolet rays. You know, those things that cause skin cancer. And they do a lot more besides, Sam. But the important point is that they're just starting to franchise, and they already have a proven idea. Nearly all new franchise companies just have a concept. It may work, more likely not. But this is already proven."

"Where can we get some shares?" Percy kept a straight face. "I expect to come into some excess bread soon, maybe even by tomorrow, and I'm always looking for a good investment."

Adolph straightened up--he looked to be nearly six and a half feet tall--and turned to look at the newcomer. "You can't. Yet. The stock isn't listed yet. But my contact at the company says the company expects to be listed, either on the Stock Exchange up there in Vancouver or on the OTC Exchanges down here. They're evidently considering both options right now."

"And where do you fit in?" As a practicing con Percy liked to see how fast on their feet competitors were.

"I will be acting as a sales rep for the company's initial offering of stock," Adolph said. "I'll get a commission from the company. The price you pay for any stock will be just the same, whether you get it through me or direct from the company. But I really think this one is going to be a winner. They have good management and good plans."

Percy was surprised at the apparent forthrightness of Adolph. Admitting he'd get a commission up front defanged a big objection right up front. Most hustlers tried to pretend they had no vested interest in selling whatever product they were touting. Maybe, he thought, there's something to this stock.

"Pap, if you can put off getting rich for a little while, what say we do some work on earning our bread and butter. You can get back to the dessert later," Shant said.

"Sure, sure, be an anti-capitalist. Destroy what has made this country strong. Okay, okay, I'm coming," Percy said, as Shant gently tugged at his collar. "Hey, do you have a card? Give me one and I may get back to you later." Adolph handed him a card embossed in what looked like real gold. As the two men left Sam was leaning over the bar, listening intently to what the salesman said, and ignoring the clearing of throats by dry regulars at the other end of the bar.

Shant headed to the rear of the bar, chose a table against the wall, and sat down in the chair facing front. Percy was forced to sit with his back to all the action, a position Shant hoped would keep his attention on the matters at hand.

"Okay, Pap, let's sketch out the pix you're going to want. Here's my tentative list of subjects." He looked quizzically at Pap, who was looking back earnestly at him. "Do you think you might like to make a note or two, Mr. Percy? I seem to recall that your memory is not as good as it once was, and now that you're approaching your senior years..."

"What do you mean, senior years? Christ, I'm barely out of my twenties. And right away you're trying to shuffle me off to some old fart's funny farm? Some friend."

"I think perhaps you have been out of your twenties for quite a while, Pap. But my folks raised me to be respectful to old people, so I won't hassle you. Would you like me to order you a glass of prune juice to get you started?"

"Finished, would be more like it. No, I require no prune juice, you young punk. Let's get on with it." He pulled a ragged notebook from his jacket pocket, flipped through it until he found a page partially clear, withdrew a ballpoint from another pocket, crossed his legs and pulled down an imaginary dress in imitation of a serious stenographer. "Okay, boss. Shoot."

"To make this easy, Pap, how be I just read through the list, tell you a couple of details about each, and you can make your usual clever determination of what kind and how many photos you're going to want."

"Sounds eminently workable, young sir. Why not do that and stop putzing around? I'd like to get laid or drunk, or even talk to that stock bullshitter, before this day ends."

"And so you shall, Pappy. Even senior citizens should have a little fun occasionally." Noting a nasty glint in the photographer's eyes, Shant became businesslike.

"First subject is Larry Mahon. About 40. Started and owns a city trucking firm."

"Three pix." Percy scribbled something on his pad. "Next."

"Jason Bourgelt. God, I hate that name Jason. He's maybe 50, 55. Took over a floundering furniture store, turned it into four stores throughout the valley. A little squirt, barely five feet tall."

"Another three bagger." Another scribbled note. "Next."

"Are you sure you know what you're doing, Pap? Those notes look pretty sketchy."

"I know exactly what I'm doing. Next."

34

Shant sighed. "Okie dokie, amigo. Next is Saunders P. Jingloter. Who makes up these names? Can you picture some sweet new mommy saying to her spouse, 'Oh, let's name him Saunders. It goes so well with Jingloter.' Whatever happened to Jack and Steve and Bill?"

"They went to San Fran, learned to like boys, and changed their names. Next."

"Here's a dandy. Arterio Goya Gonzalez. One of our Hispanic compadres, undoubtedly. He started a Spanish radio station here in town. At first he had about six listeners. Now it's the top rated station in the evening drive hours, whatever that means. I just copied it from a publicity handout I got from him."

"That means in the evening when he's driving it in to all those Latin beauties. Don't you writer types know anything?" Another squiggle was added to the notebook. "Next."

"This one is my style. Andrew Mason. He's the pres of a firm that exports stuff down to Mexico, has some work done on it, then imports it back here."

"Yeah, that's that maquilladora angle. They get their labor done down there for pennies an hour, apparently, then can bring back the finished products and sell at high prices. I'll put him down for four pix. Maybe he can get me started in that game."

The list of names went on, and Pap duly entered squiggles beside his scrawled names. Whether he'd be able to decipher them later only time would tell, Shant thought, but he knew from past experience that once Percy got started on a project he finished it, usually in pretty good shape.

"Say, old buddy, doesn't that broad over there look familiar to you?" Percy pointed to a woman standing just inside the bar's east door.

"You've still got pretty good eyesight for a senior," Shant said. "That's none other than my current research associate, Miss Linda by name." He stood up, caught the woman's eye, and beckoned her over.

"Hiya, babe. How's about a kiss for your lover?"

"Lover? I thought lovers had to be around some times. I see you so rarely I've forgotten your name." She smiled at him, then turned to Percy. "And this must be Percy Percy, the wonder photographer I hear so much about."

"Yes, that's all true, even if you knew me as well as lover boy here. Well, maybe not know in the biblical sense, but you know what I mean."

She leaned over, kissed Percy on the cheek, then turned to Shant, and stuck out her right hand. "Nice to see you again, Mr. Shant."

Shant pushed her outstretched hand down, grabbed her, and kissed her soundly. "What's this handshaking crap? You think I'm your insurance agent? How was your trip? I'd have picked you up at the airport if you'd let me know what flight you were on. How long can you stay?"

"That's four questions. Which do you want answered first?"

"None of them. What do you want to drink?"

"Maybe a little vodka and seltzer. Not too strong. I had a couple of quickies on the plane."

Shant signaled to their waitress, placed an order for three drinks, and sat down with his arm resting on Linda's shoulder. "Nice to see you, kitten."

"Kitten? What kind of a greeting is that? You've been watching Bogart movies again, haven't you?" Percy grinned.

"Well, it's somewhat preferable to its grown up version," said Shant. "You want me to address her as pussy?"

"I see that both you degenerates are up to your usual trashy form. Be nice."

"Okay. Seriously, how long can you stay?"

"For a couple of days, probably, unless the outfit I'm currently doing research for just can't get along without me. But likely they'll survive for a day or two."

"What research are you doing now, Linda?" Percy asked.

"The company is planning to start a rec vehicle subsidiary, and they asked me to find out the probable market demand for a new line of quality--read expensive--trailers and motor homes. I've been on for a couple of weeks now, and should have it wrapped up in a couple more."

"How's chances of doing a little work for me?"

"I know your idea of work, Mike."

"No, no, I'm serious, babe. I got an okay on that Vegas shakers and movers article, and I'm going to need some extra help on background stuff. Especially with the old timer here on the payroll, I'll have to make sure his senility doesn't screw up things."

"Senility my ass. I could outwork you any day of the week. Well, maybe one day out of five. But enough of that," Percy said. "Are you people hungry? Why don't we get some dinner and we can talk over this assignment later. Probably much later, if that's a gleam in Mike's eyes, not just an astigmatism."

"Good idea, Pap. And I hope it is the right kind of gleam. I read somewhere that sex is just as good as jogging. And you don't need special clothes for it," Linda said.

"Okay. Let's go and eat." Shant scribbled in midair, and when the waitress brought over the check he put some bills on it. "Have one yourself, Marie. See you later."

The three friends left the bar and headed up to the roof garden restaurant.

CHAPTER 3

"Let's give it something with real class, Lennie. Something that sounds like it's a branch of IBM or Microsoft."

"Good idea, Toro. But we want to be careful that we don't get too close to a real thing. What we don't want is a battery of legal shysters from some big company breathing down our necks."

"True. What do you think would be good?"

The Toro was great at determining what was wanted. In general. But he lacked a little something in the execution department, usually deferring to Lennie's more talented and artistic abilities.

Lennie sat silently for a few moments. "How about the Great International Universal World-Wide Development Corporation?"

The Toro looked at Lennie through slitted eyes. "You're kidding, right?"

"Yeah. That might be a little too much. Give me a minute."

Pedro "the Toro" sat quietly, watching Lennie who doodled with a pencil, jotting down names, then crossing them out.

"Something with Research in it, Toro. At least for one of the names. We'll need two. One for the research arm, another for the ad agency. Two

38

separate names will give us far more respectability. And it'll be far more versatile, too. We should be able to stiff most of the advertising bills if we play it right. And that, partner, means more for the bottom line." Lennie smiled. "And of course that bottom line is our line."

"Right, right. Good thinking, Lennie. Are two companies enough? Maybe we should have more?"

"No, I don't think so, Toro. Too many cooks, and all that. We make it too complicated and we'll be so busy trying to keep track of who's doing what to whom that we won't have time to do any doing."

"Yeah, I guess you're right. So what do we call this research outfit?"

"We've got research already. All we have to do is add a little color. Let's see. How about Assembly? Naw, that sounds too much like a high school bunch. What about Group?"

The Toro look attentive. "Group? Does that give the research part some class?"

"No. No good. Hand me that thesaurus there on the bar behind you, Pedro." Lennie often had the thumb-eared paperback book with him.

Lennie flipped through the pages of the well used book.

"Here we are, Toro. Institute."

"But doesn't that sound like some kind of reform school?" Pedro answered his own question. "No, I guess not. Yeah, it has a nice ring to it, Lennie. Research Institute. Is that enough of a name?"

"We should add some kind of qualifier, Toro. Something distinctive, yet similar to some other established outfits. Western? Nah, too common. Desert? California? North?" He shook his head at all. "Maybe something a little more specific, yet retaining a nice air of distinction. Northern? Northwestern?" He smiled. "Close. How about Northwest, Toro? Does that conjure up all kinds of nice thoughts about the forested, smog-free northwest? Sure it does. Perfect. The Northwest Research Institute. Absolutely perfect,

Pedro. Could you resist an ad from such a prestigious company? Of course not. That's our first name."

Throughout this monologue Pedro had by turns nodded, smiled, frowned, and shaken his head as Lennie detailed the possibilities. Now he grinned in appreciation of his friend's aptitude.

"That does sound real good, Lennie. Northwest Research Institute. What does it do?"

"Anything we want it to, Toro. Absolutely anything we want. That's the nice thing about imaginary companies. They can be just as versatile as we want them to be. And you can be damned sure we want them to be very, very versatile."

"I guess. How about the other name?" Pedro lacked staying power. He soon got bored and wanted to explore new fields.

"Okay. Now we need a name for an ad agency. This will be the outfit running up the charges, so it really has to sound kosher. Something that most media will assume is a big company, so they won't even bother checking out its credit. The more we can slip past those sharp eyed credit managers, the more that will fall to the bottom line. And as we said before, Toro, that means mucho mas for us." Lennie reached into his breast pocket, looking for one of his favorite smokes, a very cheap cigarillo that cost about half a dollar and smelled like a bum's dirty socks were on fire. "I forgot to get some," he muttered. "I'll pick some up later." There was only one smoke shop in the entire city that even carried the noxious cigars, and only because Lennie was a friend of the owner. Pedro exhaled, silently giving thanks that his friend had come up empty handed. The cigars reminded Pedro unpleasantly of his years spent existing in smoggy Los Angeles.

"I think we should stick with the geographical approach, Toro. What goes with Northwest? Alaska? No, too far north. I don't think they even have ad agencies up there. What would they advertise?

Eskimo pies?" He grinned at his own humor. "Yukon? No, for the same reason. Ocean? Hmm. Getting close. Toro, what's the name of the big bunch of water off the west coast?"

"You mean the ocean, right?" Pedro liked to be sure of what Lennie was asking, so that he didn't inadvertently become the butt of a joke. Lennie nodded. "Well, it's the Pacific Ocean, as if you didn't know."

"Right. And it has a nice ring to it, Toro. So let's hook it up with something. We're going to be saying it's an ad agency, so how be we call it that? Pacific Advertising Agency? No." He shook his head. "Agency sounds like some one man operation trying to look big. Corporation? Nope, agencies are never called corps. How about Associates? Do you feel like an associate, Toro?"

"Absofuckinglutely. That's exactly what I feel like. Actually, in this crummy bar I feel like a good hot bath, but next to that I feel like an associate. So we have our names?"

"I think so, compadre." Lennie got up from the stool, looked around to make certain they were alone, and spread his arms in a circus barker pose.

"Ladies and gentlemen. And Pedro. I take great pleasure in introducing you folks to two of the newest, largest, and best run companies in the western world. First we have the Northwest Research Institute, recognized throughout the civilized world as a, a," he searched for the appropriate phrase, "as a major developer of new and spectacular products which meet the needs and desires of mankind. A true benefactor of the world's citizens. And acting as its duly appointed agent in getting the good words out, the slimy but shoddy ad agency of Pacific Advertising Associates, which has an impeccable credit rating and so its ads should be run without any embarrassing questions." He bowed to his one man audience, smiled, and sat down.

"Let's have a drink. All that bullshit has dried me out." Pedro swiveled and shouted down to the bartender, who was reading the Wall Street Journal. "Hey Sam. When you get a break from your financial shenanigans, maybe you could drop a couple of drinks down this way."

Sam straightened up, feigned a look of boredom, and started to mix the drinks.

"I think the names are great, Lennie. Really classy. What do we do now?"

"First, we sample those drinks Sam is bearing down on us with. Thanks, Sam. Put it on Toro's tab. And have one yourself."

"Thanks, Lennie. And you too, Toro." Sam smiled and went back to his Journal.

"What's the idea of being so free with my money, Lennie?"

"Don't worry. If this deal clicks like I know it will, owing for a few drinks at this shitty bar won't cause you any worry whatsoever. I can honestly see a big score on this one, Toro. I mean a really big score. Like a number with a bunch of zeroes after it."

Pedro's face split in a big smile. "That big? You really think we can hit the bull's eye on this scam, Lennie?"

"Yeah. We've put a lot of planning into it. And let's face it. The only thing more popular than losing weight is losing weight without work. You've seen how many fat people there are around? Christ, it seems like every second broad is a hundred pounds overweight. Half the population are fat slobs, and most of them would like to be skinny slobs. That is, if they could knock off the blubber without actually having to do anything that resembled work or effort."

He swallowed half his drink. "Not bad. Sam must actually have put some vodka into this one. Yes, I really feel this is going to be our retirement special, Toro. I figure five, maybe six months of work, then the payoff comes, and big."

"How come so long, Lennie? Usually on these scams we wrap the whole thing up in just a couple of weeks."

"Yes, and that's why we've never hit the big one. Just like a guy who is so horny that he goes off five seconds after he gets into a whore he's paid fifty bucks for. We've always been too hot to trot. This time we'll ease into it nice and slowly, and enjoy every stroke. We'll get our fifty bucks worth, Toro."

"Hey, Lennie. Maybe if this deal works as well as you think you'll be able to get yourself a legit green card. And maybe even I could."

"Goddammit, Toro, I told you to never talk about that. Never. I should never have told you, but you promised to keep your lip buttoned. You start yapping now, and I'm going to have second thoughts about our partnership."

"You don't need to worry, Lennie. I'd never tell anyone. You know that. I'm in the same boat you are. You think I want to get shipped back to manana land? I like it here with people whose names are like Smith and Jones, not Rodriguez and Gonzales. There's no one else here, Lennie," he looked around quickly to make sure his statement was accurate, "and if there was anybody even close I'd never even mention it. But there's just the two of us, and we're partners, ain't we? And we both know we're illegals, so what's the problem?"

Lennie frowned. "The problem, Pedro, is that you should never mention it at all. There's no need to. Just file it under 'forgotten' in your brain."

"Okay, Lennie, okay. No need to make a big thing of it. I won't mention it again. I promise, on my word as a gentleman."

Lennie smiled, good humor regained. "Okay, gentleman. So let's get on with it. Now that we have the names of our two internationally-known companies, we need to get them incorporated. Luckily here in Nevada that's not a problem."

43

"Why bother with all that crappola, Lennie? If we're just going to use them for a few months, then fold them, why bother with legal problems?"

"There's always the chance that some eager beaver credit guy will check to see if the ad company, maybe even the Research Institute, is actually set up as a corp. For some reason a lot of people think that a corporation automatically means a company is more legit and more stable than a company that's not incorporated. That's bullshit, of course, but we don't want to take any chances."

"What's it going to cost us to do this, Lennie? I heard that a shyster charges a couple of grand to set up a corporation."

"They do. But we can do it a little cheaper. I'll buy one of those do-it-yourself corporation kits and use it for both companies. The last one I had cost $24.95. Think we can afford that?"

"You can actually do for a double sawbuck what a lawyer charges a couple of grand for?"

"I've set up five or six corps, Toro, exactly the same way. It takes about ten minutes to fill out the one page form, and mail it off to Carson City. That's it."

"Why Carson?"

"That's the state capital, and where the corporation records are kept. There's a fee which has to be paid to the state. Last time it was about a hundred. Probably still the same. Then in a couple of weeks we'll get a nice four colored piece of paper showing that our company has been set up and is registered to do business in the state. Then we should get a city or county business license, and that'll make everything copasetic. All we'll have to do then is rent an office, get a phone, fax, and computer for e-mail, and our two world famous companies will be in business. Counting all the bullshit deposits and fees we'll get stung for, I expect it'll run two, maybe three, thou, to get everything set up properly and legally." He grinned at Pedro. "And we do want to be legal, don't we?"

"You bet. The last thing I say to myself every night, right after my prayers and just before I jerk off, is that I want to be legal. I can't picture being anything else, Lennie. I wouldn't feel right about it."

"Yeah, except for the hand job, that's about what I do and feel too, Toro."

"What hand job, Lennie?"

"Jesus Christ, Mike. You shouldn't creep up like that. You scared the crap out of me."

"I didn't really creep up, Toro. I walked up. You two guys were so busy talking about your hand jobs that you just weren't paying much attention. So, what hand job?"

"It was just the tail end of a joke, Mike. Have a drink with us?"

"Sure, Lennie. Thanks. But I'm still interested in what you guys were talking about so seriously. Not the hand job. I can live without knowing any more about that. But I can tell that you're both up to something. Some scam, I imagine. Why not tell me all about it? Then I can do a feature on it, you guys will get famous and broads all over will make a pilgrimage here to Vegas just to get a look at your handsome faces. Think of all the ass you can finagle, Toro. And you'll be able to cut out those self-handled hand jobs."

"That would be nice, Mike, but I can't tell you about something which ain't there. Like Lennie said, all we was doing was telling each other old jokes. Want to hear about the Jewish guy who went into a meat market and..."

"Thanks anyway, but no. Well, if you weren't talking about some scam, what are all these names you've got scrawled down here, Lennie? Just practicing your penmanship?"

Lennie looked at the paper Shant was holding, with his various company name ideas.

He looked over at Pedro, then back at Shant.

45

"I was working on a crossword puzzle, Mike. You know, one of those based on corporate names. He reached for the paper, but Shant pulled it back too fast.

"I'll just hang on to this for awhile, Lennie." He smiled. "In case I want to do that same crossword puzzle."

"Sure, no problema, as our southern cousins say. What's new with you, Mike?" He was really pissed that Shant had the name list but he didn't want to make an issue of it. Probably Shant would just tire of the game and later toss the page into some waste basket.

Shant was certain that the names had some significance to the two cons and he made a mental note to get more information later. Not that he wanted to expose Lennie's nefarious activities, whatever they might be. Ever since Lennie had once helped him research a major magazine series on con games, and saved him a lot of effort after agreed sources backed out, Shant had felt a real affection for the con man. But his reporter's instincts told him there was a story here.

"I just got an okay to do a series of articles on this wonderful town, so I'll be hanging around for a couple of weeks. And I got the okay to use Pap as my photographer. That means he'll be here, goosing all the broads, too. We'll have to get together and make a night of it soon."

"Sounds great, Mike. If you need anyone to research the massage parlors, you can call on me. I'd be glad to work for nothing. Just as long as I get at least one blow job a day from the pretty lady masseuses."

"Toro, you're incorrigible. I've already got dibs on that part of the story," Lennie said. "What's needed for it is an experienced hand, someone who appreciates real culture, someone..."

"Horseshit, Lennie. I can accept a blow job just as gracefully as you, even if I wasn't raised in those Ukrainian charm schools."

"Polish, Toro, Polish. There's a considerable difference. My Polish heritage goes back centuries. Most Ukrainians can trace their heritage back at least twenty minutes."

"Okay, so I'm not a whiz in geography. I notice you're here, in the grand old US and A, not back in Poland. So much for your Polish heritage."

"You've got something there, Toro. A rich heritage is one thing, living in the land of the free where broads give it away just as freely, and money is everywhere, is certainly a better thing."

CHAPTER 4

"Five hundred on number six in the second at Fairplex. To win."

"Okay." The ticket seller punched up the bet. "How are you paying?"

"The same goddamned way I pay all my bets. Is this your first day on the job? Jesus Christ, where do they find you guys? Charge it to my account!"

Dominick Falvo, the Golden Future Casino's bar manager, especially disliked anyone who wasn't aware of his position or the fact that he was one of a fairly small group who were extended credit at the race book. Most of the reason for the credit was simply his job; employees were entitled to a limited cuff. The other part of the reason was that race book manager Richard DiBonio--Dickie or Dickhead to enemies, he had no friends--was a sloppy administrator, and Falvo had built up a big debit position before DiBonio had become aware of it. Now he either had to garnishee Falvo's wages, have his legs broken, or extend even more credit and hope that sometime Falvo's rotten horse betting would enjoy a miracle.

Two races later Falvo was down $1800.

"Gimme a Form for Golden Gate. That fucking Fairplex is a shithole. Every goddamned trainer and jock is on the take. How the fuck can you win a bet when everyone at that bullring is cheating as much as Clinton did with his wife?"

The clerk at the ticket counter passed over a Racing Form, ignored Falvo's harangue, and turned his back on him to look up at one of the television monitors.

Falvo grabbed the racing newspaper and hurried over to an empty desk next to where Mike Shant was sitting reading the Form.

"Fucking Fairplex! How can you win at that sewer?"

Shant looked up. "I wouldn't know, Dom. It's a bull ring and I don't bet tracks that small. Had a tough day there?"

"Fucking terrible. I dropped about three grand." Falvo believed in rounding up to impress.

"Ever wish you were back in the saloon business, Dom? You ran one in Washington State didn't you?"

"Yeah, Spokane. A shitty town, dirty snow on the streets nine months a year. But the bar was a real money maker. Had a bunch of big titted broads peddling drinks and the money rolled in."

Falvo's bar had employed one 52 year old waitress whose breasts would have hung to her knees without her specially reinforced 38-D bra. The bar's net profit could be shown using less than four numerals. It had actually been a corner bar catering to local unemployeds and over-the-hill hookers who made more from social security disability payments than they did from renting their pussies.

"Ever think of going back?"

"Oh, I think about it, especially when I think of some of the assholes I have to serve in the bar here." He realized that Shant was one of those customers. "Not guys like you, Mike," he added quickly, "but some of the other customers. Back before Fremont Street turned into a tourist trap with all that 'Fremont Street Experience' light show crap every night we used to get some real gamblers in here, especially when the poker world series was on at Binion's Casino up the street.

"But now we get blue haired seniors from Iowa who want a 'nice white wine'. Jesus H. Christ!

"Who do you like in the fifth at Golden Gate?" Like all dedicated horse players Falvo sooner rather than later got back to the only topic of any real interest.

Shant smiled. "Ever hear that joke about horseplayers? A bettor is looking at the Form when his buddy runs up. 'Hey, didya hear the news? World War 3 just started!' The bettor looks up. 'Yeah?' There's a moment's silence, then the bettor says 'Who do you like in the second?'"

Falvo looked puzzled. "So what's the punch line?"

"Not important," Shant grinned. "The fifth at GG? I passed on that. It's a maiden claiming, and there's five first time starters. Your odds would be better playing keno."

"Well, I think number eight is a lock. A good jock, the trainer's not bad, he's winning 21 percent of his races this meet, and the horse has had a couple of bullet workouts."

"Just having the fastest time in a workout doesn't mean too much, Dom. Many trainers give their workout riders orders to not come in first. They don't want that boldface black bullet showing up in the Form. And that trainer's record with maiden claimers is lousy. In the Stats book it shows less than five percent."

"I still like him." Falvo got up and went to the ticket sellers. "Two big ones on number eight, fifth at Golden Gate." He spoke loudly, hoping that Shant could hear.

"Two thousand?" The ticket seller looked down at his computer screen, punched a few keys, then looked up.

"Says here you'll have to get an OK on that amount. From DiBonio."

"What the fuck you mean, an OK? My credit is good."

"My computer shows an OK from Dickie is needed."

"Fuck! Where is he?"

"How do I know? You might check his office, over there behind the chief cashier's cage."

Falvo slammed his dog-eared Form on the counter, then turned and walked slowly toward the cashier's cage.

"Is he in there?"

"Yes. You can go in."

"Hiya, Dickie. I need..."

"Don't ever call me that, Falvo. M name is Richard."

"Okay, okay, don't have a heart attack. I just need your OK on a bet. This has never happened before. What the fuck's going on, some shitty clerk trying to complicate things?"

"No, Falvo, there's no clerk, shitty or otherwise. The reason your account is flagged is because of the amount of your debit. Do you know how much that is?"

"Well, I've had a bunch of bad breaks, Di...Richard. A bunch of bad beats. I'm on a losing streak right now, but that will soon change. As a matter of fact I've got a couple of hot horses today at Golden Gate, and so I want to get down on them."

"I'll bet you do. My question stands. How much are you into the casino for?"

"Aw fuck, DiBonio, I don't know exactly. I'm not a bookkeeper. Maybe a few grand?"

"A few grand? How about 22 grand, Falvo."

"That much? Wow. Well, like I said I'm on the down side of a losing streak. I'll get healthy real quick, and then those red figures will turn bright green."

"Right, just like a traffic light changing? You've got to get this debit cut way down or you'll have to start betting with hard stuff. Hard currency, that is."

"Jesus H. Christ, Dic...DiBonio, how the fuck can I clear up the nut if I can't make bets?"

Falvo turned to the only window in the room, and air punched an opponent.

"I'm the bar manager in this casino, Richard. I'm not taking a powder. Hell, I've got connections to the Family. They'd be happy to bankroll me for any amount but I don't want to waste their time on a chickenshit thing like this."

"So you're connected, are you? Well, I regularly play poker with a couple of heavy hitters myself. In fact, I count them among my best friends. But I don't recall them mentioning your name, Falvo."

"I owned a bar in Spokane where almost all the customers were wise guys, DiBonio. I have lots of wise guy contacts, so don't treat me like an asshole."

"I've got business to take care of, Falvo. I don't have time to sit around and bullshit with you." He typed a few keys into his desk computer, then looked up at Falvo.

"Your nut right now is $22,680. Against my better judgment I'll clear you up to 30 large. But that's it. Either start picking a few winners, or at that point it's cash only."

Falvo stared at DiBonio for a few seconds, then turned and left. He muttered something that sounded remarkably like "cocksucking dago bloodsucker".

In the main race book room Shant had just left the cashier's cage with a healthy stack of bills in his left hand. He held a Form in his right.

"What did you hit, Mike?"

"Caught a nice one at GG, Dom. A non-winners of two races. Had a lousy jock up but I know his trainer likes that kind of situation, especially as his horse was returning from almost a year layoff."

"What did it pay?"

Shant smiled. "26 to 1."

"Jesus Fucking Christ! Why can't I get lucky with a score like that. You had it to win?"

"Yeah, along with an exacta both ways. It paid $933 for a $2 ticket."

"Shit." Dom looked a little queasy. "I gotta go get a drink. Maybe a bunch. See you later."

Shant looked around for a cocktail waitress. He rarely drank when he was handicapping as he wanted a clear head. But after his combined $11,400 score he felt a little exception to his rule was justified. He spotted Nancy, one of his favorites, and waved her over.

"Get me a vodka rocks please."

"With lime?" She moved in close and rubbed her very firm breasts against his shoulder. "Now or later at my place?"

He laughed. "That sounds great, kiddo, but you'd better make it now. I've got a friend in from the coast and I doubt she wants to visit your place, lovely though I'm sure it is."

"Some broads have all the luck." She smiled and headed toward the bar.

Shant took his seat and opened his Form to the GG nightcap. It was a cheap claimer and he started to read down the past performances. Sometimes these cheapies could throw up a winner at healthy odds. And by the last race all the losers were dumping what was left of their bankrolls on ridiculous longshots in hopes of getting even.

"Here you are, sir."

Nancy did a little curtsy, giving him a glance at her treasure chest, and set down his drink. It was a comp as all race book drinks were.

"And Sam at the bar said you had a long distance call. The party said she'd call back in 15 minutes exactly. Are you starting your own cat house?"

"Nope. Can't imagine who'd be phoning me here. Anyway, thanks for the fast service, Nancy. I just had a good winner." He took a fifty from his pocket roll and laid it on her tray.

"Thanks, Mike. May you have many more. Don't forget the call. Use Sam's bar phone."

He took a solid hit from the vodka, then sat it down, looked at his watch, and decided he had enough time to finish the past performances for the GG nightcap.

"Sleazy Leasy looks okay," he muttered. "Up in class, if you can call a raise from $4,000 claiming price to $5,000 up. And the colt has had three winners out of five races at this distance. Morning line odds 5/1, currently 12/1. That's good, shows most bettors are looking for something that's not increasing in price. Most of them think a class drop is like money in the bank. But too often it just means the horse's racing value is actually dropping."

He finished his vodka, and grabbed his Form and headed to the sellers' windows.

"Jerry, number six in the nightcap at Golden Gate. $250 to win, $250 to place." He didn't often back up his win bets, but he wasn't all that enthusiastic about Sleazy.

He checked his watch. Almost 15 minutes since Nancy had given him the message. He took his tickets and went toward Sam's bar phone.

It rang as he approached. Sam answered, looked around, spotted him, and beckoned.

"For you, Mike. Would you like to have your business cards printed with this number?"

Shant grinned and picked up the phone.

"Mike Shant speaking."

"Of course it is. What a surprise, locating you in a bar."

"Hi, Patricia. It's great to hear from you. How're tricks up there in Canada's rain forest?"

"Hard to believe, but it hasn't rained for 17 days. The locals are muttering that this is the start of global warming. I think it's just ordinary late summer weather. This 'rain forest' image Vancouver is stuck with is undeserved."

"Sure it is. That's why if you sit down for more than 20 minutes moss starts growing on the north side of your shoes."

She laughed. "Anyway, what's happening. Have you broken the bank in Vegas yet?"

"You know me, babe. I don't even play casino games. You have about as much chance of actually beating the house in the long run as winning the lottery. I stick strictly to horses, who sometimes do run honestly."

"Any idea of when you'll be clocking in here in the city of sun? No panic, but next month's issue of Your Money has more holes than your socks. I could use some of that silver-tongued ability of yours. In the magazine, or maybe even elsewhere."

"Easy for you to say when I'm safely a thousand miles away. Actually, I'd planned to get back there by next week, but I just got a juicy assignment delivered to me from that coast mag I queried last month. At a very healthy fee, so I'll probably be tied up here for another few weeks.

"If you're really desperate, I could always do a quickie on how Canada's use of two languages, just to placate a very small minority of frogs in Quebec, costs it millions, maybe even billions, in lost revenue from firms who just won't set up branch operations in Canada because of the stupid extra costs all that bilingual crap costs."

"How soon could you get it to me, and how many words?"

"Within a week. Probably a couple of thou, unless you wanted more. Or even less."

"I always want more. You know that. But on this article two would be about right. Try to keep it readable without 'parental discretion required' being needed on the copy. I appreciate your help, Mike. Can I depend on it by, say, the twentieth, a week today?"

"Okay. I'll do it on my laptop and email it to you for sure by then."

"Great. Oh yeah. Here's one about your favorite country. 'How do the French defend France? No one knows, it's never been tried.'"

Shant laughed. "And here's one right back at you. I heard this from one of the ground troop vets who was active in the '03 Iraq war. 'Notice to France: If you don't declare war now, you won't be able to surrender later.'"

"Great. I knew you'd appreciate mine. Yours was on the cutting edge. I think most people now are sick of France's posturing, especially when it repeatedly has to be rescued by the very countries it ridicules as war mongers. An article in a national weekly that crossed my desk recently reported that France and the French are the most disliked places and people. Even the Eiffel Tower can't redeem them any longer. Okay, I've got to run. And needless to say I look forward to your physical presence in this sunny city, amigo. Take care. I'll watch for the email."

"See you soon, kiddo." Shant hung up. He pulled out his black pocket secretary, inserted the password, and entered his new assignment on his calendar. The deadline wasn't a problem. The Quebec nonsense was one of his writing hobby horses and he'd be able to write the article cold, without needing any additional research.

"Those frogs are a royal pain in the ass," he told Sam who was nearby opening a can of Corona for a poker slot customer, "but they sure add to my income." Sam looked up, familiar with Shant's comments which made no sense to him, and shrugged his shoulders good naturedly. He wished that all his customers were so agreeable.

Shant returned to the race book. The final GG race was over and the results posted on the board. His horse hadn't won but it had come second, so his place bet really had been a saver. It paid $11.50 for each $2 bet, so he cashed in $1437, a reasonable return for his total $500 investment.

Certainly enough to buy a drink for Pap and himself. He headed into the casino to find his friend.

CHAPTER 5

"Hey, you guys, open the door. Can't you see I've got my hands full?"

Lennie swung open the door. "How can we see anything when the door's closed, Hector? And what are you bringing us a bicycle carrier for?"

"Because this fucking carrier is stuffed full with mail for you guys." Hector Gibson was the manager of the Dreamland Motel, just a couple of short blocks from the Golden Future Casino. He had been a pretty bad light-heavyweight boxer for too many years, and all that pounding hadn't helped already fuzzy mental abilities.

"Well, if you're bearing gifts, come on in, Hec. Here, give me that carrier." He took it, and handed it off to Pedro who had just shuffled out of the one bedroom in his ratty housecoat. "Here, hombre, some more dedicated fans are contacting us by the ever reliable US Postal Service. Want a beer, Hector? I know Sleepy here does."

"Okay, Lennie. Just one though, I gotta do some yard work today. Say, how come you guys are getting all this mail? And addressed to these companies too? What gives? Are you guys up to something scammy?"

58

"Here's your beer, Hec. Relax, sit down for a minute. Naw, we're not up to anything off color. Pedro and me are just developing a couple of ideas for some friends who have these companies back east. They wanted to sort of test some advertising ideas, so we agreed to help them. For a little cash, of course." Pedro smiled, and took a beer himself. "Cheers, Hec. First one since the last one."

"Well, okay, just so long as there ain't nothing illegal, immoral, or fattening going on in here in the Dreamland. I've gotta take care of its reputation, remember."

"Sure, its rep. That's worth protecting." Lennie grinned. Reputation as what? A hot bed, cheap dump? Yeah, that would be about it.

"I gotta get going, guys. Thanks for the beer. See you later." Hector left, clutching the half full can. Motel management didn't pay all that much.

"Let's check the incoming, Pedro. How much do you guess is here?"

"Well, there's sure more mail than yesterday, so I'd guess, ah, maybe $1500."

"Hey, Pedro, yesterday we had about a grand, and today there's far more. My guess is $3000. I'm sure there's about 350 letters here."

"Okay, Lennie, you're on for a drink. Let's start opening the mail."

"Sure. And what a break for us, Pedro. Because this dump motel is right on the corner of two streets, we can use both streets as addresses. That means we can get Pacific Advertising Associates on Fremont, and our famous Research Institute on 5th. And all for $25 a night for this hotbed heaven. Some of the sheets actually look singed from all the screwing they've been part of."

Half an hour later the carrier's contents had been ripped open. One pile held names and addresses of customers, often on ruled scraps of paper. Another pile held $1 bills. Other piles held $5 and $10 bills.

"Well, who is closest?"

"Quiet, Pedro, let me finish counting." Lennie thumbed through the last few $5 bills, made a note on a paper, then drew a line and totaled the columns.

He looked up with a smile. "You owe me a drink, my friend. A big one. There's exactly $2990 here. A few people just put in sawbucks instead of $9, so we're averaging a little over $9 a pop. I'm a lot closer than you are."

Pedro whooped with delight. "That's fucking great, partner. It looks like our deal is really going to go. Let's head down to the Golden Future and have a drink. Several drinks. And we can really piss Sam off when we ask him to change this bundle."

"Not yet, Pedro. We have business to take care of first. Remember, we're big time executives now. We have to work at least an hour before we start boozing."

"Okay. What do we have to executive?"

"Executive is a noun, Pedro, not a verb. You got to practice your English if you want to pass as an American."

"Okay, okay. I'll practice so much no one won't ever know I came from south of the border. But never mind that. What do we got to decide?"

"Most important, Pedro, we need a slogan. We been using 'Lose weight quickly without work', but that's not really a good one. Now that it looks like we got ourselves a real winner here, we should sharpen up our pitch."

"Sure. Lemme think on it. What do you suggest?"

Lennie squinted his eyes; he thought it made him look intellectual. "When I was sleeping, Pedro, I had a brainstorm. Something using sleeping and how easy it would be to lose weight at the same time you're sleeping. You know, to show how easy it is with our fantastic 'no fad' diet. All those fatties out there, especially the broads with thighs that look like they belong on an elephant, don't want to actually do anything to lose weight. They're too busy snacking twenty times a day."

Lennie reached for another beer.

"So here's my brainstorm, partner." He paused to build the suspense.

"Okay, fatties, here's your chance to 'Lose weight while you sleep!'" He struck a Mussolini-type pose.

"That's terrific, Lennie! I like that. It's short, and sweet, and it really tells what we're selling. Fantastic!"

Lennie smiled appreciatively. "I thought you'd like it, Pedro. We can start using it right away on the new classified ads we're going to send today. And as soon as we can get that artist guy, what's his name, Switzer, to draw some new layouts, we can change our display ads to show this new headline. I think it'll really help pull in all the fatties who want to drop some flab without any effort."

"And of course that's what our fantastic no-fad diet will do for them, right?" Pedro laughed.

"Okay, that takes care of one of our executive jobs, Pedro. I been thinking, and if this scam really rolls out, we might have a blockbuster on our hands. So we should do a little planning for in case that happens."

"I thought this deal we're now doing was the whole deal," Pedro said. "You mean there's more?"

"Well, partner, if it continues to boom, maybe we should take a look at franchising this idea."

"What the fuck is franchising?"

"It's a kind of way of doing business, Pedro. You know, like McDonald's."

"I know what McDonald's is, Lennie, but what's that got to do with franchising."

"Okay, Pedro, I'll try to explain it simply. Say you had a good business idea." Lennie thought for a minute. "Here's a better example of franchising.

"You used to be a catholic, right?"

61

"Yeah, before I smartened up."

"The catholic church is a great example of franchising, Pedro. It's not just the religious part, a hundred other churches got the same thing. But what do the Catholics offer that's unique?"

"A lot of virgins?"

"Be serious. Pedro. What their specialty is is forgiveness. You can be a killer, a child molester, a terrorist, whatever. All you have to do is visit some fag in a robe who says he forgives all your sins. So presto. You can start on Monday doing the same crap, killing people, molesting kids, knowing that come next Sunday your friendly priestly homo is going to let you off the hook. That forgiveness angle is what makes the catholic church unique, and what makes it such a fantastic franchise idea."

"You mean that having a special thing, a unique thing, lets you franchise?"

"Exactly! When the Catholic Church first started, it was just one of a bunch of similar zealots. Because humans are naturally nervous about what if anything comes after death, they are real suckers for creation stories. You know, the story that after death a fantastic paradise will open up, and you'll exist for ever after as some kind of angel, floating around the sky. No body, no booze, no screwing, nothing, but still it's called paradise."

"It does sound pretty stupid, when you put it like that," Pedro said.

"Of course it is. Can you imagine anything more boring than eternity with all your relatives going back a whole bunch of years? But anyway, the creation myth meets a popular need, the need to believe that there's something better after this life which for most people is goddamned miserable. And getting back to the Catholic Church, the early guys looked around for something to make their deal stand out from the competition. Some wise guy thought up confession and forgiveness, and hey, they were away to the races. That spiel worked well, especially with people who weren't too smart. That's why the Catholics were so successful in places like France, Spain, and all the new world countries where the level of intelligence at that time was pretty low."

Lennie went to the small fridge and grabbed two beers. He threw one to Pedro and opened the other.

"The key, Pedro, is that unique thing. The Catholics have forgiveness, what do we have?"

Pedro looked at his beer can.

"What we have, old buddy, is an easy, foolproof way to lose that flab all the fatties are lugging around. None of those porkers wants to work at losing weight. They just want some magic genie to cut it off painlessly and easily.

"So our 'Lose Weight While You Sleep' is such a great unique slogan. The fatties can continue on with their slob eating habits, knowing all the while that once they go to sleep, just like the Catholics' forgiveness, everything will be eliminated and they can start over gorging when they wake up."

"Lennie, that's the most fantastic idea you've ever had." Pedro's face lit up like a child's face on Christmas morning. "We'll clean up!"

"We will. Now we have some work to do. We have to keep our ads running. The more ads we have out, Pedro, the more fatties we're going to pull in. I'll get busy on printing up some more insertion orders from this list of magazines I copied at the library."

"We use the Pacific Advertising Associates to place the ads, right?"

"Yeah. And that's where the second street address is perfect. Magazines and newspapers today are skeptical of post office boxes, even 'suites' which everybody now knows probably just means a box in a private mailbox store. So being able to use two legitimate street addresses makes getting our ads accepted, and on the cuff, a lot easier."

"What if some magazine phones up to check?"

"That's why we set up that telephone answering service downtown. Those broads take all our calls, and they say that the list of names we provided are all out, or in conference, or something. Today no one expects a phone call to go through. It's just leave your number and I'll get back to you. Telephone tag, it's called. And once we get a few more bucks we'll get some cell phones and use those numbers as well. Every company wheel has his own cell phone and of course answers it personally. The old days of having some secretary do that are gone, and no one expects it. So with our cells we'll be as good as General Motors."

"Do you think any magazines will accept those full page ads you had that commercial artist draw up for us?"

"That $300 we spent on Gary Switzer's artwork will make us a bundle, Pedro. Of course the mags will accept those ads. A full page ad on average with the mags we selected probably averages seven or eight thou, maybe more. If that space isn't sold in one issue, it's wasted. That's why the media will take almost anything. Gary's full and half page ads are professional, so is our advertising space insertion order, and our addresses and phones are covered. Sure we'll get those ads in, amigo. And when they appear, hold on to your tacos. I predict the fatties will deliver the bucks in fine style."

"I sure hope so, Lennie. It would be great to have a real winner for a change. I'm tired of all those two bit schemes we wasted a lot of our time on."

"Speaking of wasting time, how be you get busy on that miracle diet we're selling? Remember, besides our super slogan, part of our pitch is that 'no fad diets' are involved. So to keep things legal, and to stave off the inevitable bitching when the porkers find that we're not giving them a miraculous no-effort secret, make up our diet using sound nutrition ideas. You're a pretty good cook, Pedro, so just design a one-week diet plan that will lose weight if it's followed. Keep it as simple as possible. Maybe like a typical Mexican diet. Basically good food with not too much fat. Use those diet books we got at the library to help you decide on portions and stuff."

"I'll do my best. We want enough for a week, right?"

"Yeah. Then you can just repeat that week for a full month, maybe making a few small changes. That will be enough. We'll print up the recipes, along with a cover that Switzer can do for us, and we'll run off a bunch at a fast copy store. If demand grows like I think it will, we can have a commercial printer make up what we need. Besides that all we need are some mailing envelopes with our Research Institute name and address printed, and some mailing labels we can run off here on the computer printer."

"Okay. You're going to work on some insertion orders?"

"Yes. I'll try and do another 15 or 20 on the comp, then fax them off through our computer fax. That'll make about 50 we've got out. I almost forgot, remind me later to pick up those imprinted pencils I ordered at Ziggy's Imprints on Fremont. I thought they'd be funny things to pass out at the bar."

***

"See the odds up there on the big screen, Linda? Those odds numbers change every 30 seconds, and are based on all the money bet, right at Golden Gate and at all the off-track locations and online betting sites."

"Who sets the odds? The race track?"

"No. Unlike all casino games, horseracing odds are determined solely by the bettors. When I make a bet, I'm betting against all the other bettors, not the house like in a casino. The track takes a percentage of the total amount bet, usually from 16 to 20 percent or so, although on exotic bets it can go much higher."

"Exotic bets?"

"Simply a term for anything other than win, place, or show bets. It includes daily doubles, quinellas, exactas, trifectas, and the lottery-type pick three and six."

Linda looked at the odds board. "So the track takes a percentage off the top. For what?"

"That money is used to cover everything: purses for the winning horses, maintenance of the track and grandstands, advertising, and profit to the track shareholders. The reason I like thoroughbred betting is that you can beat the game. You're pitting your knowledge and handicapping skills against other bettors, not a predetermined casino edge as in craps or roulette.

"Of course that doesn't mean I win every race, or even every day, or, unfortunately, every week. But over the long run I can expect to come out ahead. For example, yesterday I had a real good day betting. But today, now that I'm showing off for you, I'll likely be a loser."

She smiled. "You mean I'm bad luck."

"No." He patted her behind. "Absolutely not."

"Okay, so now that I'm a trained handicapper, what do I bet on in the first race?"

"The race is a cheap claiming race for a price of $8,000 for 4 year old horses. That means males, females would be identified as fillies, or mares if over 5 years. The horses in it, seven of them as you can see from the list of names, won't be in great shape. Most will be on a downward spiral, and many will be older horses, perhaps 7 or even 8 or 9 years old. That's old for a racehorse. Not necessarily over the hill but not likely to improve much either, so this level of race is close to the bottom.

"To pick a winner here I'd look for a horse that has been away from racing, a layoff, for a couple of months or more. That might mean the horse is physically screwed up, and he will be a loser. But enough times it will mean the owner or the trainer has given the horse a needed rest, and the horse may now have enough renewed stamina to leave the other clunkers behind."

"Any such potentials in race one, oh professional advisor?"

"Looking in the Racing Form, we can see that horse number six has been off for about four months. See that line over top of all his races? That shows a layoff. No other horse has had a layoff. This horse's trainer is winning his races at a nice 18%, and the jock at 17%. Not spectacular figures for either, but certainly high enough figs to confirm they're pros, not hobbyists."

"You're recommending number six?"

"You got it, kiddo."

"How much do I have to bet? And what do I say?"

"Minimum bet is $2, or any amount above. When you go to the window, just say '$2 to win on number six in the first race at Golden Gate'. The seller will punch out a ticket and give it to you."

"I want to live dangerously. I'm going to bet $10. If I blow my bankroll will you lend me bus fare home?"

"Perhaps. I'll have to think about that. Meanwhile, the minutes-to-post notice up there shows 2. You'd better get your bet down. I'll go with you."

"You mean you have the courage of your convictions? I didn't know advisors actually acted on the advice they gave."

Shant laughed. "Well, this one does. Let's move."

"Number six's jockey has such pretty colors. Is that a good sign?"

"Only if you believe that all females are virgins until marriage."

"Heavens! You mean some aren't?"

***

"Whoopee! My first bet and it won. How much do I get?"

"Number six closed at 7 to 1, so each $2 ticket will pay about $16; you get your bet back plus the odds. You bet $10 so you had five $2 tickets. You'll get $80."

"Hey, this beats doing research. With my newfound wealth I'll buy you a drink." Linda waved at a waitress.

"Save your money. All drinks in the race book are comps, free. But the girls always appreciate a tip."

"I'm learning something every minute. Do you have any other skills besides picking horse winners? If you want me to get started on that overnight success research I've got to get a furnished apartment here in Vegas for a couple of weeks. I phoned Dorothy Smithers before and she said she had a unit all ready to move in, so I think I'll take it. It's near Sahara and Paradise on the east side so it's handy to the Strip and downtown. In fact, if you're not too busy looking at horses, maybe you'd like to give me a lift? Dorothy said the apartment had a nice big king size bed. Perhaps you'd lend me more of your vast experience? You could test it and tell me how it stacks up in the comfortable bed department."

Shant grinned. "I'm not too sure about my vast experience, but I'd be happy to give you a lift over there. If you wanted me to check out some of your furniture, I'm pretty sure that could be arranged."

"Okay, cowboy. Let's get going. As my dear mother used to say, 'More doing. Less talking.'"

***

"Somebody's at the door, Pedro. Can you get it? I'm still counting this money we got yesterday. I thought Tuesday would be a quiet day for mail but it sure wasn't. Maybe Wednesday will be the slow time."

Pedro opened the door and bumped into a garbage can.

"What the fuck is this? We get home delivery on garbage now?"

Hector the motel manager popped up from behind the can. "Yeah, you do. This may be garbage to me, Pedro, but it's US mail to you."

"Why'd you put it in a garbage can, Hector? Couldn't you just carry the mail over?"

"That's what I did, Pedro. The fucking can is full of your mail."

"Full? You mean the garbage can's full of mail?"

"How many different ways can I say it? Yeah, the can is full to the top with letters addressed to that Institute name you gave me. Do you want it, or should I just move it down to the garbage pickup area?"

Pedro burst out laughing and reached out to grab the can by its handle. "Okay, Hec, I'll take it. How about a beer for your effort?"

"Thanks, but I have to do some stuff. Maybe later?"

"Absofuckinglutely, amigo. Whenever you're free just drop in. You're always welcome." He pulled the can inside and shut the door.

"Lennie, can you believe this?" He upended the can and a torrent of letters poured out onto the threadbare carpet. "There's hundreds here, Lennie! Maybe thousands. We're rich."

"Looks like it, Pedro. Why don't you start opening that stuff up while I finish counting yesterday's haul? I'm afraid there's going to be too much to cash in at Dominick's bar. Too bad. That was a lot of fun, seeing him trying to figure out where we got all the cash. But with this Niagara of cash we'll have to start using a regular bank. Probably open an account in the Institute's name, in case any of the fatties start sending checks or money orders. So far we've been lucky that everybody figures it isn't worth screwing around with that kind of stuff when they're buying something for a price under ten bucks."

"I'm sure there are thousands of envelopes here, Lennie. I saw an ad one time for a letter opener thing. You just put a pile of envelopes into it, pressed a button, and it slitted open each letter. I'm going to run over to an office supply store and get one. Ripping all these suckers open by hand will take forever."

"Good idea. While you're there pick up a bunch of those things you stick on fingers to make counting bills easier. You know, like the broads in banks use. They're made of rubber I think."

"I know what you mean. When I was a kid some older kids showed me some and said they were for guys with small dicks. You know, like a condom. They said they just fit over the heads and the broads really got off on all the ribbed sections."

"Right. Now that we've had our daily sex advice session could you get on your horse?"

"Okay, okay. Get started on this new mountain of mail if you're done before I get back. See you soon."

Pedro left. Lennie looked at the mess of mail spread out on the motel room's floor.

"Keep this up, fatties, and it's Acapulco, here we come!"

CHAPTER 6

"Did you invite Harry Jukes?"

"He wasn't in the bar, but I told Dom to tell him when he saw him. He said he would. And Dom is also getting a few of the waitresses, the big titted ones, to come over for awhile."

"I'm sure you specified big titted broads, Pedro. Did you know that sometimes broads with small boobs are actually better lays?"

"Maybe so, but I like something to grab onto while I'm busy screwing. With small tits there's no handholds."

"And you picked up the imprinted pencils? We can give them out at the party."

"He finally had them ready. About two days later than promised. Here. They look pretty good." He threw a pencil to Lennie.

"They do. That Northwest Research Institute looks pretty snazzy, and that crest or whatever the fuck it is looks authentic. Your buddy did a good job. That crest makes the company look like it's been around for a long time."

"I saw Mike Shant and Pap in the race book at the Golden Future. They both said they'd be glad to come. They even asked if they could bring anything, but I said everything was taken care of. I guess they're not used to seeing us this flush."

"It is sorta nice to have the bucks to lay on a good party. Monday through Friday's mail we brought in about 28 grand, Pedro. Even knocking off say 3 thou for overhead, getting the diet booklets printed up, postage, and some envelopes and stuff, we're ahead over 25 big ones. And that doesn't even include today's mail, which old friend Hector should be lugging over pretty soon. I invited him to the party. It's important to keep on his good side. Some asshole motel managers would be skittish about all this mail coming, especially to a name like NWRI."

"You're right, Lennie. Hec may not be the sharpest guy, but he's sure treating us nicely. Maybe we should slip him a few bucks?"

"Not until after the party today, and not just a payoff. Make it for something definite. How about giving him fifty for, uh, for mail security, for making sure all mail for us is kept safe and secure."

"Sounds good. I'll do it tomorrow, or more likely Monday."

"I'm not sure we've got enough booze. Most broads like vodka and we've only got six bottles. And three of bourbon probably won't last. I'm going to run down to Al's Liquor and get some more. Do we need anything else?"

"I guess some more snack junk would be a good idea. We can order in Chinese later on, but we should have lots of snacks until then. Maybe some jars of olives and onions?"

"Good idea, Pedro. I'll pick up a bunch of stuff. Al delivers so if it's too bulky I'll do that. I better take more money. I've only got a couple of hundred."

Pedro reached out to the money piles, grabbed a thick one, and passed it over.

"Don't forget to get a receipt," he laughed. "We'll need it when we file our NWRI tax returns."

"Right. When we file from Rio de Janeiro. Maybe you could get this cash rounded up. I've got an empty suitcase in the closet. Use that and stash it away. We want to be proper hosts for this party, but let's not encourage our guests, especially the broads we don't know, to take samples home with them."

***

"Have another tequila, Mike. It's my native drink. It's made from a cactus plant. Did you know that?" Pedro slurred his words slightly but was standing erect near the fridge. The one bedroom motel was crowded with the even dozen people. Several of the casino waitresses were sitting on the sofa, which Lennie or Pedro used as a bed on alternate weeks, the other getting the real bed in the bedroom. Shant was standing in the entryway to the bedroom, talking animatedly to Dominick, the Golden Future bar manager, about the merits of pouring booze into a glass before the mix.

"No, no, Mike, it's best to pour the mix first. That way the booze floats on the top, and the customer thinks he's getting a bigger shot."

Lennie and a busty waitress were squeezed into a corner of the front room near the TV set.

"I really like your clothes, Lennie. Everyone in the bar says what good taste you have."

"You wanna have a taste of me now?" Lennie leered at her, indicating with his eyes what part of his anatomy he thought would be the best place to start.

"Not right now," Sally laughed. "But I do have a personal question. All the girls waitressing have wondered. You have so much hair on your head. Is it a wig?"

Lennie laughed. "Feel it. Pull it. But not too hard, Sally. No, it's real hair, and it's all mine. All my family has great hair. When my dad died, at 89, he had as much hair as I do now."

"You're really lucky. Most guys nowadays seem to be bald. Even real young guys. Like in their twenties."

"And my pubic hair is just as thick. How be we go into the bedroom and you could check it out."

"There's already somebody in there, Lennie." Sally peered into the bedroom. "It's Harry Jukes, your bar buddy. Looks like he's checking Myra's chest. Maybe he's a TB doctor."

Pap was sitting on the edge of the sofa, with his left arm around Gloria, undoubtedly the waitress with the biggest bust.

"Yeah, I been a photographer for a lotta years, Gloria. Been in a lotta different places, cities, countries, whatever, and I've taken pictures of a lotta people. But I have to be honest and say that your body is as attractive as any I've seen."

"Thank you, kind sir. Do you just mean my big tits?"

"Certainly them, too, but your whole body. I've seen you walk in the bar, and you've got a feline grace. You move like a big cat. Very sensual, very provocative. And more than just big boobs, I assure you. You are," he paused to take a healthy drink of something the color of mud, "ah, that's good bourbon, you are, Gloria, the very ultimate in a female. Very, very sexy."

"And what are you planning to do with all this sexy body? A great body, Pap, is only really great when it's being used for something. Or were all those nice compliments just professional photographer talk?"

"Not at all. If there was some place reasonably private I would strongly suggest we immediately start using that great body of yours in a constructive, two-person way. But alas. At the moment privacy is a rare commodity. But perhaps we could arrange to continue this stimulating and certainly erotic conversation at a later time, and in more congenial surroundings?"

"That would be nice, Pap. Just name the time and place. Here"—she scribbled her number on a coaster—"for when you want it."

***

"So what's it all really about, Lennie? I don't really believe that lottery win crap."

"Well, maybe not exactly a lottery win, Mike, but something close. I've been running scams and deals almost since the day I walked into this great land of free enterprise and opportunity way back in the 90's, and I have to say this deal is the best I've ever had. The cash is rolling in like a tide, and before it stops I, and Pedro too of course, should have enough bucks to quit this business and go legit. Maybe buy a saloon or something. Pedro's thinking about a legal brothel, maybe just outside the Vegas city limits."

"He'd have to go out beyond Clark County. Inside it prostitution isn't legal. The city fathers don't want people wasting time screwing when they could be gambling."

"Whatever, Mike. I'll fill you in on this sweet deal but let's wait until we're somewhere more private. I don't want some of these guests to learn too much about it. They're liable to want in or even start their own and that could fuck things up. Sometimes even Pedro is a problem. He likes to share his good fortune with the world and that's not a good idea."

***

"Hey, folks, here's Dickie DiBonio. Welcome to the one an' oney Golden Future race book boss." Pedro was slurring a little. "Come on in, Dickie, and have a drink."

"My name is Richard, and unlike some of us I didn't have to change my name." He scowled at Pedro.

Pedro "the Toro" Gutie had once been Pedro Gutierrez. When he had crossed into the U.S. after leaving forever his drafty peasant shack outside Guadalajara, Jalisco, the birthplace of the mariachis, he had ignored the official border crossing at Nogales in favor of the wide open spaces to the right, where there was no one to ask embarrassing questions about immigration documents. As soon as he had arrived in Las Vegas he had decided to change his obviously Mexican surname to one he felt was truly American, and he became Mr. Gutie, from parts unknown.

Because of his natural exuberance, all his friends, and some not so friendly like DiBonio, knew his story. He had a lot of unknown company in his adopted land. Estimates of "undocumented" people in Arizona, Nevada, and California alone exceeded eight million. Many thought that estimate was far short of the actual total. Because of those numbers individuals like Pedro had little to worry about from Immigration agents unless they worked in high visibility jobs. As Pedro had never had a real job in his life he had even fewer worries than the average illegal immigrant.

"Okay, Rickie, I'll call you whatever you want. Come and have a drink anyway."

"Fucking wetback asshole," DiBonio muttered as Pedro grabbed his arm and pulled him over to the makeshift bar. "If there was a reward I'd turn you in to the INS."

"Simmer down, sport. You're at a party. Try to enjoy yourself." Pap didn't like DiBonio but didn't want his two favorite con men's party spoiled.

"I understand you two yahoos are in the chips. What's going on?"

"Well, Dickie, it's sort of hard to explain." Lennie delighted in using the name DiBonio detested. "Actually it involves a unique type of high international finance." He took a healthy drink, and winked at Shant who happened to be standing close. "Let's see if I can explain it simply.

"We arrange with small basically impoverished foreign governments to purchase their entire stocks of new currency. Not the stuff in circulation, you understand, just the bills hot off the printing presses. Clear so far?"

"Keep going, buddy. I can understand anything you have to say." DiBonio's lips curled in what he thought was disdain; it looked more like an attack of heartburn.

"Okay, Dickie. Once the new bills have been purchased, we have them shipped to our currency rendering plant in the Argentine mountains. There, under the most absolute secrecy, with entrance only by fingerprint matching machines, the bills are immersed in a solution of sodium chloride and after shave solution."

"What? What the fuck does that do?"

"The particular combination of liquids does something really special, Dickie. One, it sanitizes all the currency, so all marks and fingerprints from previous handling are totally removed. Two, it gives all the bills a unique smell."

DiBonio's face registered a mixture of disbelief and uncertainty.

"What is the fucking point of after shave smelling currency?"

"After we ship the currency back to the impoverished small country, our job is done. We collect a healthy fee, and that's where our sudden riches are coming from."

DiBonio looked puzzled. "What does the small country get out of it?"

"Why, Dickie, it's obvious. If you were a citizen in a small impoverished country, you probably wouldn't see too much currency. And think of how pleasant it would be, if when you did manage to handle a few bills, they all smelled nicely of aftershave. Wouldn't that make your day?"

Several bystanders burst out laughing. DiBonio's face darkened. "You asshole. I should have known you couldn't tell the truth about anything. I guess all you Hungarian jerkoffs, or wherever you came from, are all assholes."

"It was actually Poland, Dickie, a country that was eating off silver plates when you wops were sitting on the floor eating pizza made of horse droppings and pig turds." He smiled. "Anyway, you wops have progressed nicely. Now you sit in chairs to eat your pizza. Have a drink, Dickie."

Lennie turned away and started talking to Shant. DiBonio looked around for a friendly face, found none, and did go to the bar and drink a very healthy bourbon shot.

"We're getting low on vodka and bourbon, Lennie. I'm going to go and get some more. Anything else we need?"

"Maybe some more snack things, Pedro. When you get back we'll have our grand pyramid pencil burning."

"Great. Make sure you wait for me."

***

Lennie went into the bedroom. Harry Jukes was pulling up his pants.

"You want seconds, Lennie? She's really good." On the bed the girl smiled at Lennie.

"Not right now. I just came in to get something." He pushed the curtain aside and reached into the closet, picking up a large cardboard box on the top shelf.

"When you guys get dressed come on out. We're going to have a pencil ceremony."

"What's that?" asked the girl. "Some kind of weird sex thing?" She looked interested.

Lennie laughed. "Not really. Come and see what it is."

78

***

Throwing the empty bottles into a garbage basket, Pedro cleared the end of the bar table. He took the box from Lennie and ripped off the lid.

"Listen, everybody." Lennie stood on a chair to get attention.

"First, due to the fantastic success of our most recent business idea, we're presenting each person here today with a permanent, highly useful, long lasting memento of this glorious occasion. Guard your gift well, maybe even put it away to pass on to your favorite heirs."

"What is it, Lennie? Something worth a lot?" The young waitress from the casino was impressed with Lennie's spiel.

"Maybe not in actual dollars, sweet cheeks, but in sentimental value, in remembrance of this event, and in memory of an important part of Pedro's homeland, we're today using these unique implements to construct, then destroy by man's worst enemy, fire, a pyramid like all the pyramids built by the ancient Aztecs, Mixtecs, and General Mixups. Here, everyone, here is our special gift to you."

Lennie passed the box to Pedro, who began handing out the contents.

"Pencils!" screamed one of the waitresses. "They're just pencils." She started laughing.

"But special pencils," Pedro grinned. "These pencils are crafted by poor Mexican natives in their remote mountain towns, and flown here by chartered jet specially for this occasion."

Lennie grabbed a handful of pencils and formed them into a rough pyramid shape.

"And just as the Aztecs used to burn all their young maidens, which was a hell of a waste, we today are going to burn these priceless mementoes of this grand fiesta, to make the fire gods happy. Pedro, as a former Mexican, do the honors."

79

Pedro opened his lighter and held it by the side of the pyramid. After a few seconds the wood caught fire and then the whole pyramid flamed as the paint coated pencils burned hotly.

"Okay, everybody, bow your heads and repeat after me, 'To the gire fods, no, no, to the fire gods.' And good riddance too." Pedro fell back onto the sofa, his 98 pound frame bouncing off Gloria's breasts.

"Wooee! What a party." And Pedro passed out happy.

CHAPTER 7

"Hey, Lennie. There's someone at the door for some kind of Institute." Harry Jukes slopped his drink as he turned.

"Oh shit." Lennie had just retorched the smoldering pyramid to burn the few remaining pencils. "Okay, I'll get it. He pushed through the crowd at the counter bar, opened the door and stepped out. He was face to stomach with a man who must have weighed over 300 pounds.

"I'm looking for the Northwest Research Institute, but obviously I have the wrong address. Do you happen to know where their offices are?"

Lennie knew instantly that this was either a customer or prospect from the Lose Weight ad campaign.

"No, this is the correct temporary address. We're just in the process of moving to our new building downtown, we'll have the top three floors. And this is sort of a going away party for several employees who are moving to Seattle to join our Head Office there." Even Lennie thought his impromptu spiel as unconvincing as a tanned Eskimo but he plowed on. "These temporary quarters were used to conserve company capital. We wanted to save money so we could pour more into research..."

The door opened and Gloria staggered out, her bare tits preceding her.

"Hey Lennie, Pedro says I must have had a boob job. Come in and tell him these are the real things, my mother gave them to me as a birthday present." She laughed.

The obese customer or prospect grew red in the face. "This is obviously a racket or something else criminal. I came here all the way from Long Beach California because of your ads in Healthwise magazine, expecting a reputable research institute. I can see it's anything but. I'm going to the police." He walked quickly to a taxi which was parked in the next unit's stall, pulled open the back door, and squeezed his body inside. The taxi left with a squeal of tires.

"Jesus H Christ. Now the shit has really hit the fan." Lennie put his arm around Gloria's shoulder and pushed her gently back into the motel. "Pedro, get sober damned quick. We have a problemo."

***

Forty minutes later the last of the partiers had been hustled into taxis. The garbage can usually devoted to incoming mail was pressed into service for the burned pencils, empty bottles, and two pairs of women's panties. "Someone either wore a double pair, or else two broads had the same idea," Pedro groaned as he helped Lennie move the can and dump it in the large motel bin.

"Probably both," Lennie said, realizing he wasn't making much sense, "either that or..."

He gave up on that elusive thought as a black and white police car rolled into the motel parking area. He could see the chubby Long Beach fan in the back seat.

82

"That's the man I spoke with," Long Beach said to the driver who had also exited the car. "He obviously is part of this swindle, and I want him arrested." He was pointing directly at Lennie.

The second cop, not much over six feet, also got out, stretched his legs. "Let's go inside where it's more private, and try to see what's happening," he said. Lennie had seen him off duty a couple of times in the Golden Future Race Book. That was a good sign, he felt. Anyone who played the horses couldn't be a total prick as most cops were.

The Long Beach prospect—he hadn't yet become a customer—had plopped himself down on the sofa, which smelled strongly of bourbon, vodka (it does have a smell, Lennie noted), and assorted junk food remnants ground into the cheap fabric.

Neither cop had shown any interest in sitting beside Porky, as Pedro had already silently named him. They both wandered around the room, checking the swarm of glasses in the sink, the obviously used bed in the bedroom (another smell to add to this repertoire, Lennie realized) but neither seemed unduly upset at the wild accusations being hurled at Lennie by Long Beach. They hadn't yet even taken out handcuffs, rubber hoses, let alone ticket books, and Pedro was slightly miffed at the lack of "Law and Order" dramatic action.

"Okay, let's sort this mess out," said the horseplaying cop. Lennie vowed to buy him a drink the next time he saw him at the race book; he seemed to view the Long Beach's complaints with some skepticism.

"I relied on this so-called Institute's national advertising in medical journals," Long Beach said. "That's fraud or something. And they used testimonials from people they claimed to have helped lose, er, trim their bodies of excess weight. That's got to be against the law."

The friendly cop turned to Lennie. "Haven't I see you somewhere?"

Lennie didn't want to embarrass the cop. "Yes, on Fremont Street, at the Thoroughbred investment shop."

The cop grinned. "Yeah, that's where." He turned to Long Beach. "Anything to do with commercial promises, or business-type claims in general, are civil matters, not criminal. What specifically are you charging here?"

Long Beach began a long and dreary account of his reaction to the ad he had seen, its effect on him ("my weight problem is hereditary, not of my own doing" he claimed unconvincingly), his reliance on the testimonials in that ad, and on and on. Both cops now looked bored and Lennie decided to go on the offensive.

"Those testimonials are 100 percent accurate. I'll just take my associate Peter (Pedro smiled at his anglicized name change) and retrieve a couple of them. Because of our forthcoming office move they are in temporary storage in the basement. Peter, bring that list of files with you." He pointed to the file box which held their corporate stationery and miscellaneous office supplies. "We'll be right back just as soon as we've located the testimonials file folder."

With Pedro he moved out the door before anyone could disagree. The cops both stood, looking bored as Long Beach continued his lengthy and increasingly incoherent tirade.

"You've got to write a couple of testimonials very fucking quickly, Pedro. Here, I'll jot down what you should say. Use any address that comes to mind, make them out of town, better yet out of state, maybe even one from your homeland. Use two different pens and change your handwriting just like you did when we ran that Nigerian lottery scam."

Lennie grabbed two sheets of paper and scrawled a few sentences onto each and handed them to Pedro. "You stay and do them, I'll go back and try to confuse Long Beach even more. Bring

84

them over—fold them and muss the paper a little so they look authentic, not hot off the press—as soon as you can."

***

Back in the motel the two cops were now looking irritated. Long Beach had talked for almost 20 minutes without a pause. Each time a cop tried to say something he just raised his voice to offer a fresh complaint.

When Pedro/Peter reappeared, they looked relieved at the interruption.

"You accused us of not having valid testimonials. Well, in spite of the fact that we're in the process of moving our offices, and everything has been put into temp storage, here are just two of the many, many glowing testimonials we have received for our weight loss plan." Pedro handed the two sheets to Lennie, who immediately started to read from the first.

"This one is from a John Fauntelroy (Pedro had a fondness for what he thought were typical English names) of New York City. He says, and I quote, 'By using your copyrited (Pedro's spelling was not that great) no-fad diet materials I was able to get rid of 73 pounds of fat and general flab that I had put on over the years from eating fast food junk. (Long Beach at least blushed at that.) I can recommend your valyouable (Pedro!) product to everyone in the world.' And it's clearly signed, as you can see here," Lennie flashed the letter for three seconds, "by Mr. Fauntelboy (Jesus Christ, Pedro!)." No one reacted to the spontaneous name change by the New York customer.

"And the second letter, from a Miss Angel Biggies (I'm going to throttle you, Pedro!) of Guadalajara in our friendly neighbor, Mexico. She writes, in her own sweet feminine hand" (this time the letter's exposure to the three man audience was

85

under two seconds) "about our no-fad diet, that 'before I weighed over 200 pounds, mostly ugly sloppy fat (again Long Beach blushed) and I didn't have no (Pedro!) friends. But then I bought your no-fat material and I lost 120 pounds, so now I am just 90 pounds (he gave up on mentally castigating Pedro; no one seemed to care about the glaring errors) and am very popular with many men friends, many of whom treat me like a queen.' And here's her authentic signature, in pretty purple ink."

Before anyone objected Lennie folded the letters and placed them in the file box, gave it to Pedro/Peter and moved his eyes to indicate the box should be moved to secure basement storage. P/P got the message and left with it immediately.

There was a moment of silence. Long Beach's tirade had almost put both cops to sleep and they seemed disinclined to do anything, even to talk. Finally the racehorse cop struggled back to consciousness.

"Well, Mr., ah, sir, what we have here looks like a civil matter, a disagreement or misunderstanding or something similar. There's really nothing the police can do. If you want to proceed with your complaints, I'd advise you to maybe get a local lawyer and see what he advises."

Lennie vowed to make that cop's drink a double. Long Beach protested but the cops held firm. Whatever the problem was, if one even existed, they implied, it was not their problem, and the outsider from California—California!—would have to take his problem somewhere else.

Twenty minutes later the cops and Long Beach had gone, and Lennie and Pedro collapsed onto the sofa whose remaining springs had so recently been insulted by Long Beach.

"That was great thinking, Lennie. You really are the best."

"At least on a par with Miss Angel Biggies, I hope. Don't ever have kids, Pedro. I hate to think what names you might give them."

"I'd name them after you, partner. Lennie 1, Lennie 2, Lennie 3..."

"Okay. Thanks a lot. Now let's forget our corporate troubles and get drunk again."

CHAPTER 8

"I wonder what those two assholes are plotting. Probably something I should be aware of." DiBonio was making one of his casino 'tours of inspection'. He had always been impressed by military terminology and used it whenever possible in his job, causing all employees no end of merriment at his expense.

At the moment he was watching Lennie and Pedro, alone at the end of the bar, laughing uproariously. What to do? He reached a hand to scratch his head, then quickly stopped it. His toupee was in place but he didn't want to take any chances. He'd bought it from an acquaintance who assured him that it was top of the line, quality designed to last a lifetime. Yeah, the lifetime of a fruit fly, he thought. Goddamned piece of crap. But he wasn't about to shell out the grand or two the casino stores asked for a custom fitted hairpiece, so he stuck with the "Made in Somalia" he had. He felt it was a reasonable fit. Everyone he knew thought it looked less stable than that movie actor so-called he-man, whatever his name was.

The men's washroom was on the other side of the wall where Lennie and Pedro were sitting. Maybe he could lean against it from the can side and pick up something.

Luckily the can was empty. He put his ear against the wall.

"Christ, Pedro, when those cops busted in I thought the scam was fucked. And that fatty from Long Beach. If we charged him a buck a pound for every pound we showed him how to lose we'd be rich."

"You mean with our super no-fad diet? What a gem that is. It took me about five or six hours in the library—you should see the library lady they got there, tits big enough to sit on—and we got a fantastico diet which all the porkers in the country are willing—hell, happy—to give us nine bucks for. What a great idea we had this time, Lennie."

"Actually, amigo, the idea was mine. But you did research and write that diet, so, okay, 'we' did strike it rich this time."

The washroom door opened, and a half drunk local boozer staggered in, looked at DiBonio with his ear against the wall.

"What the fuck are you doing? Too drunk to stand up? I know where you're coming from. And hey, buddy, your rug looks like it's going to fall off."

DiBonio straightened up and assumed what he thought was a commanding look. "I'm just checking the wall here for termites. If you listen close you can hear them moving around."

"Oh yeah? Well, listen close and you'll hear me pissing." The drunk chortled, pulled out his dick, and succeeded only in pissing half onto his already soiled shoes. He made an attempt to re-zip his fly, gave up when the zipper caught on something, grinned at DiBonio, wiggled his hand aloft to remind him of the slipping rug, and exited after bouncing off the doorframe twice.

"Fucking drunks. We shouldn't even serve them." But he knew that if the casino started screening out Fremont Street drunks their bar business would plummet. He tugged at his toupee and leaned against the wall.

"...I thought you were out of your mind when you started talking about testimonials, Lennie. I mean, we both knew we didn't have a single fucking one of them. Luckily that one cop you knew a little seemed to be more pissed off with the Long Beach whale than with what we were doing."

"Yeah, a lot of cops, after seeing the shitbox we were operating from, especially after that pencil burning party, would've said, 'Hey, hold on here. You're going to get some stuff from storage? Okay, I'll go along just to make sure you don't get lost. And then it would have been impossible for you to use your literary skills to create a couple of masterpieces. But I do wish you'd either learn to spell, Pedro, or remember what names you're using. Or better yet, both. But those cops were so bored and pissed off with Tubby from everyone's favorite state of California—what a cesspool!—that all they wanted was to get rid of Lardo and get back to their doughnuts. Lucky for us. And luckier yet that I'd seen the cop at the race book and didn't blow his upstanding citizen role with Gordo before he realized the guy was just a creep anyway."

"How much we take in so far, Lennie?"

"I haven't done today's mail yet, but yesterday we had 363 letters, all with at least nine, a bunch with 10, bucks in them, so that came to $3514. And as we were leaving our mailman-security chief buddy Hector told me he was going to have to use two garbage cans today, so likely we hit at least 500, maybe more, fish bites. That'll make it close to five grand. That's for one day, partner, and the take is zooming each day. At a rough guess I'd say we'll be grossing well over a hundred big ones—thous, amigo, not centuries—each month. Multiply that by 12 months, Pedro, and we're definitely in the million dollar class."

The washroom door opened again. A tourist wearing a blazing Hawaiian sport shirt and mid-thigh shorts which highlighted his skinny legs, looked at DiBonio very suspiciously.

"Fuck you too," DiBonio said, getting the first shot in. He'd heard enough anyway. More than enough. Lennie and Pedro, both of them burned out grifters who in total couldn't put together half his intelligence, were running a weight loss scam which was paying off big time. More than a mill a year! With the proper setup, and some financial backing from the mob, this could be DiBonio's ticket to stardom.

When the Golden Sands casino had opened, about the time Sinatra was still on the mob's payroll at the Sands, no one in the Fremont Street downtown area really knew much about casino games, race books, or even how to charge for drinks. DiBonio had then been operating for several years as a street bookie, taking dollar bets from winos and busted gamblers and running a book himself. Most of the bets were on football games, boxing matches, or highly publicized horse races. He was good at figures, and by consistently giving unfair payoff odds to his customers when they occasionally stumbled onto a winner, he was able to grind out a meager profit. Fremont Street then, aside from Binion's joint which always had been a haven for big betting gamblers, was little more than a handful of sawdust on the floor drinking saloons, with the odd roulette layout and a few 21 tables, along with banks of nickel and quarter slots with handles. When the eastern mob bosses, nearly all of whom were illiterate, and aside from a few like Meyer Lansky unable to understand even the simplest odds or percentage problem, decided to set up shop in the desert town of Las Vegas, they had no one who knew anything about organized gambling. Their people back east were number runners—how much brains did it take to make a profit by selling 999 numbers each day and paying off at only 400 or even 500?— and leg breakers. Guys like DiBonio, with all his faults, were needed, and so he was able to move into mob-run casinos as a part of "management".

DiBonio figured that some day, especially if he was able to get a real profitable scam or racket going, he'd be invited into the mob organization. But even with the right ethnic name the chances of that were on a par with his street customers getting a straight shake.

This deal, he thought, would be his door opener. Show the bosses how to set up and run the scam, maybe even keep Lennie on to do the work—Pedro was a write-off—and he'd have it made. He would be made, he smiled, a made man. The Promised Land!

He headed to his cubbyhole office, detoured through the race book to see how the handicappers were doing. He hated the bastards, sitting there with their goddamned Racing Forms and calculators, figuring out which horse in the fifth would finish first. And he especially hated it when one of them would pick a winner who went off at great odds because few other bettors liked it. Even though the race book, unlike all the casino table games, made its money as a percentage on the amount of money bet, and didn't win or lose on any bets, DiBonio disliked paying out $980 on a $20 win bet which went off at 48 to 1.

He saw Shant leaving the payoff cashier's window with what looked like a roll. That prick! He was one of the worst, making just two or three bets a day, but often winning one of them at horrendous odds so that he was way ahead.

"Hey, Shant. Glad to see you're winning. Hit a longshot?"

"Sort of, Dickie. Had the exacta at Turf Paradise in the sixth. Paid about three for $20."

"Three hundred?"

"Three thou. Both win and place were longs."

You fucking lucky prick. I hope you get rolled. And calling me Dickie. When I get this weight scam rolling you'll change your tune. "Way to go, Shant. I'll buy you a drink later, but now I've got a meeting." That's what they said on TV, got a meeting. Did have a nice military ring to it.

"Sure thing, Dickie. Catch you later."

Dickie again! Well, asshole, you'll see. But now to more important matters.

CHAPTER 9

"You're sure of that? These two dummies are doing over a mill a year already?"

"Yeah, I overheard them talking. They didn't know I was here, and that's exactly what Lennie, he's the brains of that pair, Pedro's just a worker, said they'd be doing. Well over a mill, in fact, about a mill two."

Solly Cantafio moved his chair back from the scarred desk in DiBonio's office, grunted contentedly as his paunch now had a little room, and turned to his lieutenant, Ramming Ray Costello, so named after he eliminated competitors in Detroit by ramming their cars with a specially reinforced pickup truck.

"Whaddya think, Ray?" The boss was a democrat, and liked to get the views of subordinates. Besides, it was good if things went bad, he could always lay the blame on them.

"It's sorta different than what we normally do, Solly, but I been noticing all the stuff on TV and even in mags and the papers about losing weight. Seems to be a real popular issue now, so maybe it would be good. Besides, it would help us spread out a little from gambling and sharking. The competition's getting tough in both areas. Some of the legal pawn

94

shops are so profitable they're even on the stock market now."

"Yes, that's it exactly. Diversify. That's the trend now." DiBonio was excited. He had one of the top bosses actually in his office, listening to his pitch for a lose weight operation.

"When I want your opinion I'll give it to you." Cantafio might be a democrat but he sure didn't extend that to hired help like this jerk DiBonio. "Ray, how much green up front to get going?"

Ray hesitated. He knew that any figure he might give, even as the roughest guesstimate, would be remembered by his boss and used against him if it didn't materialize.

"It's tough, Solly. I don't have no experience in this kind of deal. But based on what Dickie here tells us, we could get going with just a few thou, maybe 10 or so. Is that right, Dickie?" Never hurt to get others involved, he could always blame the underling for any problems.

"Yes, sure, say 20 big ones would get everything going. All we need is an office, maybe a good looking broad as front, and some advertising to rope in the suckers. How much can ads cost? A couple of grand each should cover even the bigger magazines and papers. And I got the feeling from those two assholes, well, Lennie is okay" (he planned to bring him in to do the actual work, so he didn't want to badmouth him too much) "that maybe they were going to stiff some of the bills. We could do that too, just set up a cheapo company and then fold it. Or if you didn't want to do that, for public relations kind of, then there would still be lots of cash to pay off."

Cantafio pulled out a Cuban cigar, unwrapped it, and waited for Ray to light it. Usually he smoked dollar stogies, but the boys back home had jacked a truckload of illegally imported Cubans, so now he smoked the best. He inhaled, blew a lopsided ring, and looked at DiBonio.

"Okay, say we decide to go ahead. I might give you—and Ray here, he'd be in charge—say 15 grand to start, with maybe a little more if needed. Really needed, not so you can wine and bang that broad who's the front. But there's always downsides to any deal. What're they here?" He looked at DiBonio.

"Well, I honestly can't think of any big problemos. Maybe we'd need to hire another broad or even two to actually do, uh, the work, you know, like I hear Lennie say that they were getting over 500 letters a day, and more than that coming, so we'd need somebody to open the letters, take out the money, and take cash and checks to the bank." Solly cleared his throat and DiBonio hurried on. "That's if, you know, we wanted to use a bank. Maybe just keep the cash and chuck the other stuff? Lennie said almost all of the money was cash, yokels even sending in a sawbuck for the diet they charged only nine bucks for. And of course we could raise that price. Say we increased it to fifteen or so. Right away that increases gross to maybe a mill point six or seven, even maybe two mill. And..."

"Never mind all that maybe bullshit. I ain't interested in maybes. Right now I'm interested in those problemos you said earlier. Ray, Whaddya think?"

"I can't see too many holes, Solly." DiBonio's spirits rose like an impotent's hard-on. "But (down went the erection) there could be some confusion maybe with these local jerkoffs. If they was to keep running their scam, two things. First, they maybe cut into our take. And second, and most important, whenever you get amateurs screwing around in something they likely bring heat, and that is always a problemo." He looked at DiBonio. "So maybe we should do some cleaning of the competition before we get really rolling."

"That's good thinking, Ray. Whaddya suggest?"

"I always think the easiest answer is maybe the best. How be we get one of these scammers, maybe the dumbest one—Pedro?—in here and DiBonio and me have a little talk with him? Maybe like we could convince him to return to his native land or something. If we could do that, maybe we could actually use the other guy, the smarter one, to help us get started. After we got it down acey deucy we could like pension him off."

Solly dragged on the Cuban, tried to blow a ring, and choked on the attempt.

"Godddamned spicks can't even make a decent cigar. We should a taken that asshole Castro out and choked him on tacos or whatever those greasers eat." He cleared his throat.

"Yeah, I think that's a good plan, Ray. So DiBonio, you'll get the asshole partner in here for a little talk with Ray. And you too, because remember this is your idea, and I'll be holding you on the spot for it."

DiBonio had an instant vision of what concrete shoes would feel like, but replaced that nightmare with piles of envelopes stuffed with sawbucks and fins cascading over his head, and mob soldiers looking up to Randy Richard as a made man.

"Well Dickie, whaddya say we get started? You get ahold of Pedro the wetback. Have him here in this shitbox of a office tonight, say about 10. This dump is as good a place as any to have our little interview."

"Sure, Ray. I'll get right on it. And I just wanna say, Solly, that I'm real pleased that you guys are going to run with my idea..."

"And I'm real pleased you're pleased, DiBonio. Now cut the fuckin' horseshit and get moving."

***

"So here's the deal, Pedro. I represent a big company back east and we're interested in expanding like into Vegas and your little weight scam has come to our attention. We think it has some small chance of making money and we're ready to buy you out."

"That's really thrilling, Ray. But I ain't least bit interested in selling out. Especially not to anything that has Dickie here as part of it. I wouldn't sell him my used rubber."

"Yeah, well, your likes and dislikes really ain't the subject here, Pedro. And they ain't of any interest either. When I said we was interested in buying you out, what I meant was like you are selling out. Now. You can take our offer, or."

"Or what?"

"There ain't no or. That was just what you call a, a, imaginary question like. You wouldn't understand, because you ain't a real American, and I know how little school time you greasers get. Now here's the offer. First and last one. I give you five hundred and you take a little trip to visit your dear old momma and poppa down south. Stay awhile. Like maybe a year or so."

Pedro looked at Ray, then at DiBonio. He straightened his 98 pound frame. "I may have been born on April first, but that don't make me no fool. That is the shittiest offer I ever heard. Even if you added three zeroes to it my answer would be the same. Go fuck yourself. Better yet, fuck DiBonio there up the ass. Just hold on to his rug if you don't wanna be fucking a bald head."

"I'm a little disappointed in you, Pedro. Here I make a very reasonable offer and all you do is insult my associate Dickie here."

Ramming Ray lit a cigarette and looked at DiBonio.

"Whaddya think, Dickie? Is our greaser friend here taking things seriously enough?"

"All those wetbacks are the same." DiBonio was really pissed off the way everyone was using his hated nickname. "They all sneak into this country, then go on welfare with their dozen or more kids. Fucking is about all they seem to be good for..."

"All that's very interesting, Dickie. But what about a answer to my fucking question?"

"You mean was this midget here taking us seriously? Of course the answer's no, he ain't."

"That's too bad. Pedro, my boy, you'd better consider my offer again, or else I'm gonna hafta take some unpleasant measures here."

"My answer's the same. Fuck yourself."

"Ah, that's too bad. Well, Dickie, what's to do?"

"Listen, you little spick. You take our deal or tomorrow I contact the INS. They'll be down and throw your ass back across the border faster'n you can say dos tacos."

"You really think I'm worried about the Immigration guys? Shit, they'd bounce me out at Nogales and I'd be back in at Tijuana sooner than the five seconds it takes you to comb your three remaining hairs."

"Okay." Ray moved to the door, opened it, and signaled to two hulks drinking beer nearby. "Tony, you guys get in here." They moved quickly into the now crowded office.

"Tony, this here runt is Pedro. We made a top offer to him but he can't seem to understand how good it is. Pedro, this's Tony Wagnessi. Him and his buddy here are what you might call convincers. When some jerk doesn't know when he's well off, or that he got a good deal from us, then Tony here talks to him gently and convinces him to see the light. Tony, the spotlight's all yours."

Wagnessi, well over six feet and about 270 pounds, moved next to Pedro.

"Well, little fellow, I guess the next move is mine." He backhanded Pedro across the face, knocking him backwards into the rusted file cabinet which was DiBonio's sole claim to office furniture. There was blood on Pedro's mouth.

"Fuck you too, you goddamned gorilla. It's gonna take more than some rough stuff from a moron like you to change my mind."

"Moron? Okay, asshole, let's get down to business." Ray knew that Tony's mental abilities, or lack thereof, were sensitive areas. His next move showed his anger.

Wagnessi grabbed Pedro by the hair, lifted him up, and then slammed him down onto his outstretched leg. Pedro grunted in pain, then passed out.

"Shit, I didn't say kill him, Tony. How the fuck can I talk to him when you KO him?"

"I don't like being insulted by any prick, and sure not a greaser like this. I didn't hurt him that much. He'll be back with us soon."

"I hope so." Ray pointed at the other thug. "Claude, you wait outside the office. It's too damned crowded in here. If Tony needs help we'll call you."

"I ain't gonna need no help with this dwarf. As soon as he comes back just tell me what you want him to do, or say, and that's what he'll do."

***

"Look, asshole, I can keep doin' this all night. Can you?" Wagnessi's forearms were spotted with blood. Pedro's left eye was closed, two teeth dangled by roots, his left leg looked permanently bent at an unusual angle, and his shirt and pants were coated with blood.

Pedro muffled another groan, shook and pulled out one of the hanging teeth. "I've known muscle-bound bullies like you all my life," he said. "You try to make up in punching what you obviously lack in brains. Go fuck yourself, stupid."

"Jesus Christ, Ray. My arms are getting tired. Can't I just finish this wetback off for good."

"Sure you can, Tony. Then all you have to do is go see Solly and tell him what you done."

"Okay, okay. But do you want me to keep punching this jerk?"

"Not right now. I'm as tired of this as you are, Tony. Pedro, you are one lucky Mex. If I didn't have things I gotta do right now me and Tony would keep using you for an exercise bag.

"But keep this in mind, greaser. The offer I made is our final offer. There ain't no other offer coming down the road. So I'm gonna give you a little time to think it over, and then we'll be back to get your formal acceptance." He laughed. "You like them words, Tony? Formal acceptance. Sounds pretty good, right? I always wanted to use them some time, and now's the time. So you've bought a little time here, Paco. But come manana we're gonna be back to have another meeting with you. And if you thought this one was fun, wait until the next one. I'll have both Tony and his pal Claude talk with you, and there won't be no next time. That meet will be it."

He opened the office door and motioned to Claude who was leaning against a pool table.

"Claude, get over here. You and Tony take Pedro out and throw him in the garbage bin at the back. Those smells will help him think of home sweet home, which is where he's going pretty quick."

He turned to Pedro, blood now dripping from his mouth where his teeth used to be. "See you later, amigo. Better get your shopping bag packed with all your possessions. You're taking a trip down south real soon. Real soon."

CHAPTER 10

Solly was not happy. He threw his toughest glare at Ray and Tony.

"What the fuck's the problem here, Ray? I tell you to do a simple job on a skinny little pipsqueak, and you come back and say you couldn't do it. What kinda bullshit is that?"

"Solly, I didn't really fuck up. It's just that the guy, that wetback Pedro, is so small that I was afraid Tony here would break his neck and off him before we got a signed thing from him.

"But don't worry, Solly, today we're really gonna lean on that prick."

"Get somethin' straight, Ray. I ain't worried. That ain't my job here. My job is to like make sure guys like you and Tony worry. Got that straight?"

"Sure, Solly, sure. I didn't mean no disrespect or nothing. I was just like joking, you know, trying to bring a little fun into this deal."

"If I wanted fun I would a phoned Bob Hope to come over and make me some fun."

"Bob Hope's dead, Solly, you couldn't a phoned him..."

Solly's glare froze Ray. "I know he's dead, Ray. And maybe he'll have some company pretty quick, if certain parties keeping fuckin' around stead a doing their jobs."

Ray's face whitened with strain. He nodded at Solly, jerked his head at Tony, and both left the room.

"Christ, Ray, you was taking a chance trying to joke around with Solly. Everybody knows he ain't got no sense a humor at all."

"Yeah, yeah. Can it, Tony. I know Solly better than you ever will. I was just being, like, palsy with him. But one thing's for sure. We got to lean on that Pedro prick and get him on the next bus to TJ.

"Call Claude on his cell and have him pick Pedro up. Tell him to meet us at that cabin we use sometimes out about five miles on the road to Pahrump. Tell him to make sure that the other guy, his name's Lennie, doesn't come along. The boss said to lay off him. At least for now."

***

"So we start again, greaser. But this time it's a little different. There ain't no next time this time, prick. You remember the offer? Good, so that'll speed things up a bit. And you'll prob'ly notice that this time we have both of these big gentlemen with us. You remember Tony, I'm sure, and this other guy is Claude. His specialty is moving bones to where they ain't supposed to be. In fact he did that so successfully one time that some fag judge said he had to have free state room and board for 4 years."

Pedro's eye was almost closed and his mouth still looked battered but he still shook his head when Ray asked him to accept the offer.

"Well, now, that's really too bad. But luckily we're out here in the boonies where our party won't be interrupted, so I guess we'll just start off. Seeing you're already familiar with Tony, how be we start things off with cousin Claude?"

Claude picked Pedro up like he was lifting a marshmallow, shook him like a terrier shakes a rat, then hurled him clear across the one room shack. Pedro hit the opposite wall with a sickening crunch, then dropped to the floor. Claude was on him instantly, picked him up, and this time windmilled him above his head three times, then released him. Momentum smashed Pedro's body into a brick fireplace. He slid to the ground and lay motionless.

"Okie dokie, Tony, you have a turn." Claude aimed a satisfied look at Ray and grabbed a can of beer from the table.

"I guess I better wait until numb nuts there wakes up," Tony said. "Ain't no point in putting on a show if the guest ain't awake to appreciate it. Throw me a beer, Claude."

Ray was lost in his thoughts. He wondered how he could deke out that asshole DiBonio on this job, and take over to be in charge of the scam. He'd heard the jazz that DiBonio had used to sell the idea to Solly. If those figures were even close to the truth there's be a lot of loose cash floating around, and a smart guy like him should be able to peel off a bunch for himself. Then he could dress in style, maybe even get a hot convert, and really show both the broads and the bosses how cool a guy he really was.

Just a break. That's all he needed. Then he could put some space between himself and assholes like these two leg breakers here. By hanging around with them he was lowering his star with guys like Solly, who drew a solid line between hired muscle like Tony and Claude and guys who were smart enough to successfully run one of the mob's many businesses.

Yeah, he needed to move up. This deal could be just the answer. Get this Mex Pedro to take the offer, ship him outa town, and report back to Solly that he really handled the job, quickly and with no troubles. Shit, he might have to go through that asshole DiBonio. The bosses were sort of fanatic in that way, they expected the troops to follow channels, so he'd have to go along with that, at least until he could find a way to ease DiBonio out of this deal. Maybe out, period. Yeah, he grinned, that would be the best thing, find some way to get Dickie to put himself in a box with a lid so tight he couldn't wiggle it loose. Then he'd be the main man in the Golden Future casino. Hell, if he played it right, and he knew he could, he could end up as the Vegas kingpin, somebody who had respect. And the big bucks and broads that went with the job. And the cars...

"Hey, Ray, you ever going to answer that cell? It's been ringing like 10 minutes already."

Ray threw a frown at Tony and picked up his cell phone.

"What're you guys doing there? Having a fucking party when you're supposed to be on the job? This fucking phone has been ringing for half an hour." DiBonio sounded irritated.

Half an hour. Ten minutes. What a bunch of complete jerks. "No, nothing like that, Dickie. It's just we're having a little problem convincing our amigo Pedro that he should like take our good offer."

"Three guys and you can't do that? What're you doing, smacking him with a feather? Look, Solly was just on to me, and that means I'm on to you knuckleheads. Incidentally, Ray, my name is Richard. Kindly knock off with the Dickie. So when're you going to finish the job?"

Ray had held up the phone for the last bit and now he looked over at Tony, who looked at Claude, then back to Ray and shrugged his shoulders.

"It's sorta difficult to say exactly when, Di.. Richard," he said. "At the moment our star guest is taking a little snooze. Just as soon as we can get him wakened up again we'll really work on him.

"I think I can definitely promise you that we'll have him in the bag within a couple of hours."

"A couple of fucking hours! Solly said he wanted to hear back from me within the hour."

"Okay, okay. We'll put the pressure on. I'll give you a call just as quick as possible, within an hour anyway. You at your office number?"

"Where else would I be, when Solly's around? And pissed with you guys, I might add. So you better make sure I get that call no more than one hour from now. Got that?"

Fucking prick. How he would kick his ass out the door when he got control of the Golden Future. "Yeah, okay Richard. Call you soon." He pressed the disconnect button and threw the phone onto the table. "Richard! You're a Dickie, now and forever, asshole."

He walked over to where Pedro was slumped. He kicked at his legs but got no response. He bent over and slapped his face hard. Still nothing.

"That was some professional working job, Claude. This prick is still really out. And you heard me on the cell with Dickie—he wants us to call him Richard, can you imagine that shit?—and we have to have this thing cleared up within an hour. Evidently Solly's right there in the casino and he's getting a little upset. So this time, Tony, you do the job. Get him up and conscious, and let's get him to take the offer. Then we can put the greaser on a Greyhound to TJ, report back to Solly—fuck Dickie—that the job has been done right. Right?"

Tony nodded and grabbed Pedro by the hair, hauling the slight body upright. He shook it like a maid shakes a dust rag.

"Shit, he's really out. Claude, fill that bucket there with water and give it to me."

With the filled bucket on the table Tony pushed Pedro's head down into it until only the crown of his head was visible.

"There ain't no bubbles coming up," Claude said. "That ain't a good sign."

Ray pushed Claude aside and reached down to pull up Pedro's head. "Claude, grab that piece of mirror there over the fridge."

Ray held the mirror close to Pedro's nose, looked at it, then moved it down slightly over his mouth and looked again. He straightened up.

"God damn it to hell. You jerks have killed the fucking wetback. Whadda we do now?" He sat down hard on a kitchen chair.

Tony and Claude looked at each other, then both shrugged. What was the big problem, Tony thought? So one wetback gets offed. Big fuckin deal. This kind of thing happened alla time.

As if reading his thoughts, Ray said, "Usually this wouldn't be no problem. But Solly was pretty definite on this. He wanted this guy out of the picture in a kinda legal type way. And now he can't. So we're going to hafta cover our asses on this." He sat with eyes unfocused for a minute. "Okay, here's what we do.

"Everything happened just the way it did. When DiBonio phoned Pedro was just out, not dead. After the call, at DiBonio's orders, remember that, we was gonna put the pressure on but Pedro said he'd take the offer and sign a piece of paper, but first he started to puke, so we told him to do that outside. He looked like he was really in bad shape but after he was out there just a second or two the prick started to make a run for it. Claude, you chased him but he wouldn't quit and finally you had to chop him ina neck. But you hit him a little hard, he was such a scrawny punk, that he conked."

"Why do I have to be the bad guy?" Claude said.

"Why? Because you were the guy who creamed him, Claude. Can you remember doing that?"

"Yeah. I guess." Ray started to shout something. "Okay, Ray, I mean that story's okay."

***

"I know, Di... Richard. Claude didn't do it on purpose. The greaser was trying to run away and we, that is, Claude didn't have no choice. A normal guy would justa been dropped but the greaser was so scrawny that he popped."

"Solly will not be pleased, Ray. He was counting on getting Pedro outa the way without problems." His grip on the phone tightened.

"I know that, Richard." You weasel prick! "But we can't do nothing about it now. It's like they say. You know, what's past is dead."

"That's not the way it goes, Ray. It's what's past is past. Or something. Anyway, we'd better make the best of this. I'll dummy up a note Pedro left, showing he wanted to go back to his home in Mexico, and that he wanted outa the weight loss deal. That may satisfy Solly.

"But we can't have old Pedro floating around, so you guys take him off the highway there and plant him deep enough so he won't be found. Then make sure there's nothing of his in the cabin and after you guys can come back to Vegas. Even though you guys didn't really earn it I'll get Solly to okay a few bills for each of you."

A few bills! You cheap prick. Acting like it's your own money. You skim that much every day. "Sure thing, Dickie. See you later." Fuck Richard. He won't be around long enough for me to worry about what asshole name he wants to be called.

***

"So I cleared things up with DiBonio. I even insisted you guys get your regular pay in spite of the fuckup. So when you get back to Vegas you'll each be getting a couple of C's for your time.

"But first you gotta plant old Pedro so he can rest in peace. Claude, you get the honor of planting as you offed him. So Tony and me will take the Buick. There's a shovel in the Pontiac" (Ray could hardly wait until he got in the Lincoln or Caddie class; once DiBonio was out it wouldn't take him long) "so do a good job. This desert sand's easy to dig. Once you've done that we can hook up at the casino and have a drink."

"Why can't Tony help me?"

"Because I need to talk with him about some company business." (He had nothing to say to Tony, but Claude was hired help, he shouldn't be questioning his orders.)

"Claude, take off and get the stiff under. Tony, you and me will check this place for anything our friendly Mex may have left, then we're off to the big city."

***

"I thought you were going to bet Golden Gate today, Mike."

"I was, Pap, but the track conditions there are listed as sloppy, and I can't pick winners on an off track. San Fran's a nice city but they get too damned much rain. So I'm giving my business to Santa Anita. The city of angels is nice and sunny today."

"Any luck so far?"

"Nope. Had a place in the second—my first bet—but I had him on the nose. This mare in the fourth looks pretty good, though. Been off for almost a year. Her trainer's done that before and brought her up through weekly workouts the couple months before he raced her again, and she won by five lengths. He's following the same pattern so if the odds stay long—they're 15 to 1 now—I'll jump on her."

"Good luck, amigo. I'm going to have a late breakfast, then do a little touristo bit. Maybe walk down the Boulevard just like all the folks from Plum Creek, Iowa. I'll be back before Santa Anita ends, so

109

if you find anything good in the later races put on a sawbuck for me. I'll pay—or maybe collect from—you later."

***

After a short stroll down Las Vegas Boulevard, the well known "Strip", Pap got tired of playing dodge ball with the garishly dressed tourists and headed back north to Fremont Street. He decided to drop into the Golden Slipper for a change of pace. In the main bar he spotted Harry Jukes over at a corner table talking to one of the thugs that hung around DiBonio and his mob bosses. He decided not to join the table although he knew Jukes pretty well, mostly from the Golden Future casino.

Just finishing his Kahlua and coffee Pap saw the thug get up and leave. Jukes sat there, looking pissed off. Or depressed. Pap walked over and sat down.

"How're they hanging, Harry?"

Jukes looked up and nodded but said nothing.

"Something the matter? You look like you picked a 50 to 1 longshot but didn't bet him and he ran away from the field."

"Something like that, Pap. I just heard some shitty news. You knew Pedro, right, the Mexican who partnered with Lennie, that Polish guy."

"Sure I know Pedro, he's a buddy." He looked sharply at Jukes. "What do you mean, 'knew' him? Why the past tense?"

"That's the point, Pap. I just heard from, from a pretty good source, that Pedro's been snuffed. Out in the desert somewhere."

"Jesus Christ, Harry! Are you serious? I just saw him, last night, I guess, or earlier, at the Golden Future. What do you mean snuffed? You mean killed?"

"Yeah, that's what I hear. Murdered, I guess. Why I don't know but apparently he's definitely past tense. And that's a bummer. I didn't know the guy much, but he seemed like an okay guy."

"He was. Fuck! Who could a wanted to hurt Pedro? He never got mixed up with those mob creeps, never even talked to them as far as I know. How did you hear about it?"

"You know I can't say anything, Pap. I don't want to join Pedro."

"I saw you talking to the mob asshole, what's his name, Tony something, Wagner or something."

"It's Wagnessi, he's a dago like all the rest. Even if I heard it from him you know I can't say anything, Pap. And please do not say anything about this, or about talking with me. I already said too much. Don't put me on the spot, buddy. I'm not part of those guys, you know that, I just hang around and pick up a little small change doing odd jobs for them. But nothing heavy, and nothing more than running errands or getting them some broads. They wouldn't hesitate to take me for a ride in the desert if you told anyone about this. Pap, please give me your word on this. It's really important."

Pap paused. "Okay, Harry. This conversation's already forgotten. But that is really bad news. You're sure about it? Yeah, I guess you are. I've got to go. Does anyone else know about this or do I have to keep a lid on it?"

"As long as you don't involve me, it don't matter. I understand that a state highway cop noticed a fresh bunch of sand piled up just a few feet off the Pahrump road and stopped to have a look. He found Pedro's body buried under just a few inches of sand. So the news is official. Just please remember, you didn't hear nothing from me."

***

"Just in time, Pap. In the eighth at L A I had a real sleeper. A colt who hadn't won in 16 tries was in a maiden claimer with seven others who were even

111

worse, but he'd never been tried at the route distance, and all the others had. And in all those previous 16 races, whenever he got to within third or second, in sprints, he was always picking up on the race leaders, so I felt he showed promise for a first time mile distance. He hung back till the stretch, then his jock—that hot apprentice Billy Sharpels—put him in gear and he won driving by almost two lengths. Paid 22 to one, so your sawbuck made you just over two hundred. Here it is."

"Thanks, Mike, nice handicapping. And the money is always welcome."

"Then how come you look like your best friend died?"

"Well, he wasn't my best friend, but he was a friend, and one a yours too. Pedro."

"Is this a bad joke, Pap? We both saw Pedro, just yesterday I guess. What are you talking about?"

"I just heard from a guy, then I phoned our buddy Sandy Klook at the NHP, and he confirmed. Pedro's body, apparently with a broken neck, was found barely covered in a makeshift grave just off the Pahrump Highway. Some highway cop spotted it when he was cruising the road."

"Broken neck? As in accident?"

"Klook said they wouldn't know until after the autopsy, but based on the bruises all over his body they now figure Pedro was beaten up, then either accidentally or intentionally killed."

"By whom? Any suspects?"

"Just the usual, Sandy said. He thinks it was a mob hit. Apparently they use that Pahrump road a lot because it's so deserted, few tourists ever use it, and the locals are mainly early morning and late afternoon commuters into Vegas, so most of the time it's really empty. The road to Pahrump from Beatty off the Reno highway used to get a lot of action, Sandy said, but the Highway Patrol started cruising it more, so now the mob has moved over to the Pahrump strip."

"A mob hit? Pedro didn't have anything to do with those assholes. And that's what he thought they were, assholes. I heard him say that a bunch of times. But I don't think even mob jerkoffs go around killing people because they call them assholes."

"Neither do I, Mike. But they must have had some reason. And there's something else. The guy I heard about Pedro from, and before you ask I can't tell you who, because I promised him I'd keep his name out of it, and I'm sure that he had nothing to do with it, but he did get his info from that mob guy Tony Wagnessi. You remember, that big ox who's been hanging around here the last little while, especially with that other moron, Claude something, who looks like he failed grade two and dropped out forever. If his IQ beats 55 I'd be surprised."

"But it still doesn't make sense, that the mob would be interested enough in Pedro to whack him. That little guy never moved in their circles."

"I know, but that's what the cops figure, and it makes sense. Who else would get Pedro out into the desert, beat him up, kill him, and bury him? In a sloppy grave so that he was found far sooner than the killers wanted. And remember that Pedro, skinny little guy that he was, could take care of himself. To beat him up would take somebody a lot bigger. Someone like Wagnessi, for example."

CHAPTER 11

"C'mon, Lennie. Open the goddamned door. It's the police."

Lennie struggled awake and rolled off the sofa where he had crashed early this morning. It was Pedro's turn with the bed.

"Okay, okay, I'm coming."

He slipped the door bolt and opened it. Two Las Vegas uniforms and a guy in a suit stood there. "What time is it, and what do you guys want?"

"It's about time you got up. Why don't you get a respectable job, like us?"

"Sure, and start paying taxes and all the other fun things. Maybe tomorrow. You haven't told me what you want yet."

"Don't you know, Cichecki? Or are you just acting dumber than usual?"

"I resent that, occifer. And I don't have a clue why you boys in blue are rousting a respectable citizen at this ungodly hour."

The suit answered. "It's noon, for chrissake. And a respectable citizen? Where?"

"You're Dan Thorsen, aren't you? Last I heard you was with homicide. Did you get busted down to serving parking ticket summons, or whatever you're here for?"

114

"Yeah, I'm Thorsen, and still in homicide, Lenny. Where were you yesterday, from about one o'clock right through to midnight?"

Lennie paused in doing up his shoelaces and straightened up. "You're serious, ain't you? What I have to do with your department I haven't a clue. But for your information yesterday I spent most of the afternoon in the Golden Future casino bar. And after that I was with a friend. At her place. In fact I just rolled in here about an hour before you guys disturbed my slumber."

"Can anyone vouch for that alibi?"

"Alibi? What the fuck you mean alibi? I ain't done nothing to need an alibi."

"Never mind the editorial crap, Cichecki. Just give me a couple of names that can verify where you was."

"I still think this is bullshit, but if you're serious, Dom, the bar manager at the GF can confirm I was a paying guest at his crummy saloon all afternoon. As to the friend, I'd sorta prefer not to, she's got a regular long distance trucker boyfriend who's built like King Kong."

"Prefer not to or not, you'd better give us the broad's name. This is official homicide business."

"Who was homicided?"

"You show me yours, I'll show you mine."

"Okay. The lady was Julie Crandall, she lives in the Mountain Towers. Number 433. But I'd really appreciate if you'd see her at work, she deals 21 at the Riviera on the afternoon shift. Call her at home and King Kong's liable to be there."

"Yeah, I guess I can do that for such an upstanding citizen. I'll drop by after we finish here. She's a good looker?"

"Great T and A. Superb! And now you're up to the plate, officer. Who departed this vale of tears?"

"You really don't know, Lennie?"

"Haven't a clue. I wasn't able to check in and get the latest comedy news on that 24 hour so-called news channel that never shuts up or never says nothing useful either, for that matter."

"Well, I'm sorry to tell you, but it was Pedro Gutie, your..."

Lennie sat down heavily on the edge of the sofa. "Pedro! You're kidding."

"No, a Highway cop found his body last evening just off the Pahrump road, hardly buried in the sand. He'd been beaten pretty badly and his neck was broken."

Lennie sat there silently. After a full minute he sniffed loudly and coughed to cover it. Then he stood up and walked over to the open door where one of the uniforms looked questioningly at the suit. He shook his head.

Lennie turned to the homicide detective.

"Do you have any idea who did it?"

"At this point, no. But because of the location we think it was a mob hit, or at least something to do with them, they use that road a lot for quickie burials. But the crappy way it, he, was buried indicates if it was a mob kill then it was someone not very high up. It, the body, was barely covered, like the guy doing it was an amateur and in a hurry to get somewhere else.

"Lennie, can you think of any reason the mob would a been interested in Pedro?"

"There's no fucking way Pedro would have got mixed up with the mob. He thought they was all assholes and wouldn't even bullshit with the soldiers who sometimes drank at the Futures. I remember one time he was really busted, down on his luck, that was before we got together as sort of partners, and one of the Fremont Street wiseguys offered to loan him some cash. On the usual 20 percent vig a week, of course. But even though Pedro was literally down to eating at one of the soup kitchens, he knew that his luck at the slots would turn. He didn't want anything to do with them.

"No, there's absolutely no way that Pedro would have gotten in bed with anyone even remotely hooked up to the mob."

The suit closed the notebook he'd been jotting things in.

"I'm sorry about Pedro, Lennie. On the way here Jolson"—he indicated one of the uniforms—"told me you guys were pretty close, but there's a procedure to follow in murder cases so I had to do it. Assuming your alibis check out you're off our list of suspects."

"What about the mob? Will you follow up that angle?"

"Make book on it. In this town both the Chief and the Mayor are down on the mob and we have standing orders to do our damndest on any cases involving wise guys. There won't be any punches faked on this case, or any other mob case. With the apparent lack of evidence it may take a while, but we will get the people responsible."

***

About an hour later the phone rang in Lennie's motel unit.

"This is Sergeant Dan Thorsen, Lennie. We, more accurately you, got a problem. I talked with your friend Julie Crandall at the Riviera. She says she may have met you around town somewhere once or twice, but she says she definitely wasn't with you last night."

"Aw, fuck, Dan. She's just shining you on. I told you about that hulk of a boyfriend, she's prob'ly scared of what he would do if he found out she was sharing her very considerable assets with another guy. But take my word, I was with her all night, in fact from late afternoon right until just before you rousted me."

"Well, Lennie, the ball's in your court. Dom did confirm you were in his bar at the GF all

117

afternoon, although he's not sure when you left. He did say he saw you hitting pretty seriously on some broad just before he got busy and lost sight a you, but he couldn't confirm who the broad was. If I was you I'd have another talk with your friend and convince her that you really need her confirming your alibi, Lennie. Without it, you ain't got any alibi at all for all the time before and around when Pedro was killed; the ME says it was about nine when his neck was broken.

"I'm not going to pull you in right now, Lennie, because personally I don't think you were involved. But I'm just a cog here, and if nothing else breaks soon, and if you can't get friend Julie to go to bat for you, routine will mean we'll have to bring you in for at least a interrogation.

"So best you firm up that broad, Lennie. Or maybe get yourself a shyster."

***

"I know you're busy, Mike, and I ain't gonna lay out no 'old friends' crap, but I could use your help. I have a great alibi for when Pedro was killed, but unfortunately the lady in question won't give the good word to the cops. I think she's afraid of what her boyfriend might do, he takes about a size 20 shirt and I guess she's telling him he's her one and only."

"I'd like to help you, Lennie. I liked both Pedro and you, but what can I do? I'm a freelance writer, not a lawyer."

"I know that, Mike, it's just that you're pretty good at talking to people and you know the words to use. I get all screwed up when I try to sell an idea, especially if it's the truth; I'm more easy with some scam. I just thought maybe if you was to drop in at the Riviera this afternoon, and get my friend, her name's Julie Crandall, and she deals 21, to understand how important her confirming my alibi is. Dan Thorsen, the homicide sergeant handling the case, is a pretty good guy, and he said if Julie just confirmed the alibi he wouldn't have to even talk with her hulk boyfriend. But without that alibi Thorsen said I'm right at the top of his hot list, because I was sorta in business with Pedro and maybe had a reason to whack him, especially since we was both seen with some healthy bankrolls recently with this lose weight scam. As if I'd whack a friend for a few bucks. Or anyone, for christ's sake, I'm a scammer, not a fucking murderer."

"Yeah, I know that, Lennie. Okay, I'll cab up to the Riviera and see if I can get this Julie Crandall to talk with me on a coffee break. What about if this hulk boyfriend happens to be floating around? I don't relish talking about his girlfriend's romantic adventures with a guy who wears size 20 shirts."

"No problemo, Mike. When I was with her last night, she said he was on a haul to Chicago, and won't be back till the weekend."

***

"Julie? Would you happen to be Julie Crandall?"

"Right first time, handsome stranger. How'd you know my name?"

"From a friend of yours, and mine, Julie. Could I buy you a coffee or whatever on your next break? I just want to talk with you for a few minutes."

"Who's the friend?"

"Lennie."

Her face darkened. "You with the cops?"

"No way. I'm just a friend. But Pedro, the man who was murdered, was also a friend of mine, and I'm just trying to help Lennie so that the cops won't waste time on him, and will try to find the real killers."

"Look, I can't talk any more here. That prick pit boss is throwing me a stare. I get a break in about 15 minutes. I'll take that coffee in the coffee shop on the second floor, you know the place?"

"Yeah, that's great. And thanks in advance."

"I haven't done anything yet, whatever-your-name-is."

"It's Mike, Mike Shant. I'll see you upstairs, I'll get a booth."

***

"Look, Mike, I already told the cops that Lennie wasn't with me. I'm not trying to screw him, well, you know what I mean, but I just can't take the chance that Doug, my boyfriend, finds out. He's getting serious, and I'm sick and tired of dealing cards and having every tourist yokel bet a buck just so he can stare at my boobs."

"I already talked with Dan Thorsen, the homicide sergeant who's in charge of this case. He understands your situation, and he's already convinced that Lennie wasn't involved. All you have to do is drop down to the station, dictate a short statement confirming that Lennie was with you the whole time, and that's it. The statement will be put into the case file and probably never be seen again. But it will clear Lennie of any suspicion and let Thorsen stop wasting time and try to get a real lead."

"I'm not being a prick for the fun of it, Mike. It's just like I said downstairs, this boyfriend looks pretty serious and I think he's going to actually offer to make an honest woman of me." She smiled. "He's not the greatest catch, maybe, but you'd be surprised how few of those there are around. My life looks glamorous if you're from Small-town, Iowa, maybe, but it's not. I stand on my feet far too much; when I get older I'll probably have varicose veins big enough to chin yourself on. And every guy I meet is either married and just looking for a quick lay, or

120

else is already so screwed up with ex-wives and ex-girlfriends that I'd be number ten in line.

"So I'm really concerned that my little fling with Lennie doesn't get known. I'm not going to be wearing white if the current BF does pop the question, but I'm not an easy lay either. I've known Lennie on and off for a couple years, and he's always treated me right. So I feel real bad about screwing him up on this, but I just can't take the chance of my boyfriend finding out."

Shant sat and thought for a moment. His logical approach was obviously going nowhere. While he detested people who used threats to win arguments, he owed Lennie as a friend; he'd probably never see the lovely Julie again.

"I know exactly where you're coming from, Julie, and I sympathize with you. But on the one hand you have the very slight chance that your BF will find out you're not perfect, and on the other that Lennie, a friend, could be in serious police trouble. We all know from TV that someone proving he didn't do something is damned difficult."

He took a drink of coffee, signaled to the waitress for refills. "And there's a down side to not clearing Lennie now when it's quick and easy, Julie."

The waitress came with a coffee pot, refilled their cups and left.

"What's the down side?" She looked less friendly than she had a minute before.

"Well, if you don't clear Lennie now, what might happen? He can't prove he's innocent, the cops run into a wall and can't lasso any other suspects, and finally Lennie is actually charged with something, maybe even the big one, murder. What's his lawyer going to do? The first thing, I imagine, is to issue subpoenas to everyone involved who could help his client. Those kind of subpoenas are served anywhere, and if the people served don't show up they're immediately on a 'Find and Apprehend' list."

Shant hoped that Julie didn't know any more about the subpoena process than he did.

"So you're happy in some LA suburb, maybe even with a family started, and you're ordered to appear in a Vegas courtroom. No ifs or buts, just be there. Under oath Lennie's lawyer asks you about his alibi. Even if you deny he was with you, and that would be perjury, a pretty bad deal in itself, in a murder case he would be free to pry into every facet of your life, and could make you out to be, well, almost anything, because he would be trying to discredit you, and confirm Lennie's version, with the jury. To me that would be a helluva lot worse than taking a 10 minute trip to a police station now and signing some form which will probably never be seen again."

He drank his coffee and sat back. He'd given it his best shot, helped along by scattered memories as a kid watching Perry Mason do his legal tricks on TV.

"When you put it that way, stranger, it seems pretty clear. I guess I hadn't really thought it through. Okay, Mike, you can tell Lennie—and I hope he knows what a good friend you are—that I'll do the right thing. I'll buzz this Thorsen on my next break, and if it's OK I'll go down tomorrow before I start shoveling the cards to eager losers."

"That's great, Julie. I know Lennie will be happy. And on his behalf I throw you a big kiss."

"If I'd met you before I got hooked up with my traveling trucker, you could do a lot more than that, Mike. Like they say, life isn't fair."

CHAPTER 12

"How're the pix coming, Pap?"

"Everything is in my steady hands, and events are unrolling as the universe dictates."

"Does that mean that you have actually started taking some pix of the people I'm interviewing?"

"That's exactly what it means, Michael. I have photographed in all their glory the first four people on that list you gave me, have appointments set for the next three, and will finish up the rest by Tuesday, Wednesday at the latest. Incidentally, as you requested, I am taking about twice as many shots as I really need, just so that you and your friendly editor have plenty of choices."

"I'm impressed, Pap. I think that calls for a drink. On me, of course. Or more accurately, on my expense account."

"I accept and thank you, your expense account, and most of the western world."

Shant signaled to Marie, indicated two drinks. She nodded and went to the bar.

"Are you having any problems with these subjects, Pap? From my side they've all been pretty cooperative so far, actually overly friendly."

"Yeah, that's what I've found too, Mike. Whether it's just Vegas being turned on to free publicity, or whether these guys are abnormally friendly, I dunno, but they've all gone out of their ways to accommodate whatever posing instructions I gave, and most have asked if they could see some proofs for personal purchases. If they come through, I'll probably make as much on pix reprints as I'll get from you. Or the magazine, actually."

"Good for you, amigo. Glad you're able to double your fee. Capitalism at its finest."

Marie arrived with the drinks, Shant asked her to tab it, and Pap made the motion of patting her firm behind. "Only because you're a gentleman of senior years, Pap, do I let you fondle the merchandise. Anyone younger would get slapped," Marie said.

"Or dated," Shant laughed.

"Yes, that would be a distinct possibility," Marie agreed and left to serve another table.

The two men nursed their drinks for a moment.

"Pap, what's your reading on Pedro's killing? Do you think it was a mob, or at least a mob-related, murder?"

Pap lit one of his el cheapo cigars and blew out a noxious cloud of smoke. "It sure looks like it, Mike. Burying his body along the Pahrump road, which everyone over the age of 12 knows the mob uses as a cemetery, certainly smacks of a mob hit.

"On the other hand, almost anyone could do that to throw suspicion on the wise guys."

"Yeah, that's a point, Pap. But then again, who would want to hurt Pedro? He was a nice guy, never got involved in anything to do with the mob, and kept strictly to his scams, usually with Lennie, that had nothing to do with those people whose names end in vowels."

"But is that necessarily true, Mike? You know, I've heard street talk that this current losing weight scam that he and Lennie were running—remember that wild party with the pencil pyramid burning at their motel?—had somehow caught the eye of local wise guys. According to the gossip, one or two locals figured that Pedro and Lennie were making so much money, and showing it so publicly, like coming in here with literally bags of small bills for Sam or Dom to change in bigger bills, that it'd be worth their while to get in on the action."

Shant frowned at this new information.

"Any names attached to those mob guys, Pap?"

"Guess whose name keeps cropping up? Our old buddy Dickie DiBonio. I've heard that he's got a hard-on to show the mob oldies that he can do more than run this casino race book."

"Hard-on or not, Pap, Dickie hasn't got the balls to beat up and kill Pedro, even though he outweighed him by a bunch. DiBonio's a talker, not a doer."

"That's true. But consider this. We think of Dickie as a jerkoff, but he is manager of this book, and he is hooked into, even if just barely, the mob. That old time mobster Solly from the east has been floating around here for a couple of days. What about if DiBonio went to him, trying to get accepted further into the organization, and told them about Pedro and Lennie's new scam that was paying off big time? Isn't there a chance that Solly might give him the okay on at least a trial run?"

Shant nodded. "Sure, that's a possibility, Pap. But how do we get from there to Pedro's murder?"

"We have DiBonio talking to Solly, and Solly giving at least a lukewarm go ahead on the scam idea, right? So what would be next?"

Shant finished his drink, caught Marie's eye, and signaled two drinks.

"I guess that Solly, or whoever was in charge, would tell DiBonio to give him complete details on the scam, so he—Solly—could decide if it was worth doing on a bigger scale, maybe even back east or on the west coast."

"That's about what I figure too, Mike. And that means talking to Pedro, or Lennie, right?"

Before Shant could answer Marie put the two drinks on the table, made a point of aiming her behind in Pap's direction, smiled, and moved off.

"Yeah. And DiBonio would probably prefer Pedro. He's smaller and less sharp than Lennie. But good old Dickie wouldn't get involved himself, of course. He'd ask Solly for some muscle to do the Pedro 'interview'. And Pedro, being the stubborn, proud Mex he was, would tell the muscle boys to fuck off. That your reading, Pap?"

"Exactly. The muscle, either with DiBonio or alone, gets Pedro somewhere quiet, try to pump him, he refuses, the muscle gets pissed off, and either accidentally, or more like intentionally, breaks little Pedro's neck."

"Has your street gossip supplied any names of goons who might have been involved?"

Pap hesitated. "This info is really sketchy, Mike. But there have been a couple of hulks new on the local scene the past coupla days. The boss of the muscle crew appears to be a Chicago hood named Ramming Ray, so called because he evidently polished off people by literally ramming them with a truck. And he has a couple of goons with him, a Tony Wagnessi and a guy named Claude, no last name apparently. Both these guys are really bad news. Street talk has both them involved, indicted in a couple of cases, but never convicted, of murders back east. From what I hear all of these heavies could a been involved, and probably were. The way Pedro was apparently badly beaten, and had his neck broken, smacks of the way those assholes operate, strictly in the old school mob way of 'If you can't make 'em talk, kill 'em.' Not very sophisticated, but effective."

"Is this street talk sound enough to go to the cops, Pap?"

"Not a chance, Mike. Even if the guys I've talked to had pictures of Pedro's death, which they don't, they wouldn't talk to anyone in blue. They know they wouldn't last a day if they finked on mob guys, no matter how stupid those guys were. The mob would protect them then get rid of them themselves if they were a liability."

"So there's nothing we can do?"

"Legally, no. There is one small chance of getting some kind of payment for Pedro's death."

"And that is?" Shant asked.

"It's gonna sound a little flakey, Mike. But hear me out before you start laughing."

"Pap, you know I respect your opinion far too much to start laughing at what you say. Once you've said it, however, I'll probably collapse onto the floor in a laughing jag."

"Thanks a lot, buddy. Well, anyway, getting back to local street gossip, the word is that all three of these jerkoffs—Ramming Ray and his two muscle boys—are really hooked on weird sex parties. Not just a hooker at a ranch doing her usual suck and fuck, but heavy stuff. Young girls tied up and attacked by all three morons at the same time, that kind of crap."

"So we should line up some of this action for them and hope they fuck themselves to death?"

"Not quite, but in the ball park, Mike. Here's what I think we could do.

"None of these three guys is local so they aren't familiar with what's happening here in Nevada. You've probably heard me talk about that really crazy motorcycle bunch who have taken over the old ghost town northwest of Beatty, a couple of miles in from the Reno Highway?"

Shant nodded.

"That bunch is from hell. Really. Even the state cops won't go near the place unless they have armored cars and SWAT teams with them. The only reason that they're not actually attacked in force by the law is that they keep strictly to themselves. Any broads they have are derelicts from LA or San Fran, runaways or young hookers who nobody cares about. These guys go into Beatty to buy their grub and other supplies but they're on Sunday school behavior when they do. They don't even talk to locals. And they apparently have an out of state source for guns and ammo, of which cops say they have an arsenal like the National Guard. Some day the law will have to move against them, but everyone right now is acting like they don't exist."

"So there's a motorcycle gang from hell only a short way from Vegas. Pap, how does that help us avenge Pedro?"

"Remember what I said about these hoods' liking for weird sex stuff. How be we get them convinced that just outside Beatty is the hottest sex camp of young, fresh broads from LA, just waiting and eager to satisfy every perverted desire of our friendly eastern gangsters?"

Shant's eyes lit up. "You mean we sick them on the crazy motorcycle gang? Would that really work?"

"Here's the way I think it might play out, Mike. We paint a great wild sex picture for the eastern lads. Being the mobsters they are, we can be sure they won't even go to the can without all their artillery, right? So they drive out to Motorcycle Motel, nice and remote in the desert. The cycle mob welcomes them, especially if they have been pre-warned that a small party of three, loaded with guns they probably would like to add to their collection, is on the way to ravish their pet hookers. Three mobsters would pose no threat to 20 or even 30 bikers, all armed."

"That's absolutely Machiavellian, Pap. It's fantastic. Do you really think the hoods would get into the cycle camp?"

"I do, if, as I said, the cycle guys were aware that it was just three guys coming. Otherwise they might think it was a cop raid, and they'd start shooting too soon. But if the mobsters get in, I really feel the chances of them getting out alive are slim enough to cause a life insurance salesman a real dose of ulcers."

Shant smiled, then broke into a real belly laugh.

"That's the most fantastic plot I've ever heard of, Pap. And you know, it's just crazy enough to work. At worst the mobsters will get the shit kicked out of them. At best, they'll start a shootout at some point, and they, plus probably a few crazy bikers, will, just like in the old time western movies, bite the dust. How Pedro would have loved it, he would have chortled at the almost Mexican style of revenge."

"That's what I thought, Mike. Rough justice, maybe, but justice nevertheless."

"The only fly in that ointment, Pap, is that it takes care of the actual physical killers. But it doesn't even touch DiBonio, who from what you said was probably responsible for the whole thing."

"True, but remember, Mike, we don't know that Dickie was behind the plot. It sorta stands to reason that he is Mr. X, but we don't have any firm proof.

"What I think we should do, Mike, is proceed with the biker-mobster party plan. Meanwhile, I'll keep picking up what street gossip I can, and you do the same in the race book, you know some of those regular players there know more what's really going on here in Vegas than the vice squad dicks do.

"Then if, more likely when, we get some hard evidence tying friend Dickie to Pedro's death, we can work out something to see that he pays. Probably not a legal solution, because we can't go up against the mob, nor get anyone else in Vegas to do that, but maybe some variation of our party plan idea might work. Not the sex party bit, as I don't think DiBonio is so inclined, but something to grease his skids with the mob. They start viewing Dickie as a liability and his days are not only numbered, but ended."

"You should have been a mystery writer, Pap. You have a very devious, twisted mind. You probably could have written best sellers."

"Too much work. I like talking and drinking too much to sit down at a hot typewriter. Or computer these days, I guess."

"Yeah. Well, let's get the party underway. How do we actually do it?"

"We can't get involved even indirectly, Mike, or else we become possible targets in the mob's crosshairs. I'll plant the word about the crazy pussy camp with a couple of jerks I know. They're usually so doped up they'll immediately forget who told them. But they're on the far fringes of the mob, and if I know them, and I do, they'll try to turn their hot tip into cash or a fast fix. They'll probably end up with Ramming Ray or one of his muscles, they're the new boys here and most likely to pay for a hot sex orgy tip.

"At the other end, I know a guy in Beatty who does some repair and service work on bikes, and I know the bikers do fairly regular business with him on their 'Sunday school' shopping trips. He owes me a big one. A long time ago, when he was young and wild, he got involved in a B&E that went bad. I figured the kid just made a one time mistake, so I alibied him for the cops and he slipped through. He turned right around and as far as I know hasn't even approached the line since then, and he will be happy to let slip to some of the bikers the news about a probable visit by some eastern hotshots who plan on visiting and ravishing their personal pussy stock.

"And I know that my Beatty friend will keep me outa it, he'll just say a straight biker passing through gave him the word.

"I think it'll work."

Shant smiled, waved vigorously at Marie. "I do too, Pap. The whole thing is brilliant. If it works out, maybe someday I'll write a feature article about you and make you famous."

"Yeah, famous and dead. Thanks anyway, Mike, but wait until I've cleared this mortal coil before you start singing my praises about the time I conned the mob."

"Okay. Marie, how about a couple of doubles. My old pappy here said just a couple more shots and he'll work up enough nerve to really grab a handful of your beautiful bum."

"Keep hitting me with tips like you always do, Mike, and both you gentlemen"—she winked at Pap—"can grab my ass anytime you want."

***

That afternoon Pap phoned his friend in Beatty, and tersely explained the rumor he wanted planted the next time the bikers came by.

"No problem, Pap, you know I owe you big time. If you hadn't stepped in that time I'da ended up just another street punk stealing hub caps. Those bikers are due in anytime, prob'ly tomorrow, maybe even later today. So my story's that I got the tip just today from a biker out of Vegas on his way to Idaho, and he said he overheard the news from what looked like one of the mobsters himself spouting off in a mob drinking spot. They started to hassle him, and he had to take off pretty quick, and he was really pissed off, so that's why he was talking about it.

"How's that sound, Pap?"

"Excellent, Steve. Just make sure you credit the rumor to the passing biker. I don't want you to be involved in any way."

"That's easy. When these guys come in it's usually for some repair, and that often takes me an hour or so. The guys hang around and shoot the shit, and it'll be easy for me to drop in the passing biker story. Sort of as a joke, if you know what I mean, but serious enough so that the bikers will believe it."

"Next time in Vegas, Steve, dinner's on me. And I've got a good job going with this writer, so that means steaks and cocktails, not the usual burgers and beer."

"You're on, Pap. And even if it was just B&B I'd still consider it a pleasure."

***

Pap saw Shant in the race book when the nightcap at Fairplex in LA County was just finishing.

"I thought you didn't bet Fairplex, Mike."

"Normally I don't, Pap. It's just a bullring and some of the trainers and jocks here hit so infrequently that they're open to boat race fixes. But in the final there was what I thought was a standout, a mare down from Emerald Downs in Washington state. Anything from up north, in Washington or even B.C., is considered low class by the locals at Fairplex, even though those horses win more than their share. And this mare was dropping from a $6,000 claimer there to the bottom level at Fairplex. So I bet her to win and also hooked her up to the other six in the quinella. She placed, I lost the win end but tripled my bet on the Q."

"And I also am a bearer of good tidings," Pap said. "I've planted the party idea with two different dopers, one of them is sure to make contact with the eastern thugs.

"And my Beatty friend is geared up to planting the story, heard from a passing biker, about the mob guys' planned invasion of their personal pussy stocks.

"All we have to do now is wait."

"And keep on looking for ways to tie in DiBonio," Shant added.

CHAPTER 13

"You're Leonard Cichecki?"

"It's Lennie. Yeah, I am. Who are you?"

"I am Thornton Withers, Investigative Agent with the Fraud Division, United States Postal Service."

"I buy my stamps at the post office."

"Very funny, Mr. Cichecki. I'm not here to sell postage stamps. I am here to talk to you about this Northwest Research Institute you're promoting."

"I'm not promoting it at all, Mr. Smithers. I am merely marketing some of its products."

"My name is Withers, not Smithers. And what are the products you are marketing?"

"Sorry about the name, Mr. Dithers. As to the products..."

"It's Withers, not Dithers!"

"Well, I guess you can call yourself whatever you want, although I'll need to see some ID before we talk further."

The agent pulled out a billfold, flipped it open, and held it out to Lennie. He peered at it closely then looked up.

"Ah, yes, you do appear to be the individual shown on that photo. Although I must say that in person you look much younger than your photo. In fact I would hardly recognize you from that ID picture. You really should have a new one taken, one that really shows you as you are. I'm sure the federal government would gladly pay for the new photograph, as it would make their agents, in this case you, Mr. Withers, look far more presentable. And of course looking presentable is important nowadays for everyone, certainly for those who hold positions of authority in civil service positions, as you do, Mr. Withers. Wouldn't you agree that you do occupy a position of some importance, that you are in fact an important cog in the overall wheel of government?"

The agent looked puzzled. "Well, yes, of course, my position is of some importance and...Mr. Cichecki, I'm here to ask you some questions, not answer questions. I am a duly appointed agent in the Fraud Division, and as such I would appreciate your co-operation."

"Of course, Mr. Withers, you can rest assured of that. I always co-operate fully with duly appointed personnel of our friendly federal government. In fact, when I was younger, sort of like you look now in comparison to that unflattering photo in your little wallet, I had dreams of serving our great Uncle Sam in some capacity, maybe even in the honorable Postal Service, whose workers toil in winter, and summer, who slog through storms, who leave no stone unturned...."

The agent held up his hand like a traffic cop.

"Mr. Cichecki. Please. I must ask you to refrain from going off on these tangents. I do appreciate what you're saying, sir, and I do think your dream of joining this Service was most commendable, but I must insist that we return to the subject of this meeting."

"I'm only too happy to do whatever you think is best, Mr. Withers. As they say, I'm at your service." He laughed. "Your Postal service, if you get my meaning." Lennie laughed again. "So just feel free to carry on with whatever your superiors have told you to do, Mr. Withers."

"It's not what my superiors have told me, Mr. Cichecki, it's just my regular job. My division has received a number of complaints, well, let's just call them inquiries at the moment, concerning this Northwest Research Institute. All the comp...inquiries, seem to be concerned with a claim that you, or at least this Institute, is making, that what is being sold is a, and I quote from an advertisement in a national magazine for handymen and homeowners, according to the official slogan on its cover, a quote no-fad diet unquote. Is that correct, Mr. Cichecki?"

"That the magazine you're holding in your left hand, and showing me, is a magazine for handymen and homeowners? Yes, according to what it says at the top of that page, really the cover, I guess, that you're showing me. Yes, sir, that is what the magazine says it is for."

The agent looked blankly at Lennie, then down at the magazine he was holding, then back at Lennie.

"Well, yes, I guess that's true." He paused. "But what I really meant to say, it wasn't about the magazine I was holding," he quickly dropped the magazine onto the sofa, "but the question was more about, well, on the subject of the no-fad diet, I guess."

"You have certainly chosen well, Mr. Withers. Too many folks nowadays just want to lose weight quickly and they don't care how the diet they choose will really affect their long term health. I do have to say, Thornton—may I call you Thornton? Or do you prefer Thornie? And please call me Lennie, all my friends do, and although we've just recently met I can tell that we're going to be friends—and as I said, I really do have to stress that people everywhere, not just here in Las Vegas, or even Nevada, but in all the wonderful states of this great country, that of course you and your colleagues serve so well, so very well,

Thornie, in that great Postal Service you represent so well." Lennie paused for breath. The agent's mouth was partly open and his eyes looked as glazed as those of a roast suckling pig.

"But as I was saying," Lennie continued "people are putting their health at risk every time they even consider using a diet which is not structurally and nutritionally sound, one that has been created lovingly by people who have a vital interest in this great nation's health and who are concerned that all the citizens of this fine country do not put at risk the most valuable commodity everyone of us, rich, poor, white, black, red, tall, short, fat, skinny, whatever, and that valuable commodity, Thornie, is none other than our health. Our personal health, which without it the richest man alive is poorer than the poorest, for without good health, the ability to do whatever you want and whenever you want, whether that's jogging a mile or doing pushups, or even," he smiled coyly at the agent, "indulging perhaps in some good old sexual congress. Of course that's only for properly married folks, and only in the privacy of their own bedrooms. And probably only at night after the children are sound asleep. And that fad diet they are following can be the end of all their dreams and hopes, both for themselves, their children, even their grandchildren. So, Thornie, it just proves what we both know, and agree on, that these fad diets are destroyers of the American way of life. They break up families, they cause parents to separate, children to leave home, old folks to spend their days in loneliness, businesses to fail, even giant conglomerates to split apart. All those woes as a result of endangering their health, taking chances with the most precious commodity they have, their personal health, just by being led astray by these awful fad diets. Thornie, I think we should have legislation, hard hitting, really powerful, legislation which regulates, no, eliminates, such sneaky and vicious attacks on us. Wouldn't you agree with that, Thornie?"

The agent sat down heavily on the edge of the motel sofa. "Could I have a glass of water please?"

***

"Nope, haven't seen Mike since early this morning, Pap. He said he was off to interview one of the hotshots for that article he's writing on Vegas biggies. He said he'd see you later, after three or so, in the race book. Want a drink now or should I hold it till later?"

"It's almost 4 now, Marie, so hold it. I'll go check in the race book to see if he's there."

***

"How's it going, Mike?"

"A little quiet, Pap. I'm playing Golden Gate and Santa Anita but so far I've only had two bets between them. Lost the first, had a place bet on the second. It won, paid $18, but only $7 for place, a lot of money was on it. What're you up to?"

"I just finished all the shooting for your article. Got the last guy out at the construction of that new mega resort way south on the strip. I can remember when the strip started at Sahara and ended about a mile south. Now they're so far south on it they're getting close to the California state line."

"Not quite," Shant laughed. "But the strip sure has stretched out. How did your shoot go?"

"Great. Got a couple of pix with Jackson perched on a giant crane, waving to the crew below. Caption will be something like, 'Big construction magnate on current big project'. Or whatever your editor decides on, of course."

"Sounds good to me. So you have them all in the bag?"

"Yep, every one on your list is photoed and cataloged. How's your end coming."

"Aside from a little editing, it's also in the can, Pap. This assignment has gone remarkably smoothly. Remember all the hitches and glitches we had on that celebrity article in Hollywood. Working with those fabricated 'stars' is a helluva lot harder than working with real people who've actually done something concrete."

"No doubt about that, Mike. Phonies always are a pain in the ass."

A cocktail waitress came by and they both ordered. Although drinks in the race book, as in most of the casino, were comps, both Shant and Pap always tipped the girls generously. They worked long hours on their feet, made poor wages, and had to take a lot of verbal abuse from loutish losers and/or drunken customers.

When the drinks arrived, very quickly, both men sipped, then sat back in the comfortable padded chairs. Shant leaned forward and turned off the sound on the small cable TV set into the desk of each race book seat. Patrons could dial up any of the tracks running in the U.S. or Canada and see live coverage, including the local track odds, which sometimes were a bit of information smart bettors used if the odds diverged strongly from the overall race book odds which reflected the total of all bets made everywhere.

"Any news on our little morality play, Pap?"

"Nothing much yet, Mike. My friend in Beatty did phone to say that two of the bikers had been to his shop the day after I contacted him, and he was easily able to plant the 'rumor' about the Vegas hoods planning a pussy raid. He said they were real excited about it, and he heard them saying to each other that they planned a hot reception for the dagoes when they got there. So that end seems solid. I also got the info out to a coupla dopers about the wild sex orgies out there but haven't got any feedback yet about whether our intended marks got the message. But I expect that nature will take its course, that those dopers will try and turn their hot tip into cash or dope, and sooner rather than later."

Both men sipped their drinks. Pap lit one of his vile cheapos. "I'm glad the air conditioning here in the book is as effective as it is, Pap, otherwise half of these seniors would likely drop dead from those fumes."

"You exaggerate, amigo. They wouldn't take out more than one or two oldies."

The men sat in companionable silence for a few minutes.

"How're things with you and Linda?"

"Pretty good, Pap, considering that I do a lot of travel and most women don't like faraway boyfriends. Or husbands either, I guess."

"You've never talked about your one experience with married bliss, Mike. Was travel a problem then?"

Shant was silent for a minute. Pap thought perhaps he had stepped in where he shouldn't have.

"I'm sorry, Mike, that's none of my business and I shouldn't have brought it up. It may bring back bad memories for you."

"No, that's not it. I've never talked about this before with anyone. There are memories, of course, we were together quite a few years. But really bad memories, no. And that's maybe a large part of why we eventually split. In all the time we were married I was freelancing, just as I am now. Never really wanted to do anything else, although over the years I did once or twice get involved with the corporate world—my major at college was business—like publishing a big company magazine, and acting as PR honcho for another biggie. But I'm far too private, too individual, for the kind of team playing you need to do, so I never lasted long. But in all that time together, you know I can't remember once where she even asked me what I was doing, or how the writing was going. I recall when I first started out, and money was really tight because we already had a coupla kids, I used to type out my stuff, on a typewriter of course, with none of these lovely 'delete' and 'move' keys around, so when I got done the manuscript was often messy and had to be retyped. I had to use an outside woman who did the retyping at her home. She did a great job, always met whatever deadlines I gave, but of course she had to be paid. The money paid her could have been put to good use in our family. My wife had been a professional secretary before marriage. To be fair, she had the kids to look after, but we did always have a house, and even then had a good sized and fenced backyard so watching them wasn't a minute by minute chore." Shant paused, his gaze on some faraway place, and sipped his drink.

"In all that time never once did she offer to help me with the typing. And I don't think she ever read a single article that I wrote, even when they were edited and published.

"That's what I meant about bad memories, Pap. They aren't really bad at all, they're just, well, just memories of an earlier time.

"Toward the end of our relationship, our marriage, we drifted apart, and finally I moved out, although I kept seeing the kids and sending money. Not a single note, letter, or even phone call from her. About a year later I was served by one of those rent-a-cop guys with a notice of divorce action. We were divorced and I never heard from her again. It was like our marriage had never existed."

Shant coughed, rubbed a hand across his eyes, and took a healthy slug of his vodka. He turned toward Pap and smiled.

"So that's the complete story of Mike Shant's Soap Opera. Not dramatic, not bloody, just sort of nothing, I guess."

Pap stayed silent. He knew his good friend was in pain, but it was pain he couldn't help him with.

After a few minutes Shant looked toward the large closed circuit TV screens behind the sellers' windows. "Hey, the sixth at GG is coming up. I have a pretty good layoff angle colt in there, Pap. Not close to a sure thing, but will probably go off at pretty fair odds. Want to do a double sawbuck bet with me?"

"Absofuckinglutely, amigo." Pap was glad his friend was back in the here and now. Reminiscing was okay, especially if you were pleasantly loaded and singing old college songs, but it could be painful. 'If only' dreams were just that, dreams. As an old wino acquaintance of his often slurred, 'The past is passed, an' that's where it belongs'.

Shant and Pap both walked up to the sellers' windows.

***

"Mr. Cichecki, Lennie, we just have to talk about this North Inshitute thing." The agent was slurring quite well, considering he'd only had four full glasses of Lennie's 'very weak, hardly any alcohol at all' brandy. "I mean, shurley we should be able to agree on that, couldn't we?"

"Of course we can, Thornie. Let me just top up your glass there. Of course we can talk about anything you want, after all you are the official agent of our wonderful postal service, those guys in blue or whatever the color is who deliver only bills and letters from ex-wives demanding more of our hard earned money. I think they must shred any letters bearing good news.

"But be that as it may, Smithers old boy, we most certainly can talk about any subject you like, at any time, and at any place. There is absolutely no topic which is off limits. You wanna talk about diets, fad or otherwise, the international monetary

141

situation, good looking broads, or the price of condoms in China, all of it is on the table."

The agent raised his glass, took a swallow, dribbled some on his chin, and placed his glass securely on the table which was about five inches short of where he put it. The plastic glass hit the threadbare carpet and spilled its potent contents.

"I'd suggest we adjourn to my favorite corner bar, just around the corner, sorta cross from that famous Pacific Advertising Associates office," Lennie giggled, "but I'm afraid that you, agent Thornie, wouldn't quite make it.

"So p'raps you should just sorta slide down there on that sofa bed thing and catch a few winks. After you get a few zees we can carry on with this enlightn'in conversation at Sam's Bar, where only the most respectable winos, and authentic federal agents from the postal service, drink reg'larly. How does that sound to you, Agent Thornie Smithers?"

"It's Dithers," the agent mumbled. "Not Smithers, it's...." his voice trailed off as his eyes closed and he began to snore,

Lennie laughed.

"An' the score, folks, at half, or even full, time is research an' institute type stuff one, postal service zero."

CHAPTER 14

"Hey, Shant, didya hear about my promotion?" DiBonio smiled like a croc eyeing a fat calf. Shant looked up from the Racing Form he was using.

"Promotion? No, I haven't heard anything."

"Well, I have been moved up in the organization. I'm now in charge of, well, I guess you could call it new business development." DiBonio liked to use current business terminology, even if he used it incorrectly.

"I guess management is finally realizing your true abilities, Dickie." DiBonio missed the sarcasm. "What exactly will you be doing?"

"My new responsibilities include finding new businesses for the, uh, organization to get into. You know, new fields where we can use our existing abilities to, uh, explore new fields. So I'm like the CEO of this new division."

"Is that what they're calling you, Dickie, the CEO? That sounds like you're right at the top of this new endeavor. Do you have a business card with your new title, I'd like one to impress my friends at home with the important people I know in Vegas." Again the sarcasm was wasted.

DiBonio looked a little crestfallen. "Uh, no, I don't have no cards yet, I mean this promotion is official and all, but the head guys, they're back east you know, don't want to affect the morale of the local employees, so for the time being they thought maybe it'd be better to just keep my current title as chief of the race book division of this casino."

"Chief. Is that what you are? I sort of thought you were just the race book manager."

"No, no, I'm more than just the manager here."

"Then why does it say that on that sign over there?" Shant pointed to a small wooden plaque which hung on the wall behind the sellers' windows.

"It's like I said, the bosses don't want to rock the boat here too much, they want to keep the workers happy, so I agreed that they could use that manager title for the time being, until my new position makes it necessary to put the true title on everything." DiBonio's eyes pleaded for Shant's understanding of this complicated corporate maneuvering.

"Exactly what will your new job entail, Dickie?"

DiBonio paused, then his need for celebrity status overcame his mob-bred reluctance for specifics.

"We, I, have decided that the, uh, organization should expand its interests beyond just gambling. I mean, gambling is all well and good, and nice and profitable, but there are so many casinos now, almost every state has some kind of legal gambling, either on Indian land or rivers or like here in Nevada and Atlantic City, everywhere, so I mean how much more can gambling grow?

"And you add in those damned lotteries with their ridiculous big jackpots, and you can see that competition in the gambling field is heavy, and prob'ly going to get a lot worse." Unlike younger mob members, DiBonio still used the word 'gambling' instead of the now preferred 'gaming', which was thought by some to be less disreputable.

"And those new fields are exactly what, Dickie?" Shant prodded.

"I did a lot of research and checking like, and I came to the conclusion that a lotta people now are interested in their health. Like there's a lot of fat slobs out there, you know, and now doctors and even scientists are saying that too much flab ain't good for anybody, especially as you get older, and of course we're all doing that, right?" DiBonio laughed at his original finding.

"So if there's a lot of tubbies looking to get more healthy, wouldn't it be a good business to help them get more healthy? By losing some of their pork. And so I figured we, the, uh, organization, could like start a business showing people how to get skinny. Or at least get rid of some of their blubber."

"You mean like the dozen or so national dieting clinics already do?"

DiBonio eyes opened wide. "There's that many? Are you sure? Well, anyway, that's a different thing entirely, Mike. I'm not talking about a place where fatsos go to strip down and run ona exercise bike for 20 minutes. That kind of setup takes a lotta front, you gotta keep things looking neat and clean, you know, and there's lot of employees needed. Naw, what I had in mind was a business where we could just offer, sell, the info that the lardasses needed to lose weight themselves.

"That way, we don't have no big front money needed, just a small one broad office and a few office things like computers and phones. And we advertise in the big magazines, like, uh, well you know the ones sold at the newsstands. Then guys, more likely broads, they're always saying they weigh too much—and usually they do, don't they?—buy the magazines, see our ads, and just send us the money. We, the broad in the office, opens the mail, takes out the money, and sends the schmo the info we sell.

"That's it. Nice and neat. No big overhead, no lazy employees always trying to screw and steal from you, and a big bunch of people out there who can be customers. Ain't that a great idea?"

Shant looked at him. So Pap was probably right. This little weasel was likely behind Pedro's death, simply because DiBonio wanted to claim the lose weight scam idea as his own. He was tempted to smash the prick in the face, then immediately realized that would do more harm than good. To properly avenge his friend Pedro's murder would take more brains than brawn.

"Yeah, it sounds like a pretty good idea, Dickie. Seems to me it's sort of like the idea Lennie" (he deliberately omitted Pedro's name) "is working, isn't it?"

"Lennie? Naw, his idea is completely different. And his scam is just chickenshit, nothing at all like what I have in mind. And to tell you the truth, I had this idea long before those guys, Lennie, I mean, had it. You know, I used to shoot off my mouth sometimes in the bar when I'd had a couple too much, and I wouldn't be surprised if Lennie overheard me, then started a sorta same deal on his own. Yeah, that's prob'ly it, Shant. That jerk Lennie and...I mean Lennie, overheard my idea and sorta stole it."

"Are you two gentlemen," Linda emphasized the last word, looking at DiBonio as she did, "engaged in a major international deal, or can a poor girl interrupt?"

Shant smiled and gave her a hug. DiBonio looked at her, especially her prominent breasts in her pullover pink sweater, and said, "Baby, I'm never too busy for you. How about a hug for me?" He opened his arms in anticipation.

"Dickie, if you were the last man in the world I'd become a lesbian."

"Jesus, you don't need to be like that, Linda. I was just being friendly."

"And so was I, Dickie. You ought a see me when I'm not. And incidentally, it's Miss, or Ms if you prefer, Johnsen to you. My friends get to call me Linda."

"Okay, Miss Johnsen," Shant laughed. "What can I do for you?"

"Or to you," DiBonio muttered, again fondling her with his eyes.

"I guess we'd better adjourn to a less public place, Linda," Shant said. "Let's go see if Pap has our table reserved. And best of luck, Dickie, with your new business scheme. I'm sure you'll do as well with it as you have with your other enterprises."

"Yeah, there's Pap. Let's join him."

"Hey, Mike, how are you. And Linda, like always, you look good enough to eat." He smiled with what he thought was his lascivious look.

"Be careful, Pap, one of these days I may take you up on your offer, and then what would you do?" She smiled.

"Probably have a heart attack," he laughed.

"Sorry to interrupt this foreplay," Shant said, "but I was just talking with that prick DiBonio, Pap, and your reading of Pedro's murder looks right on the money. DiBonio was running off at the mouth about his new business idea, and it was a total takeoff on Pedro and Lennie's scam. He apparently has talked the mob bosses into fronting some kind of business selling lose weight info, using ads in national mags."

"Exactly like the boys' scam," Pap said.

"Exactly. He didn't even have the brains to vary it a bit, just copied it from what he heard, and probably from what the leg breaker was able to get outa Pedro before they killed him."

"What's all this about? You guys know who was responsible for Pedro's murder?"

"We're almost positive, Linda. Pap figured it out..."

"We figured it out, Mike."

"Well, whatever. The thing is that it looks very much like DiBonio got wind of the big bucks Lennie and Pedro were pulling in from their lose weight scam. He's always wanted to be more than just a race book manager. He's wanted to get into the mob for years but never made it. The mob bosses, like everyone else, have probably been bitching about all the competition in gambling now, everything from casinos everywhere to state and regional lotteries. Those are nothing but the old mob numbers game jazzed up. They even pay off less than the mob used to, they usually paid off at 500 to one for what was a 999 to one gamble, and the lotteries today pay off at far below that."

"They're the biggest rip-off around," Linda said, "but the worse the chance of winning, and the bigger the payoff, the more the suckers flock in."

"That's it," Pap said.

"Anyway, I guess Dickie felt that some scam outside the mob's usual gambling stuff might appeal to the bosses who were already moaning about the drop in their skims. Lennie and Pedro's scam seemed like the answer: almost no overhead, no employees to speak of, and a big fat payoff, at least until some authority cracked down, and the mob has never worried too much about legalities.

"So Dick the prick sells his idea to the mob, probably that old timer Solly who's out here now from Chicago or Detroit, and pitches it on the basis of him handling the whole deal, sort of in charge of the project, at least in his mind. I'm sure that Solly, or whoever, figured to let DiBonio get it going, then turn it over to a family member, probably a made guy."

"I sure can't see the mob bosses, ignorant as they mostly are, actually leaving Dickie in charge of almost anything," Pap said. "They gave him the race book because when it was first started none of the mob guys knew squat about the mechanics of running a race betting business. Their so-called race books back east were basically just you pick a horse's number, and if it wins we'll pay off at half the

148

real track odds. Over time they couldn't help but make money. But putting in communications equipment to get the track signals, running a fairly extensive banking operation, that kind of stuff was beyond their knowledge, and likely abilities, so street bookie DiBonio was brought in.

"But he's never been more than just an employee, and I doubt if he'll ever get into the mob itself."

"Yeah, that's the way I figure it too." He turned to Linda.

"But Dickie had a problem. He knew in general what the scam was, as did everyone in the bar here, because Lennie and Pedro used to come in literally with sacks of small bills and have Sam the bartender change them for big bills. But he didn't know the details.

"And now we're into guessland, but our reasoning seems solid. DiBonio tells mob boss Solly, or whoever, that he needs a little more info, and he picks Pedro as the smallest and dumbest of the pair. He might even have thought of keeping Lennie on as an employee or something but that we don't know. Anyway, he gets Solly, I'll use his name for convenience, although it could be any boss here or back east, to supply a couple of leg breakers to get the info from Pedro. They snatch him, maybe DiBonio even gets him to a normal type meeting, and the goons go to work. But little Pedro is a lot tougher than he looks, or than Dickie thinks he is, and he refuses to spill the scam's details. After a brutal beating, where he doesn't talk, one or more of the mob goons leans on him too heavily, and breaks his neck. So they plant poor Pedro just off the highway, even doing a lousy job of that, and Pedro's body is found almost immediately."

"That sounds just like what that DiBonio scum would do," Linda said. "You know he's been hitting on me ever since I've been coming in here with you, Mike, and each time his approach, when you're not around, gets more aggressive and insulting. If he had bigger balls I'd almost expect him to take a physical run at me some time. Although I'm pretty sure I could handle that punk."

"I hope so. If you ever need help, kiddo, Pap and I are as close as the phone. Don't ever hesitate if you think that prick is really up to something."

Pap nodded vigorously. "I still have my .357, Linda, and I wouldn't hesitate to use it on trash like Dickie."

"Thanks, you guys. I really appreciate it. And Mike, the real reason I'm here today, I just had a call from that company on the coast. They confirmed they want that series we talked about a couple of days ago, the one on stealing credit cards and lifting their numbers from internet files."

"Hey, that's great, Linda. That was a four or five part series, right?"

"Yes, they said they'd take five, even six if warranted, articles, about 3000 words each. They also said they'd handle photography and research costs directly, as authorized and verified by you. And," she smiled, "they also agreed to the quoted fee." She stopped and looked around, as though her conversation was over.

Shant reached over and mock throttled her.

"Speak up, sweetie, or your days are numbered."

Linda laughed. "Okay. They left the pix and research fees open"—Pap clapped his hands loudly— "and they agreed to the two bucks."

Pap looked confused. "Two bucks? You're doing articles for a couple of bucks, Mike?"

Shant grinned. "Not quite, amigo. That's two bucks a word. That means they went for my quote of $6,000 per article, or maybe 36 big ones if they buy six."

"Great. And I assume Linda and I are into the green stuff too, on the pix and research?"

"Well, I thought I might get quotes on that stuff from three or four people I know, just to make sure I'm getting quality work, you know." Shant was laughing.

"Quality work, right? I'll give you quality work on the end of your nose, you young pup." Pap gave Shant a playful poke, "Barkeep. Send over a bottle of your best champagne. As long as it doesn't cost more than ten bucks. We're celebrating."

***

"What bar is this?" Pap's voice was thin.

"Bar? What town is this?" Shant's voice was even foggier.

"Town? What country?" Linda's eyes were half closed and she peered around like she had just awakened.

Pap picked up a matchbook from the table. "Says the Hilton. On Paradise. So I guess we're still in Vegas, Mike, and that means Nevada, Linda. Any other questions, anyone?"

"Yes, why do we drink? I'm never gonna drink again. Ever." Linda sounded serious.

"Me too," Shant said. "At least until the next time."

The three friends sat there for a few moments in silence. Then Shant signaled for the tab, paid it with a credit card, and gave the smiling waitress a healthy tip.

"So what's next, gang?"

"Well, I don't know about you guys, but this girl needs some sleep. I'm still half boiled and with any more booze spontaneous combustion would turn me into a human torch. So I'm grabbing a cab and heading home. Maybe we can get together later. It's"—she peered at her watch—"four thirty. Is that am or pm?"

151

"Must be am," said Shant. "I don't think we've been drinking for 24 hours, although it does feel like it."

"Assuming you're right, and I'm not at all sure," Linda said, "how be we get together for dinner, maybe about eight?"

"That sounds good, I need about a dozen hours to recharge batteries which are so depleted they may never even start again," Pap said. "Linda, you're going east from here, Mike and me are going back down to Fremont. Are you okay to get a cab by yourself?"

"Sure, there's always plenty outside the Hilton, so no problemo. See you guys later. And thanks for the drinks and stuff, Mike. I think."

"My pleasure. Pap, let's get going. I need a little sack time too."

***

Feeling magnanimous after her night of revelry, Linda gave the cab driver a twenty for the $14 ride and told him to keep the change. She was too bushed to worry about change.

Inside her furnished bachelor apartment, which she rented on a weekly basis when she was doing Vegas research for Shant, she dropped her keys and coat on the chair and headed into the bedroom. Cleaning up could come later.

She kicked off her shoes, pulled off her dress, unsnapped her bra, and decided to leave her panties on.

She pulled the bedspread and sheets down, flopped down, and was halfway asleep when the intercom went.

"Those guys. Must have decided to come here for another drink. I should just ignore it. But I won't of course." She went to the door switch by the front door, pressed it, and didn't even bother to use the intercom. Those guys knew the way. She opened the door slightly, went back into the bedroom, put on her housecoat, and lay down on the bed again. She'd get up when they got to the fifth floor. She looked to the windows, still dark out. Why didn't Mike and Pap go home like they said they were going to?

But what the hell. Pour them a drink and say goodbye again. No problem.

She heard the hall door open, and footsteps. Sounded like just one person, maybe Mike had come alone. Maybe for more than a drink. If so, I hope I can stay awake. No man wants his lover to fall asleep in the act.

"Well, baby, I'm glad you're ready for me. Thought you'd be in the mood after your wild night drinking like a lush with those two jerks. I'll be ready ina second."

He started to unzip his pants.

That wasn't Mike! She forced her eyes open.

"DiBonio! You asshole, you'd better get outa here right now, or I'll call the cops..."

"Sure you will, baby. Just let me show you what I got first, then you won't want to call anybody."

Linda tried to get off the bed. DiBonio backhanded her across the face and pushed her back down. "Here, let's get that housecoat off, baby. That's the way." He pulled it off her shoulders.

"And now just those panties left. Let me help you with them."

He put his hand into the waistband and ripped them off.

CHAPTER 15

"Have you heard from Linda?"

"No, Pap. I sort of thought she'd have called by now, it's almost nine. But maybe she slept in. I don't want to wake her, she was pretty stewed last night," Shant said.

"Seem to me we all were. You off to the race book?"

"Yeah, I have a couple of possibles at Turf Paradise. Where you going?"

"To get an eye opener in the bar. If I get human again I'll drop into the book later."

***

"That did half the trick, Sam. Try doing it again and see if it finishes the job."

"You got it, Pap. Had a little rough night, did ya?"

"Rough night? That's like saying the Rockies are a big hill. Yes, I fell into the sauce and barely got out alive."

"This'll fix you," Sam laughed as he poured a very healthy shot into Pap's coffee cup.

"Hey, bartender, how about some service down here." The speaker was a very large man, and

Pap was fairly sure he'd seen him before. But he couldn't remember where.

"Hell, I'll move down here next to this old guy. You seem to be taking pretty good care of him." The hulk slid onto the stool next to Pap. "Hey, old-timer, my name is Claude. Who're you?"

"Pap."

"That's a funny name. What does it mean?"

"It means old fart in Estonian." Pap saw Sam hide a grin.

"Estonian? What the fuck's that?"

"It's an ancient religious cult engaged in by south sea natives," Pap said. "A big advantage is that old timers in the tribe get their pick of the youngest, prettiest virgins."

"Hey, alright! Maybe I should join."

"Too bad, Claude, the enrolment rolls are all filled up." Then it came to Pap. Claude. That was the name of one of the leg breakers who had materialized when Solly blew into town. Yeah, this jerkoff was likely knee deep in Pedro's murder.

"So Whaddya do, Claude? Work here in the casino?"

"Do I look like one a those assholes who stands around dealing cards or somethin? Not me, old timer. I'm with the casino in a way, but not like some busboy. I'm a lot higher up." Claude looked around conspiratorially, then leaned over to Pap, almost knocking him off the stool with breath untouched by anything other than cheap booze for a week. "I'm in the, ah, sorta executive area. I handle tricky things that top management wants taken care of, professionally, like."

"You mean like an accountant or some office flunky?" Pap goaded the thug.

"Fuck no! I ain't no office pipsqueak. I'm out in the field, handling tough jobs. You may," he smirked, "have seen about some of my recent work in the paper, yesterday there was a big write up. Course they didn't mention me by name. Ain't good in my

155

business to be too much a celebrity." He laughed and downed his bourbon. "Hey, barkeep hit me again. And give Pup here another too. He's a good listener."

Pap noted that Sam poured Claude's drink from the bar bourbon bottle, but used good stuff for him.

"I still don't know what you mean, Claude. You're some kinda fixer?"

"Yeah, that's it exactly. I'm like a fixer. The big boys—in the organization, you know—got a problem, then they ask me to fix it. Yeah, the main fixer, that's Claude."

"Sam, do it again," Pap said. Maybe he could get some hard info from this moron.

"So you fix problems. Is that a one time thing, or do you keep doing whatever you do to fix things?"

Claude laughed loudly and smacked Pap on the back, nearly upending him over the bar. "Lissen, old timer, when Claude here fixes a problem it stays fixed. The problem's over, you know what I mean? You could sorta say that my fixin' is a permanent type of thing." He drained his glass and waved at Sam. "Like dead and buried permanent."

Pap realized he was on dangerous ground here. Get too much information from Claude and he might put himself in a very precarious position. But perhaps he could get a little more.

"Sounds like you might be a funeral guy or something."

Claude laughed, and emptied his glass. "Shay, barkeep, this glass's got a hole in it. Fix it. Fix it. That's good." He laughed loudly. "That's what I do. No, I ain't in the funeral business direcly, but let's jus say I bring em business." His eyes now were unfocused.

"I did see something in the paper a day or two ago," Pap said. Caution was really needed now. "Some guy was found in the desert along the road to, I think it was that town up north a here, Pahrump maybe. The paper said his neck was broken, by a

156

real pro they said, some expert who really knew his business."

"Expert? They got that right. That's eggzactly what that dip stick DiBonie or whatever his fuckin' name is, wanted, was a pro."

Claude slumped forward on the bar, knocking over his almost empty glass. He started snoring immediately.

Pap looked at Sam and motioned him to the far end of the bar. Pap followed him.

"Sam, I wasn't here with that asshole. He ever wakes up and remembers anything, just say that some old desert rat was talking to him for a few minutes but left when Claude stopped buying him drinks. Some guy you never saw before. Okay?"

"Good idea, Pap. I could hear most of what that thug was saying and I've already forgotten it too. Obviously our former friend Pedro had a run in with Claude, prob'ly the last in his life."

"Yeah. Okay, Sam, I'm outa here for now. If I was you I'd stay as far away as possible from prick Claude. When he comes too he'll probably just stumble out of here. For your ears only, Sam, I think the gods are aware of Claude, and retribution may be in the works."

"That would make my day, Pap. See you later."

***

"Mike, I was just in the bar drinking with a scum named Claude. He got loaded and he verified what we already knew, that DiBonio ordered the hit, or at least was responsible for the leg breakers working over Pedro, and scummy Claude was probably the guy who actually killed Pedro."

"It's good to know, Pap. So now when our morality play kicks in, and Claude and his buddies, including Ramming Ray and likely Tony Wagnessi, head into what they think is going to be a wild sex orgy, we can feel good that the right bad guys are spotlighted.

"You didn't put yourself at risk with Claude?"

"Naw, he was wasted before he started to give out with the real info, and when he finished he passed out. Sam was the only person in the bar besides Claude and me, and he's going to say, if Claude even remembers someone next to him, that it was some old desert rat sponging drinks, and Sam never saw him before."

"Good. Okay, on to nicer business.

"Here, in this next race, Pap, we got a bunch of allowance horses running for a sixty grand purse at Phoenix. That's a good purse at Turf Paradise and the ten horses entered are from all over, even a couple of shippers from back east. The conditions are non winners of three races other than maiden, claiming, or starter allowance. Take a look at Dandy Dan's past performances. He's been running at Santa Anita. Not winning but coming close, placing or showing most of the time. Then they ship him north to Golden Gate, put him into a hundred grand stake, and he finishes up the track. But it's a sprint and he's never won a sprint in the last three years. Today at Turf it's a mile and an eighth. He's run this distance seven times, and won twice, placed twice, and showed once. He hasn't run before at Phoenix, but note he has worked out there three times. He's got a leading jock up today, but because of that last crappy ride at San Fran his morning line odds are 15 to one, and I'll bet the locals at Turf drive him down even further."

"You're saying he's a lock?"

"I never say that, you know that, Pap. There's no such thing in horse racing. My favorite picture of all time is that one showing the winning horse just crossing the finish line. Then you notice that there's no jock, the horse has thrown him but kept on running and won. The bettors who had that horse may have had a lock, and the horse won, but of course he was disqualified. So no, this Dandy Dan is not a lock. But I think he's a solid bet, especially if he goes off at least 10 or 12 to one."

"You sold me. I assume you're betting him? Here," Pap reached into his money pocket, "here's a twenty. Not as big as you'll undoubtedly bet, but this poor old timer doesn't get 10 dollars a word either."

Shant laughed. "Neither do I. But I'll gladly add your twenty to my fifty, and we'll see how it plays out."

"Fine with me, amigo. Incidentally, did Linda ever get in touch with you?"

"Nope. I guess she's just really catching up on her sleep. I imagine she'll crash through today, and tomorrow she'll be as fresh as a spring flower."

"Wish I could do that. Okay, give me your fifty and I'll go make the bet. On the nose?"

"Almost always, compadre. And certainly this time."

CHAPTER 16

"Mike, this is Linda. Could you come over to my apartment? It's pretty important."

"Sure thing, sweetie. I'm free right now so I'll grab a cab and be there in 15 minutes."

***

"Jesus H Christ, Linda! You look terrible. What's wrong?"

"Don't worry, Mike. I feel worse than I look."

She took his left hand and guided him into the small living area, and gently pushed him down into the grey sofa.

"Mike, I want you to promise me you'll hear me out before you do any Sir Galahad stuff." She looked at him seriously. "Your word?"

"Sure, sure. Now what happened?"

"Yesterday, was it just yesterday, seems longer, when I left you and Pap at the Hilton, I got a cab home, right?"

Shant nodded, a puzzled expression on his face.

"Well, when the cab pulled up, I guess someone was watching, saw me stagger into this building. Just a minute, maybe a couple, after I got in here, and just after I got mostly undressed and ready to flake out on the bed, the door buzzer rang. I thought it must be you or Pap, checking up to make sure I'd made it okay. When the door opened I got the surprise of my young life, Mike. It was none other than the king of sleaze, DiBonio."

Shant jumped up. "That prick attacked you? I'll break the motherfucker in two..."

"Please, Mike, you promised."

He slowly sat down, this time just on the edge of the sofa. "Okay, I'm still listening."

"He pushed his way in here. Like I said, I was down to my panties, I figured I didn't need more than a robe for either you or Pap. He'd obviously been boozing, although not as much as we had. He pushed me back into the bedroom and shoved me on the bed. Then he started mouthing all kinds of obscenities, saying that I was a slut, just waiting for my 'trick', you, to come over and screw me silly. I have to admit that even though I was pretty scared at that point—I didn't really believe that he'd do anything more than talk—his graphic picture of you and all you were going to do to me was pretty interesting. But I guess I shouldn't have laughed at him.

"I sat up on the bed, and reached for my robe on the chair by the bed. And started laughing, thinking what a complete asshole he was.

"But I guess that set him off, because right away he jumped onto the bed, smacked me hard, pushed me back down, and rolled on top of me. He's short, you know, but he has to weigh over 200, and half bombed as I was I just couldn't budge him. He got my arms together and grabbed the belt off my robe and wrapped it around them and tied them. Then he pulled off his own belt and tied my legs.

"He was almost frothing at the mouth, Mike, he was really nuts. Then he pulled his pants and shorts down, piled back onto me, ripped my panties off, and, as they say on the soap operas, had his way with me. Not much of a way, but it was rape."

"Have you called the cops?"

Linda stood up and moved to the window, then turned to face Shant.

"No. Here's why, Mike. I was almost totally drunk, the bartender at the Hilton could easily confirm that. And the cab driver too. So I stagger to my apartment, and DiBonio buzzes me. He had probably been parked on the street somewhere, waiting until I got home; he easily could have phoned to learn I was out. For that matter, he might have seen us in the Hilton, Vegas is really a small town. So he splits just before I do, realizing that at some point I'll have to come home. It's fairly common knowledge that I have this short term furnished apartment whenever I'm in town working for you."

"None of that matters a damn. Rape is still rape, Linda."

"Think about it, Mike. He tells the cops, yeah, I was near her apartment, figured I'd drop in and try to get lucky. I buzzed her on the intercom, identified myself, and she said sure, come on up. So I did, she was horny like me, and we got it on."

"The cops say, how about them torn panties, DiBonio?

"He says, sure, she couldn't wait to get them off, she just tore them off."

Shant started to speak but Linda interrupted him.

"Mike, I hate that prick, and I would like to see him in jail for a long time. But this is Vegas, where there are very few virgins. It would be strictly my word against his, and the fact that I let him— thinking it was you, of course—in would make his probable story look logical."

"So you're prepared to let DiBonio get away with this?"

"I don't see that I have much of a choice, Mike. I know from a couple of articles I've researched that unless the evidence is overwhelming, cops generally tend to believe the man's story. Often, I guess, it is true, and some girl is just aiming for a payoff or even publicity. So I go ahead and press charges. What happens? DiBonio is talked to, maybe even arrested. He, or his mob bosses, could make bail in 20 minutes. He gets a shyster lawyer—isn't that unnecessary repetition?—who proceeds to paint me as the original easy lay who now just wants to tarnish this upstanding Vegas businessman's reputation."

Shant also got up, went over to Linda, and put his arm around her shoulders.

"Hell, Linda, I guess you have this figured out better than me. You're sure you don't want to bring the cops in?"

"Yes, I'm sure, Mike."

"Okay. So what are our alternatives? We hire a hit man and take DiBonio out? We get him over here, 'It was so good, Dickie, I just have to have more', then throw him off the balcony? We get Sam the bartender to put cyanide in his next drink; Sam would agree I'm sure."

Linda smiled. "Yes to all of them, Mike. But surely a couple of intelligent people, three counting Pap, should be able to come up with something just as drastic but not resulting in long jail sentences for us all."

Shant grinned. "That's the spirit! Sure, we can find some unpleasant way to get DiBonio to pay for this. You remember the scheme Pap and I, mostly Pap, cooked up for those thugs who murdered Pedro?"

"That was brilliant, Mike. That's what I mean, fix that son of a bitch in some way, good, but so that we're not involved. Although I'd personally make sure he knew what it was payoff for." Linda laughed. "You know, I feel better already, Mike. Before you came I was just feeling sorry for myself, but what the hell. We'll make that rape quickie the most expensive lay Dickie has ever had."

"Right on, sister, to use an expression from the olden days—probably before you were even born, kiddo—when all the hippies and dippies were saying it every second sentence.

"How be we do this? I'll get together with Pap late today and bring him up to date. Then this evening, after we've all had a little time to mull the situation over, we get together and start plotting. Not here, though, and not at the GF. For the time being we don't want DiBonio to know that we—Pap and me—know anything about it. We can get together at Pap's place on the east side, no one even knows where he lives so we'll have good privacy."

"That'd be great, Mike. And that'll give me a little time to catch a few winks and clean up, with the door closed and locked, of course."

"I'll phone you here about, say, seven. We'll cab from downtown and pick you up on our way to Pap's."

"I'll be here. And Mike, thanks for being such a good friend." She kissed him on the cheek, he turned his head and kissed her soundly on the lips. "Cheeks are for granddads and uncles. I'm not either."

She smiled. "You sure aren't."

***

"So that's the story, Pap."

"That cocksucker DiBonio. I say we just hijack him, take him out in the desert, stake him to a cactus, and leave him for the buzzards."

"Would be nice and simple. Even neat. But Linda really believes that the three of us should be able to come up with something just a little more sophisticated, and even more perplexing to our favorite prick. Maybe something along the lines of our morality play for those eastern hoodlums?"

Pap grinned. "I have to admit, that scheme really brightened my day. You know, I think even

164

Pedro would have liked it. Well, let's see what we can dream up."

Pap, Shant, and Linda were sitting in Pap's studio apartment. Linda was sitting on the bed—"It's the most comfortable, and this is all about my adventures, or lack of them, on a bed anyway," she laughed—and Pap and Shant used the only two chairs in the compact quarters. Mike had brought a bottle of vodka with him, and all three were sipping cautiously at their vodka and water with a lime thrown in. Linda had added a splash of tomato juice to hers.

The three had been talking and plotting without much success since about 7:30. It was now nearly nine and the day had closed down. From Pap's apartment there was a good sized slice of desert visible, and occasionally a coyote's wail could be heard on the night air. "It's hard to believe that just a mile or so west of here is the Strip," Linda said.

"Yeah, downtown Vegas seems like such a bustling city," Pap agreed. "But just a few blocks away from LV Blvd. you're in open desert.

"So far we have zilch," he said. "Maybe our reputations for skullduggery are overblown."

"Maybe. But I'm getting just a ghost of an idea," Shant said. "The other day in the race book I overheard DiBonio whispering to one of his hanger-on bums. DiBonio said he had a real boat race coming up at Fairplex, so good he wanted to run the pool himself through the race book but without clocking it in to the regular mutuel pools."

"What's a boat race, Mike? They actually have boats at some of the tracks?"

"A boat race, Linda, is a race where the winner has been predetermined. In short, it's a fixed race."

"In this day of computers and cameras everywhere, is that still possible?"

"It's not easy, but it is possible, especially at a bullring—where a circuit of the track is short, under a mile—and some of the trainers make so little in the way of legitimate purses that they may be open to a little cheating."

"How can it be done, Mike?"

"All the cameras, and all the computers, can't spot when one, or more, horses are not being ridden honestly. Say one trainer has a horse that looks bad in the Past Performances. Hasn't won in one, maybe even two, years, and is getting old for a racehorse, could be eight or nine years. But the trainer—let's call him Joe—has been working this horse out at a private training track, of which there are many in the greater LA area. He now has the horse ready for what will probably be his last win.

"But nothing in horse racing is a lock. The trainer knows that his horse will go off at big odds, in the 20 or 30 to one region, maybe even higher. That means a moderate bet, say just a couple of hundred, will not be enough to drive down the odds, but at say even 30 to one there'll be a few thou collected. That's not much money, but at a track where the majority of trainers are earning a gross yearly income of ten grand or less it's big enough to be interesting. If you can make several such bets without affecting the odds then it gets even more interesting."

"But wouldn't say seven or eight hundred bet on the nose at a small track affect the odds?" Pap asked.

"Yes, even allowing for all the simulcast money being bet away from the track, a grand or so could bring the odds down. That is, if the money was put into the regular betting pools. But if the money was bet, privately in effect, the odds would stay high and more money could be dumped on the boat race kid."

"And you heard DiBonio talking about such a boat race, Mike?"

"Yes, and he mentioned the date and race. As usual he was showing off, trying to impress his jerk listener how 'connected' he was. Seems Dickie's plan is to simply take that race right off the mutuel pools at the Golden Future. All bets will be accepted and other horses that place and show will be paid off at the closed circuit odds, so no one will notice anything."

"So aside from having some private bets, which apparently he's supposed to win, where is the payoff?" Linda looked puzzled. "I can't see that he's going to be ahead."

"So far you're right. The only way for DiBonio to cash in is to accept only bets on losing horses in that race. In short, he has to convince all the bettors of that race at the GF casino that the horse preselected to win will finish up the track."

"Is that possible?"

"Sure, Pap. DiBonio will get all his shills and goons promoting another longshot in the race, assuring one and all that it's a lock. At the same time he'll steer anybody who likes the boat race pick onto another horse.

"When all is said and done, DiBonio, or the casino, pockets all the money bet on that race, pays no lion's share to the track and the TV operators, and merely pays a few token place and show bets.

"DiBonio himself would also collect from the bets made legitimately through the common pools, and the odds would have stayed high on the boat horse due to the small totals bet on it.

"Here's how it plays out. DiBonio bets a thou on the horse, and gets 35 to one. That's 35 thou. He, or the casino, depending on whether he's cutting them in, collect the average Fairplex race pool of say 40 thou, with total place and show bet payoffs of a couple thou. Net to someone about 70 or 75 thou, possibly considerably more if the odds skyrocket on the boat horse. I've seen payoffs of 80 and 90, even 95 to 1. That would double or triple the take.

"Now this isn't a seven mill heist, but Dickie ain't James Bond either. Pulling in a quick hundred thousand could increase his value in the eyes of the mob; they're always impressed with financial scams, probably because they can't think up any themselves."

The three conspirators were silent for a few minutes.

"Okay, I think I understand how the scam would work," Linda said. "But aside from us being able to make a few bets on a sure winner, how do we pin DiBonio on this deal?"

"You just said the magic phrase, Linda. 'Sure winner'. Remember what I said before? There ain't no such animal.

"Now suppose everything goes according to DiBonio's plan. He makes all his personal bets through dummies, either on the internet or even at the track. He figures to collect the 40 or so thou on those, less a few bucks for the dummies.

"He cuts in the GF casino on the scam, because he wants the mob bosses to be aware of his financial expertise. The casino stands to make maybe a net of another 40 even 50 thou. Not fantastic, but it would show that Dickie boy is more than just a race book manager, he's a financial genius like their late Meyer Lansky, the only Jew who came through all the mob wars unscathed simply because he was a financial hotshot, and like I said before the mob respects anyone who can add up a column of six numbers without a calculator."

"Yeah, I think I understand the picture you've painted, Mike. I still can't see how we can avenge Linda's problem with that prick DiBonio."

"Remember I said a few minutes ago, Pap, how the whole scam works. If the boat race horse wins, right?"

Pap jumped to his feet. "Now I got it!" He turned to Linda, gave her a quick hug. "Look, babe. That's it. If DiBonio's horse doesn't win, then the whole house of cards collapse. Right, Mike?"

"A cigar to the gentleman in the front row. That's it. All we have to do is make sure Dickie's horse loses. Then what happens?"

Linda jumped in. "I think I can answer that, Mike. First, he loses all the money he's bet, probably borrowed because everyone knows he blows every dime he gets. That means a shylock and his 20 percent interest every week."

"Even better," Pap interrupted, "is what he faces back home at the GF casino. He not only hasn't made a profit, but some of those other bets he privately booked will be on the actual winner, and that money comes directly from the mob's pockets, it's not even in the regular mutuel pools. And mobsters hate more than anything else giving back money they thought they already had."

"Both you guys get cigars," Shant said. "I think the problems DiBonio will have with his mob bosses will far outweigh his personal losses.

"In fact, with any luck, and with say another longshot winner, maybe at 20 or 30 to one, the casino would have to come up with probably 80 to 100 thousand. They couldn't welch because that would bring the Nevada Gaming Commission into the act, and even the mob is scared of those guys; they can put them out of business in a heartbeat. And who would be personally and directly the cause of all the casino's problems? And more than likely a few of the bosses would have been seduced—sorry, Linda—by DiBonio's impassioned spiel and would have made personal bets on the boat race horse. So to repeat, folks, who could be in really, really deep shit?"

"Prick DiBonio," both Pap and Linda shouted simultaneously.

"Right. So all we have to do now," Shant said, "is to make sure DiBonio's boat race springs a leak."

CHAPTER 17

"You got hold of Jimmy Cranston in LA, Pap?"

"Yeah, I left a message on his machine and he called me when he got home from the track. He's a nice guy."

"He is, and mostly honest, which in the horse race industry is high praise indeed. What did he think of our plan?"

"At first he thought we were out of our collective minds. But as I explained it to him in more detail, he started to come around, and by the time I finished talking he burst out laughing."

"That good or bad?"

"Good. Jimmy said that it was possible our scam of a scam might work. He agreed with what you'd said, that Fairplex was probably the only track in the western U.S. where it could be pulled off. He said he personally knew of half a dozen boat races there in the last four or five years. Usually, he said, it was just the way you'd explained it to Linda and me. Some of the trainers at Fairplex are really scraping bottom, they may enter 30, 40, even more, entries at a meet, and are lucky to win a couple of races. With the lowest level claiming purses bringing in just a couple of thou to the winner, and the trainer getting just 10 percent of that, it's clear that a bunch of them can't make a living from legitimate racing."

"Yeah, it's unfortunate, but like everything in life there are the rich and the poor. Top trainers at Santa Anita, Hollywood, even Golden Gate or Turf Paradise, can hope to have gross trainer earnings of from 50 to maybe a couple of hundred thousand. The very top ones, of course, make even more, often well over a million, plus they sometimes get to share in the horse owner's syndication or stud fees.

"But," Shant continued, "the vast majority barely make ends meet, and sometimes the two ends never do get together."

"So what happens then, Mike?"

"The trainer either gets a rich girl friend, starts selling plastic dishes on the side, or looks into the possibilities of a boat race. He knows—95 percent of trainers are men—that if he's caught, the least he'll get is thrown off all tracks in North America, probably for his life. The worst is jail time, but especially at the smaller tracks it usually isn't worth anyone's time and expense to go beyond throwing the bad trainer out.

"So it's not hard to see how some of the poorer trainers are ripe for a little larceny, especially when some crook like DiBonio makes what looks like a rich payoff offer for just a little work."

"How does a boat race actually work in practice, Mike?"

"It requires at least a couple of trainers, more likely two trainers and a couple of jocks. Everything I said earlier about trainers applies equally to jockeys, in one sense even more, because in addition to making ends meet, the jocks have to watch their weight. Closely. If they get even a pound over the minimum weight the trainer is allowed for his horse, some trainers just move on to another jock. That's even though most good handicappers, and most good trainers, agree that weight is vastly over rated as a factor. Sure, put an extra 10 pounds on a horse, and that may slow him a little. But a pound or two, which poor trainers think is all important? That's like adding 3 or 4 ounces to the average man.

"Anyway, to get back to the boat race. In any race there normally are just a few real contenders that have a good chance of winning the race, depending on factors like racing luck, jock ability, and track condition. In a nine horse field there will maybe be three possible winners.

"Of course, longshots do win, but not that often, and especially not if you discount those times that the trainer has done something to actually change that long shot's chances, like maybe trained him at a private track so no one is aware of his speedy workout times, or put him on a new legal medicine, or just instructed the jock how to really race him.

"For example, if the horse normally runs sprints, distances under a mile, but his breeding indicates that he should do great at longer distances, the trainer says, 'Don't push him for the first five furlongs. Then start to let him out and close up on the leading but tiring leaders.

"Once you pass the mile post, give him gas. Few handicappers follow a horse's breeding, and if the current race appears different from where the horse has run and won before, in sprints, today's route distance will be overlooked, and the 'longshot', who really isn't that but a strong win contender, passes all the tired leaders and cruises to a four length win."

"I'm still in the dark about the boat race," Pap complained.

"Yeah, sorry, but I get carried away sometimes."

"For a writer who gets a couple of bucks a word I guess that's understandable," Pap smiled.

"Okay. In a boat race the trainers and/or jocks of those two or three contenders get together and agree that their horses will be given a workout, not a real race. Nothing that can be spotted by the stewards watching the race, nor its reruns on tape. One jock will just take his horse a little wide at the start and cost him precious feet and seconds in getting back closer to the middle of the track, or even the rail, where the horse does his best.

"Another will let his horse get boxed in behind a couple of front runners where his horse, a late-in-the-race, come-from-behinder, has no place to go.

"The net result, Pap, is that the logical contenders are effectively held back, just slightly, and in a manner which cannot be disputed by the stewards. The boat race pick, then, has the opening he needs, and away he goes to a totally 'unexpected' win."

"I see how it works, Mike. But how about that occasional longshot you mentioned. What if one of them gets into the race, isn't part of the overall conspiracy, and starts to head for home ahead of the boat race pick."

"That's where the jocks involved decide in advance that they'll keep an eye on the rest of the horses. If one not part of the plan starts to look too good, one or more of the jocks will take some kind of action to slow him up. That could mean boxing him in, deliberately bumping the horse and putting him off stride, or accidentally hitting the longshot horse in the face with his stick."

"Wouldn't that last action bring some kind of disqualification to that jockey's horse?"

"It might, Pap, but so what? That horse wasn't supposed to win anyway, and accidents do happen frequently in a race. Unless the stewards were dead sure it was intentional the most the jock would get would be a reprimand, maybe a couple of days suspension. But when weighed against his possible profits that's a small cost."

"You make it sound simple, Mike. Is it really that easy to run a boat race?"

"No. Otherwise every down on his luck trainer or jock would be doing it all the time. It's difficult for several reasons, Pap.

"First, it's always hard to get two or more people, particularly individuals like trainers, to agree on anything. Add in a couple of jocks, who may or may not be too bright, and that's a big problem in itself.

"Second, in a horse race you are always dealing with animals, and at least some of these thoroughbreds, all highly bred, will be temperamental and more moody than a woman with PMS. The trainers, even the jocks, may plan to do one thing. The horse or horses may have entirely different ideas. A horse that hasn't run better than fifth for months may all of a sudden wake up and decide to see what it's like to finish in front.

"Or worse, the boat race horse may just get moody and not respond to any of the jock's handling. It might just not want to run that day, in spite of the jockey's whipping and kicking."

"So planning and executing a boat race are two entirely different things?"

"Exactly, Pap. And even DiBonio will be aware of that. But his basic greed, in this case his desire to profit personally and also to show his mob bosses his talent for criminal acts, looks like it has overcome any doubts he may have.

"As long as we don't rock his boat, by letting word of our own scam slip out, or by too obviously making bets against his boat race selection, we hoist Senor DiBonio on his own petard, as Shakespeare would say."

"I've always wondered, Mike. What exactly is a petard?"

"Haven't the slightest, Pap. I just remember that quotation, not what it means."

Pap laughed. "I guess one out of two is pretty good. Okay. So now I understand what DiBonio is up to, and basically how we plan to screw up his plans. What do we do first?"

"You've already done that, Pap. You have Cranston at the track lined up, and he's agreed to get at least two, maybe three, of the non-conspiracy jockeys in the boat race to do what they can to thwart it. Remember, all we have to do is make sure DiBonio's boat race selection loses. It doesn't matter by how much, or even who wins, because we'll have all our bets spread on all the logical contenders once DiBonio's horse is eliminated."

"We just have to make one horse lose, and any one of the other horses win, right? And DiBonio has to do just the opposite?"

"You have it, Pap. Providing our bets are placed smoothly, and carefully, DiBonio has by far the hardest job.

"If Cranston comes through, and we both know that his word is as solid as you can get at any race track, we should be able to push Dickie DiBonio from the frying pan right into the fire."

"When do we start making our bets?"

"We should wire the money to Cranston today, the boat race is for Saturday. Weekends are good betting total days and DiBonio is well aware of that. The online mutuel pools will be open anytime, but their big coverage of Saturday races will start when the past performance data is posted, either late Thursday or early Friday. So our bets online can be made anytime. Those are just to give DiBonio a false sense of security. The only way we can really snare him in our spider web is by placing bets live at the Golden Future casino race book. That's where he plans to make his big score."

"All bets there will in effect go into a special account, not recorded in the official mutuel pools?" Pap asked.

"Right. And that's where we're most vulnerable. For the online and bets right at Fairplex there's very little problem, they can be very anonymous. But at the GF we have to use as many different bodies as possible, and scatter the bets among all the ticket sellers."

"Usually on weekends there will be five or six seller windows open."

"Yes, so if we have say six different bodies—you and I can make a few bets, but nothing too conspicuous—and six sellers, that gives us about 30 or 36 separate betting opportunities without repeating.

"We want to lay at least ten thousand on this race at the GF casino, Pap, so each bet should on average be for around three, even four hundred. Actually, we don't want to have things too organized, DiBonio might spot something.

"So let's say that each other bettor of ours will make bets of about $500, the other bettor about $300. Those amounts won't raise any doubts, certainly not in the different sellers, and even DiBonio won't find them suspicious. If anything, he'll be rubbing his hands anticipating his big payoff."

"And our payoff, I realize, is just to hurt DiBonio. And the GF bosses, of course."

"If we get lucky, and a long shot does ace out DiBonio's selection, it could easily pay 30 or 40 to one. Our ten grand won't even show up in the official mutuel pools, of course, because DiBonio is in effect just taking it. At 40 to one, the GF casino will owe us 400 thou, Pap."

"Fuck me," Pap exclaimed. "I didn't think we were talking about that kind of money."

"That's if a real long shot hits, Pap. But with at least two Cranston jocks being honest, and DiBonio's two or three screwing up things, there's a real good chance that some poor nag who hasn't won this year will cross the line first. Keep in mind that none of our money bet at the GF will drive down the odds on whoever wins, because DiBonio won't be entering those bets into the legal pools."

"If things work out as we hope, and are planning for, Mike, what do we do with all that money we win?"

"First we take off our expenses: about ten grand to friend Cranston, who will take care of his jocks. Then maybe a flat $500 to each of our friends who make bets for us at the Golden Future race book. The rest, I think, should be split up equally among our team, and you, me, and maybe a double or even triple share to Linda who is the reason for the whole thing. I know she wouldn't take more than a single share, that's just the way she is. But I could sneakily get her to take a three share. If we end up with even 300 grand, and excluding Cranston who has been paid, and there are 11 total shares, that means each share is well over twenty five thousand."

"Wouldn't that be great! Screw that prick DiBonio at the same time that we three and our good friends who helped us share in a nice pot of cash created solely by DiBonio's greed." Pap laughed loudly. "Fanbloodytastic!"

"It sure will be, Pap. Talk about poetic justice."

"By your rough time line earlier, I guess we can get going on this almost immediately, Mike?"

"Yeah, there's nothing to be gained by hanging around.

"We've already agreed on the friends we'll use, so maybe you could start meeting each one individually, telling him exactly what to do, and when.

"I've already talked with my editor at Your Money magazine, told her I had a situation here, and needed 10 thousand fast. I promised to put up my next 5,000 words against it. She said okay, and that she'd wire the money to me care of the Mirage Hotel. I didn't want it to come anywhere near Fremont Street.

"I'll go down there and get it, and meet you back here in an hour or so, so you'll have the cash to farm out to our betting friends.

"After that it's mostly your job, Pap, to see each friend, give him the cash and make sure he or she knows exactly what to do.

"Then I'll go and pay a visit to Linda, make sure she's feeling okay.

"I think after I tell her how our plan is progressing she'll feel a lot better."

"Okay, Mike, I'm on the way. How be we three get together for a late supper, say around eight or nine?"

"Good idea, Pap. I'm sure Linda would like to. I'll make a reservation at the Sands for nine, just to give us all plenty of time."

***

"You're looking great, Linda. Has Mike filled you in on our little Dickie operation?"

"You look good too, Pap." She kissed him soundly on the lips. "And Mike gave me all the gory details. I think it's great. And I can't thank you guys enough for what you're doing for me."

"Well, baby," Pap affected a smarmy smirk, "you could always say 'Come up and see me sometime'."

"You mean to play a game of rummy?" Linda laughed.

"At my age, that would be about it," Pap laughed back. "Do you really think our plan will work?"

"I've gone over it in my mind several times since this afternoon when Mike told me all about it, Pap, and I can't find any flaw in it. Of course it's all based on DiBonio's greed, but we all know that's a given. Barring any horrible luck at Fairplex I think it should work just like you two guys planned it."

"It may be too early for a champagne celebration," Shant said, "but I do agree that at the moment our plan looks very practical.

"Pap, you got all our friends lined up?"

"Without a hitch, Mike. We ended up with seven people to place bets. Georgie Wittenbrut got back in town earlier than we thought, and he was overjoyed to take a crack at DiBonio. You may remember Dickie screwed him royally on that disputed 'after the close' bet he made, even though it was clear he had it in with a minute to spare. DiBonio just screwed up and shifted the blame to Georgie. It cost Georgie almost five grand."

"Great. And they're going to start betting...."

"The first bettor will hit the seller windows at the Golden Future race book about noon tomorrow. I didn't want to start too early and catch DiBonio's, or a seller's, attention."

"Good thinking. Well, fellow scammers, by this time tomorrow we should have most of our bets laid at the GF." Shant raised his glass. "To our friends and their bets."

Pap and Linda echoed the toast. "To our friends and their bets," they said.

CHAPTER 18

"Gimme two hundred on number seven in the fifth at Fairplex tomorrow."

Wally Sawchuk checked his computer screen. "Mike, you know that dog shows 80 to one in the morning line?"

"That's the way I like 'em, Wally. The longer the better."

"It's your money, Mike. He punched up the numbers and a ticket spewed out on Mike's side of the counter. Good luck."

"Thanks, Wally." Shant checked it, then pocketed the ticket. That makes about a grand for me, he thought. Better hold off on any more bets for awhile. Or better yet, stick in a couple of regular, non-boat trip bets, so that if Dickie the Prickie—he smiled to himself—did any checking, everything would seem normal.

He went back to his reserved seat in the third row of nine-seat wide rows and opened his past performance paper. I'll check a few races at Santa Anita, see if I can get a small bet down to distract from all the action already in, and with more coming, at Fairplex. Yes, there was a maiden allowance in the fourth for three year old fillies.

He had an angle which worked well with that specific age group of females, his win rate was almost 40 percent, and at his average odds of just five to one, below what he normally preferred, he did over time more than double his investment in this class of non-winners.

He scanned down the list of nine horses entered, each listing showing a maximum of the horse's last 10 races. In the case of maidens, many of them just showed a few outings, several were making their first race starts ever. With such an unproven field, not one by definition had ever won a single race, the odds on several would be sky high. Shant had found that such races usually had winners paying about $4, meaning the track favorite had won, or over $60, indicating one of the longshots, sometimes even a first starter, had surprised most of the bettors.

He finally chose a filly with two previous races. Both had been in the money, both shows, so she wouldn't be a favorite with amateur handicappers who thought two third place finishes showed a horse of little talent. But Shant saw that in both races, at six furlongs, the same distance as today, she had closed from far back in the field to finish third.

The trainer had a new jock up. Not one of the top 10 at the current meet, he nevertheless had an excellent record in getting non-winners across the finish line first; Shant estimated he won almost a third of all such races he competed in, and that was a high win rate indeed.

Okay, Silly Suzie, you've got my twenty bucks. Make me proud.

He got up and selected the same seller who had sold him the Fairplex boat race bet ticket. This bet would help him forget Shant's earlier apparently longshot bet.

"I've got a lock at S A, Wally." Shant never used such foolhardy terminology, but he wanted to make Wally pay attention. Tickets sellers were among the worst handicappers, second only to jocks and trainers, who except for their own horses had little idea of what pro handicapping was all about.

Shant knew that Wally was one of the sellers who placed his own bets strictly on hot tips from bettors, most of whom were regular losers. But Shant had a pretty good rep at the GF race book for winning frequently, and he knew that Wally would likely jump on his pick at SA, especially since Shant had promoted it.

He also knew that like many ticket sellers, Wally picked up a few extra bucks from other bettors to whom he gave winning tips. Even though his overall success rate was probably under five percent, the occasional longshot winner was enough to qualify him as an expert. He would soon be passing on Shant's filly pick, and that would help to defuse or confuse the action at Fairplex.

***

"Dickie, Solly wants to see you. Now. In his office." The mob errand boy loved telling DiBonio when to jump, and how high.

"Listen, shrimp, my name's Richard...aw, fuck it. Okay, I'll go see the boss."

"Sure you will, Dickie. And fast." DiBonio's precarious status with the mob bosses was a current rumor. Until or unless it was disproven, flunkies like the errand boy delighted in taunting him.

"Hey, Solly, you want to see me?" DiBonio smiled with his mouth.

"Shut the door." Except with those higher in the organization, Solly wasted no time on good manners.

"And siddown. Tomorrow's the day you're making us all rich. Right?" His eyes, already mere slits, almost disappeared completely. DiBonio couldn't tell if they were even open.

"I didn't exactly say we were all gonna get rich, Solly. What I said..."

"I heard you say we'd all of us get rich, DiBonio. You saying now that ain't gonna happen?"

In his alarm DiBonio jumped up from his chair, then sat down as Solly reached into the top drawer. DiBonio knew what was in there.

"No, no, Solly, I ain't changing nothing. But if you remember"—he immediately decided to change that word, Solly's eyes had slithered open at the insult to his recall abilities—"not remembered, Solly, but, ah,"—he couldn't think of another word, goddammit!—"uh, I mean, I didn't really, uh, mean exactly that we'd be rich. Like what I said, uh, meant to say, Solly, was that there would be a nice, a real nice, payoff between the house booking all those Fairplex bets ourselves and the payoffs on the winner."

Solly sat up straighter in his chair. At least his hand was no longer near that fucking drawer, DiBonio thought. "What's this Fairplex?"

"Remember"—oh shit, that fucking word was stuck in his mouth now, what was another word for remember?—"uh, thinking back, Solly, rem...uh, I mentioned about Fairplex at that meeting, rem"—double fucking shit! Would he never stop using that word?—"uh, and, anyways, Solly, Fairplex is the track, the race track, where we have the race fixed."

"We? What's with this we? I ain't got nothin' to do with nothin' here, DiBonio. This race deal, or whatever the fuck it is, is yours. **Yours**." DiBonio could vividly see the boldface type used by Solly to emphasize that last word. "So don't try no screwing around, making out this deal was cooked up by me or anyone else in the organization.

"It's **yours**."

This time DiBonio saw the boldface word, twice as large as before. "Got that?" Solly started to reach that hand toward the drawer again, but then slowly let it fall back to the desktop.

"Absolutely, Solly, absolutely. I just meant that all the profits, like, the phony bets booked, and the bet payoffs, would go to the organization."

"Where else?" DiBonio knew the question was theoretical. Solly expected everything, from everywhere, every time, to go to the mob. Unless it went to him directly.

"And don't try to fuck up the issue with a lotta shit about racing crap. I always figured that anybody betting races is dumber than those jigs betting numbers, so I ain't impressed no how with that jive crap." Any language more recent than the Great Depression was jive to Solly.

"Got that?"

"Yeah, sure, Solly, absolutely. Maybe I should get back to the race book now, just to make sure everything's on track."

"What're you doing there, running a train?" Solly laughed uproariously at his joke, his eyes opening wide enough that DiBonio could actually see his pupils. "And why wouldn't things be okay? You said there was no way this deal could go wrong."

"Yeah, but rem..." Mother fucker! He expected that Solly would have the word 'remember' engraved on his tombstone. That's if they just didn't weight him and drop him in a river somewhere.

"I did say that, like nearly all deals, Solly, there was a chance, a very, very slight chance, of something going wrong. But to be honest," he laughed aloud at the irony, Solly didn't even smile, "well, I don't think there's no chance of that. It's best to be careful, though, ain't it, Solly, like the high school kid said when he put on a condom before the cheerleader blew him."

"Don't talk so fucking dirty. One of my grandkids is a cheerleader an' I don't like those kinda perverted jokes."

"Sure thing, Solly. Look, how be I go and check things out, then get back to you a little later?"

Solly started to reach for that drawer again but changed his mind. He didn't like flunkies to end meetings. That was his prerogative as boss.

"Okay, Dickie." He knew from casino scuttlebutt that DiBonio hated the nickname. "So get back to me. But not later."

Solly rolled his shirt sleeve up, letting DiBonio get a good look at the Rolex he'd received from a grateful trucker who regularly found crates of expensive watches just standing around in bonded warehouses.

"Be back here in two hours. On the nose, as you horse race assholes say." Solly actually smiled at his word play but his eyes didn't move.

"Right. In two hours, Solly."

DiBonio wished he could fly, like Superman, so he could pick up that fat slob Solly, get him about 50 stories high, then drop him. Splat! DiBonio was also smiling as he scuttled from the boss's temporary office.

***

DiBonio started with Smitty, the ticket seller at the far end of the row.

"How's things, Smitty? Anything unusual at Fairplex tomorrow?"

"Whadda you mean, unusual?"

"Just what I said." These goddamned sellers were dumber than shit. "Unusual, outa the ordinary like."

"I'm doing just what you told all us sellers to do, Dickie. I'm taking all bets on Fairplex tomorrow. To regular customers, guys I know, I'm putting out hints on your special fifth race, picking any number but the one you gave us to avoid. Most of these guys," his nod took in all the bettors in the large room, "don't know their ass from a hole ina ground, you know." DiBonio laughed silently. Talk about the blind leading the blind!

"So they're ready to take any tip, and they do. I've put a whole bunch on the field in that race, keeping your pick out of it. By race time tomorrow I should have a bunch a money riding on all horses except the nine, yours. That's what you wanted, right?"

"Exactly, Smitty. Good work."

DiBonio worked his way methodically up the line of ticket sellers. Each had much the same story. They were all passing out hot tips to known faces, advising them of a lock situation at Fairplex. Nearly all the recipients of the tip had immediately bought tickets on tomorrow's fifth race, ranging from five bucks from winos trying to win enough for a bottle of dago red, to big time spenders going on the hook for several hundred. A couple, from different sellers, had even received the tip, thought about it, then said they didn't like that post position number, and changed it to another number, but not DiBonio's pick. These bettors had pushed across several hundred each, and one or two, Dickie couldn't get an accurate count, had bet a thou or more. But the numbers chosen had no pattern, and DiBonio just chalked off their actions to typical stupid horseplayers modifying a hot tip to their own ridiculous handicapping.

The more the merrier, he thought. Every dollar bet is going to impress that slob Solly just that much more.

***

"It's about time for that pre-prandial drink, Mike."

"You believe a pre-prandial drink is called for once breakfast is out of the way," Shant laughed and took Pap's arm, steering him to a corner of the GF bar far from any occupied table. Marie appeared as if by magic, smiled at Shant, affected a leer for Pap, then followed that with a warm smile, and ducked her behind away as Pap made the traditional grab for it.

"Well, gents, and you too, Pap, what'll it be?"

"If you serve drinks in here with any real alcohol in them, young lady, then I'll have a martooni, time I got some class, and for my father here I imagine he'll have vodka and lime. And a little water, if it's clean." Pap leaned back expansively, then suddenly sat forward, and grabbed for and got a full handful of Marie's posterior. She jumped back and laughed.

"Old age is making you faster. Well, now you've had your thrill for the day, probably the week, you can snooze off again." She left laughing.

"She does have a remarkably firm bum," Pap said, "especially seeing that she's over the hill, must be 36 at least."

Shant grinned and said nothing. He was one of the few people to know that Pap and Marie had had a torrid affair, lasting almost a year, not so long ago. It had ended with both still friends, somewhat remarkable in high turnover Vegas.

Marie brought the drinks, got Shant's air signal to tab them, and went to a far table where a Wyoming cowboy dressed as a city slicker was trying to impress two young street hookers, both of whom looked bored almost to tears.

"How's it going, Pap? Any word from Jimmy Cranston at Fairplex?"

"Talked with him about an hour ago, Mike, just before I came in here. He said everything's like silk there. He has two jocks definitely on our side, and a third guy has agreed to ride herd on DiBonio's chosen pick and tie it up in traffic, ride him into the rails if need be. He's another guy who has been burned by DiBonio's dealings. He was set down for six months one time after Dickie claimed he had offered to throw a race. Evidently DiBonio was pissed because the jock wouldn't throw a race and cost Dickie a bundle."

"And the betting?"

"Like a young girl's breasts, Mike, smooth and firm. His contacts are getting bets down on any and all longshots in the morning line, and as you know at Fairplex the closing odds are usually remarkable close to it; they have a real good oddsmaker there.

"Jimmy said they'd have at least all the money we wired into tickets by early tomorrow morning, and he might even get a few more thou down if it didn't screw up any odds. If he does, I assured him we'd wire the extra, plus a little bonus, as soon as he called us. I gave him the number of a street phone booth on LV Boulevard, just so there's no record tying in to us."

"Good thinking, Pap. If Jimmy is able to unload a couple thousand more, that means we may be able to clean up big time at the track and online. And here at the GF, DiBonio will have to match the official tote odds, so if one of our longer shots romps in, Dickie and company could lose a bunch. A big bunch. Let's hope it's enough to put a crimp in his career path."

"Even sorta stop it completely, Mike. That would be even nicer," Pap said.

"Is it necessary to check in the book, just to make sure our pals are on the ball?" Shant stretched his legs, then bent them back under the table. The GF bar tables were designed for adults of about five feet; anyone taller had to fold up like a Playboy calendar.

"Probably wouldn't hurt, Mike. I'll take a spin through there. I told the guys to not act any different than usual, and at least a couple of our friends spend most of the day in the book, so they'll be there.

"I won't say more than hello to them, but if there're any problems they'll get the message to me. And you've already been in there several times making bets, so why don't you just hang out here with that great assed Marie. I'll be back in 30 or so."

***

"I said two hours, DiBonio. It's over that."

"I'm just a few minutes late, Solly, and that's because I hadda solve a little problem in the race book. Otherwise I'da been right on the button."

"A problem? About your deal?" Solly's hand strayed toward the drawer again.

"No, no, just a complainer who said one of the payout cashiers shorted him. On a five buck bet, can you imagine? Anyway, I just told the asshole to fuck off, and he did."

"That's how you solve problems, DiBonio?"

"No, no, I mean not alla time like that, Solly, but this guy was just an asshole, trying to cheat us out of a few bucks, you know the kind. It wasn't worth screwing around with him, I mean he bets about five bucks on good days, and we don't need that chickenshit action."

"So what about your deal?"

"Everything's going great, Solly, real great. I have all our ticket sellers promoting hot tips at the Fairplex race and most of the suckers are biting. They're putting their money everywhere, except on who we know is the winner, of course. The way things are moving now, we'll take in at least forty, maybe more, big ones, and pay out just a few token thou for the horses placing—coming second, Solly—and third.

"We'll net even more than I said when I pitched you the idea, Solly. It's going to be a real bonanza."

"And if that horse don't win?"

DiBonio's face lost color. He watched closely to see where Solly's hands were. But they hadn't moved towards that damned drawer.

"Don't win? He will, Solly, our horse will win. I've got his jockey in our pocket, and two more jocks to run interference, you know, stop any other horse from winning."

"Ain't that illegal?"

DiBonio laughed at Solly's unintentional joke. "Sure it's illegal, Solly, but so what? I mean, those other two jocks ain't gonna take out a rod and shoot the horses, you know. Those jocks have been around a long time, they know how to slow up a horse trying to win. They can get in his way, or even bump into him, so that the horse is knocked off his stride, even give the jockey on the horse that's trying to win a smack with their riding whip, something like that. That kinda stuff happens all the time, especially in cheapo races at a bull ring track like Fairplex, and no one will even think twice about it.

"Don't worry, Solly. Our horse will win."

"Listen, DiBonio, like I keep telling you, it's 'your' horse, not 'our' horse.

"And I ain't worried. You're the guy on the spot. And you know what that means."

DiBonio knew all too well. But, hell, he had nothing to worry about, the race was in the bag. There was no way his horse could lose. No way.

***

"My round for drinks, Mike. Hey, Marie, if you have a free moment sometime maybe you could bring us a couple of drinks?"

Marie made an obscene motion, smiled at Shant, and headed to the pickup section where Sam was already mixing the drinks.

"I just went up the street to that Greek joint, had an ouzo, and phoned Linda," Shant said. "She said everything looked good. Cranston had just phoned her about 15 minutes earlier. He said action at the track was great. Because none of DiBonio's bets that he's handling off the tote board are showing up, the odds on the morning line longshots, there's three of them, Jimmy said, are staying pretty firm. Only one has buckled a little because of a couple of large bets that Jimmy's friends made, but then they dropped again as a lot of money, probably from Dickie or his track pals, went onto the boat race pick.

"With just any luck at all, Pap, Cranston's jockeys should be able to let one of those longshots through and then we'd have a fat winner at 30, 40, maybe even 50 or 60 to one odds. With even ten thou on it, DiBonio would have to cover over half a million."

"I sorta doubt that fat Solly and his Chicago friends figure DiBonio is worth half a mill as an employee," Pap laughed.

"Neither do I, amigo. I think that prickie Dickie would then start to pay for his attack on Linda. Like the poker guys say, he might even go all in."

"And wouldn't that be a nice, fitting finale to his jerkoff career, having the very mob thugs he's always trying to suck up to, decide that Dickie was more of a liability than asset?"

***

"Solly, you wanted to see me?" Again? DiBonio said silently.

"Yeah. I been sitting here"—DiBonio saw that both his hands were on top of the desk, not straying towards that fucking drawer—"and I still ain't real clear on this race deal of yours. So explain it to me again, DiBonio, in real simple words."

"Sure, Solly." You ignorant slob. "It's like this." DiBonio pulled out a daily scratch sheet, which showed last minute scratches at the various tracks, and turned it over to the blank side.

"Here we have us." Solly started to object but then changed his mind.

"We invest fifteen grand on number nine, our pick in the boat race. Okay so far?"

"Listen, asshole, I ain't stupid. Just keep going. If I don't understand somethin' I'll let you know."

"Sure, sure. Okay, now that money is put through the regular tote board channels, so we have it as a legitimate bet. When number nine wins, we get it back, times whatever the odds end up as, and I expect they'll be maybe two or three to one."

DiBonio scrawled a big $45,000 on the sheet.

"That's fifteen grand times say the low two odds, okay?"

"So how come it's three times, not two?"

"On race bets you always get your original bet, plus the odds, so here we got our fifteen grand back, plus two times odds of thirty grand."

Solly nodded, and kept his hands in plain sight. "That ain't much of a payoff."

"You're right, Solly, it isn't. But then we add in another figure, and that's the amount of money bet here in the casino, on all the hot tips we been floating on every horse except number nine. It wins, all that money is ours, less a couple of thou for those second and third place horses."

"So what's that magic figure, Dickie?"

DiBonio flinched as Solly used the hated nickname, he knew it meant the boss was pissed off with his smartass explanation. He'd have to slow it down or the fat asshole could get mean.

"I don't have it right up to the minute, Solly, because the money continues to flow in. Each ticket seller is putting all those bets into a separate drawer, and every half hour or so I clean it out and put it into our safe room."

"When'd you last count it?"

"About an hour ago." He was tempted to drag out the suspense but Solly's pig eyes were almost closed so he figured he'd better keep going.

"Then it was thirty-seven thou and change, Solly. And remember"—that fucking word again, why couldn't he delete it from his memory—"anyway,

Solly, it'll keep coming in until just before the race tomorrow. I think, based on what we already got, we might hit 60, maybe 70, thou, all profit. Except for say four or five thou to cover the payoffs on the second and third place horses, but with our horse the likely post time favorite, those payoffs will be small. So," he took the sheet and wrote a large $65,000 under the first figure, scrawled a line across, and said, "for a total of," he added the figures as slowly as he could, the old mob boss would not likely trust the answer if he put it down too quickly, "a hundred and ten grand!"

Solly looked at the figure.

"That's the amount of cash we get?"

Dammit, maybe he shouldn't have been quite so specific. Now Solly would expect that actual amount. Of course it could be more, and that would be good, but if it was even a few thou less greedy Solly might not like it. Fuck it, he'd handle that problem later.

"Right, Solly. That's the amount we should have just as soon as the race is declared official and our bets are cashed. None of the local bets, those we handled ourselves, will be paid out, of course." He grinned in what he hoped was a friendly, non-smartass way.

Solly ignored the grin. "When is that?"

What the fuck was he talking about, when? When what? Oh, of course.

"When is the race official? Just a few minutes after it finishes, Solly. The stewards, there are three of them at each track, will likely look at tape replays of the race, have a drink, and then say it's official. It's just a formality."

"It better be, DiBonio. And I want you here every two hours from now until the race is official, as you call it, with a up to date total of those bets."

"But the race isn't till tomorrow, Solly, you don't mean every two hours..."

"You telling me what I mean, DiBonio?" Solly's right hand edged toward that fucking top drawer where everyone knew he kept his personal .38.

"No, no, Solly, a course not. You want a report every two hours, you'll get a report every two hours. No problem."

"That's right, Dickie, there ain't no problem. Right now, anyways."

***

"I sorta like that number five at Fairplex in the fifth tomorrow, Dave. You got the morning line?"

"Yeah, just a second, Mike." He punched numbers into his computer, then looked up.

"Forty to one." The seller leaned forward conspiratorially. "But you know, Mike, I heard from a guy who knows Fairplex, that horse has a pretty good chance. Evidently his trainer has been priming him for that race."

Dave didn't like to bullshit Mike, a good guy who tipped generously on winners, but DiBonio's orders had been simple and direct: "In the fifth at Fairplex tomorrow, put everybody on anything but number nine. I want no money at all on nine. Clear?"

Yeah, it was clear. Dave didn't like it but he also liked his job too much.

"A good chance, Dave? Okay, put four, hell, make it an even five, bills on the nose, Dave. A toke for you if it wins." And I know you don't like shilling for DiBonio, Dave, but a job's a job.

Dave punched up the ticket which dropped out on Mike's side. "Thanks, Mike. Good luck."

The money was going in nicely, Shant thought. And because none of this action at GF was going through the official tote machines, the odds wouldn't be affected at all. Come on number five. Or any number, actually, except number nine.

***

Solly was using the private telephone in the top floor office. The mob had its own electronics security guy check it for bugs and taps twice every 24 hours so he knew it was safe.

"Lemme talk to Berrini."

Berrini was the Chicago sub boss, in rank on a par with Solly, but because he had been made earlier than Solly he actually outranked him.

"Tony? Solly. I jus wanted to bring you guys up to date. You know DiBonio, right, he's that street numbers guy we put in charge of the race thing here at the Golden Future. Yeah, Dickie.

"Well, anyway, like I told Steve yesterday, he's got some fancy crooked race thing going. We had to put up about fifteen big ones, but he was just in here guaranteeing that by tomorrow this time, here in Vegas, not Chicago time, we'd have a pot of over a hundred thou."

He listened for a moment.

"Yeah, it sounds like that to me too, Tony, but Steve gave the okay on this deal if we didn't get more'n twenty into it. He figured that a five to one return wasn't a bad deal. And he wanted to see if DiBonio could actually do more than handle bets on horses. Like you know, Tony, we're a little short on manpower out here. Ever since that fuckin' gaming commission got active a bunch of our pros have had to lay low, they had too much of a history, you know.

"So Steve thought this crooked race thing would be a good way to check out DiBonio.

"If he comes through like he said was a lock, then Steve might move him up a little. He could be useful because he's got no real record, just a bust or two on nickel numbers charges which don't amount to fuck all."

He listened again, rubbing his right hand over his almost invisible hair.

"That's what I think too, Tony. If he performs, okay, even if I can't stand the smartassed little prick.

"If he don't, then we pocket any profit there is, chalk the deal off to experience, and maybe get rid of one asshole at the same time."

He listened as Tony's laughter came across the line.

"Right. I'll keep you posted, Tony. By tomorrow we'll know one way or the other."

***

"Well, Pap, you're looking sharp today. What's your pleasure?"

"I heard something about a lock at Fairplex, fifth tomorrow. You hear anything, Wally?"

"Interesting you should mention that, Pap. I did hear a pretty strong rumor about that race. Let me think a minute."

The race book was in one of its infrequent quiet periods. With the three hour difference all the eastern tracks had finished their days' racing, and most of the Midwest tracks were either through or on their last races. Only the Pacific tracks, from Santa Anita up through Portland Meadows in Oregon and Emerald Downs in Seattle were midway in their race programs.

Wally pretended to think about the Fairplex race tomorrow, the fifth. He knew damned well about that race, hadn't asshole DiBonio been on to all the ticket sellers at least half a dozen times just today alone, stressing the need to push any and all horses in that race as a lock. Except number nine, of course, that was the boat race special, and DiBonio had promised each seller a two percent bonus for all tickets sold on all horses in the fifth, less five percent for any sold on number nine.

Wally thought of Pap as one of the good guys. He never tried to past post, buying a ticket after the race had closed, and he usually tipped the ticket seller when one of his longshots came in.

196

But DiBonio's orders were clear. Push the fifth to anybody and everybody, just not number nine.

"Yeah, it's coming back to me, Pap." As if it had ever left. "It's the fifth, Fairplex, tomorrow, right?" Pap nodded.

"Well, what I heard from a couple different guys, one at least who seemed to know what he was talking about, said that the three horse was a lock. Something about having the jock in the bag on an overdue gambling debt or something like that."

As if, Wally thought, anyone with a genuine lock horse would pass that info around. All it would do is put more bettors onto it, and thus drive down the odds. Absolutely no advantage at all.

"The three horse? Yeah, that's the tip I got too. So I guess I'd better act on it, Wally. What're the morning line odds?"

"Hold on." Wally punched his computer and looked up with a big smile.

"You're in luck, Pap. I guess they're really keeping mum about this horse, cause the track handicapper has it at 40 to one. Course, those odds will come down once a little money is put on it, depends on how many guys get this tip, and I won't be passing it on after you, Pap."

Sure you won't, Wally, Pap thought. DiBonio must really be putting the screws on you sellers, because I know you're basically pretty decent. Oh well, just makes our scam easier to run.

"Forty to one? Fuck, they got a lock on that horse and it's showing such odds? Well, you can't look a gift horse in the mouth, can you?

"Let's see what I got here." Pap dug out his betting roll. Like most pro gamblers he kept it strictly separate from his "living" money. If he hit a big score he'd move maybe half of it to the living roll. If he hit a bad breaks period, having longshots come in second when he had them on the nose, or having a winner disqualified by the stewards, he'd just operate on the balance until he could build it up again. Amateur bettors didn't separate their funds, so they would live high when they were winning, then go bust on a losing streak. That's when they got involved with money shylocks, often mob run, and that's when real trouble started; paying vig of twenty percent a week broke even lucky gamblers.

"Four, five, six, six fifty, seventy, eighty, even seven." He looked up at Wally.

"You think this boat race is pretty solid?"

"Course I can't guarantee nothing, Pap, but like I said one of the guys involved has done this kinda action before, and always came through."

I'll bet, thought Pap.

"Okay, Wally, I was gonna just buy a couple of hundred, but I'm going to shoot the whole roll, seven bills. Put it all on number three's nose.

"And if it hits, Wally, it'll be a double sawbuck for you."

"Great! Thanks, Pap." He punched out the ticket, making sure he hit the "disable tote entry" button first. Ordinarily that button was used only when the casino ran a little in-house race book promotion, now it was being used to keep all Fairplex fifth race bets out of the official tote figures.

Even at just two percent, that's another fourteen bucks from DiBonio for me, Wally thought. Just today I musta earned over two, maybe three, hundred.

Pap scooped the ticket, made a big show of stowing it in his inside pocket protected by a Velcro strip. He had been pickpocketed early in his gambling career, and ever since he had used the noisy Velcro to foil the quick finger artists.

He turned from the window, caught sight of one of his friends working this scam for him, and didn't even nod. No point in taking any chances at this point, he reasoned.

In the bar he saw Shant in the rear corner talking lazily to Marie. He snuck up behind her, cleared his throat and simultaneously grabbed a full handful of her ass.

She squealed and jumped.

"You old fart. Never was that horny when we were going together. You taking some of those penis vitamins?"

"Don't need to, sweetie. I'm getting into my second youth and everything's just working naturally."

"You mean second childhood. Soon you'll be dribbling your drinks and forgetting where you are. I suppose you want a drink?"

"That would be lovely." He made a fake pass at her behind and she inhaled enough to slide by him.

"You've had your excitement for the day, Pap. What else is new?"

"Just dumped another seven bills on Wally's hot tip, Mike. Number three. That means we've got every number in that race covered with at least a thou just between you and me, and our friends will be doing the same. Zero on number nine, natch. Let's just hope that Jimmy Cranston's jocks can take it out, otherwise you and me may have to get jobs. The nine to five kind."

"Perish the thought, Pap. That would be, as foolish virgins say, a fate worse than death."

***

"So? Whaddya got to report?"

"Same as last time, Solly. Everything's going just like it should. I think we're going to be well over the hundred thou figure."

"For your sake, DiBonio, I hope you're right. Shouldn't we be putting some dough on that horse you got?"

"It's number nine, Solly. And yeah, we are. I got some guys at the track laying down some bets, and a computer geek doing that on the internet. We can't put too much on nine, a course, because that would drive the odds down too low."

"Never mind the number bullshit, Dickie. Just tell me you've got all the bases covered."

"I have, Solly."

"And nothing can go wrong?"

DiBonio hesitated. Of course he had all the problem areas covered but how the fuck could he make a statement like that, that nothing could go wrong? Did that asshole Solly, who couldn't even figure a simple percentage, think he had some kinda magic wand, to make every possible fuckup disappear?

"Well?" Solly's eyes had almost disappeared into his fatty folds, and his hand seemed to be inching toward that fucking drawer.

"That's it, Solly." Might as well assure the fat slob, because if things did go wrong...well, he probably wouldn't have to worry about it.

"I've got every angle covered. Our deal's a shoo-in. Nothing can screw it up."

***

"I was just thinking about Pedro, Mike. I sorta miss that guy."

"Me too, Pap. He was a good one. He and Lennie made a great team, didn't they?

"Did you ever hear the story about Lennie's escape from the Soviets?"

"No. Tell me."

"Lennie was originally from Poland, Pap. And during the cold war years, of course, the Ruskies invaded Poland, as they did to all the so-called soviet socialist 'republics'. Lennie was drafted into the Polish army but like all Poles he served in Russian units, even wearing Russian uniforms and using Russian-marked equipment."

"Yeah, I can remember those years. We all thought someday we'd be fighting the Russians.

Nobody realized what a false front they were showing."

"Anyway," Shant continued, "also like most Poles, Lennie wanted to escape to the west but all borders were tightly guarded.

"Lennie ended up as the commander of a four man tank unit. There was a driver, radio operator, and two gunners.

"One day the whole tank squadron is doing military maneuvers near the West German border, remember that Germany was divided into east and west?"

Pap nodded.

"So Lennie checks with the three guys in his tank. They all agree that if they're ever going to break out to the west, this will be their best opportunity. Lennie checks their map, sees that there is a small West German village, looks really small, just over the border, maybe two clicks from where they are right then. The rest of the tank squadron is doing deployment and camouflage drills and Lennie is able to slow down and let the rest of the tanks get off to the east."

Shant started to chuckle, he always enjoyed telling this story.

"He tells his crew that this is it, then guns it and heads for the German border. There's some fencing and barbed wire but no problem at all to the tank, so Lennie just crashes through it. Half a click inside West Germany Lennie's tank, well marked with the Russian hammer and sickle emblems, hits the town. Lennie roars up the main drag, all of a block long, and grinds to a smoking halt in front of what's obviously the town hall. In front half a dozen old guys are sitting drinking and schmoozing.

"Lennie opens the tank hatch, and jumps out yelling 'We surrender! We surrender!' But in Polish, something these people don't understand. They see the Russian tank, now four armed Russian soldiers leaping out of it, and they all jump to their feet, screaming 'We surrender! We surrender!' In German of course.

"Both parties jumped around shouting for what Lennie said seemed like half an hour—he was afraid the other Russian tanks would chase after him once they saw where he'd gone—and finally Lennie had to take off his pistol and hold it out to the oldest German, who could barely stand up he was so scared. Then, finally, the old Germans accepted the surrender of Lennie's tank and the four Polish soldiers, telephoned through to the nearest German army barracks, and eventually—Lennie said he lost ten pounds waiting for them—came and formally took the men into custody as 'refugee claimants'.

"Lennie said he had never had as tough a job surrendering anything in his entire life."

Shant laughed and Pap joined him.

"Yeah, that's just like Lennie. And I bet that if Pedro had been there he would have complicated things even more. Can't you just picture Polish soldiers in a Russian tank surrendering through a Spanish mouthpiece to an old German who thought that WW 3 had started?"

Both men laughed again.

"Let's drink a final toast to Pedro," Shant said. "To a good friend."

***

"How's the fifth action, Wally?"

"You mean at Fairplex?"

"Of course I mean Fairplex." Fucking idiot! "What else am I interested in right now?"

"Not much, I guess." And that's an understatement, Wally thought. One thought at a time is about all Dickie can handle.

"So?"

Wally made a production of leaning forward over his computer, and punching several keys. He rubbed his jaw, cleared his throat, and shook his head.

DiBonio's face grew red. "What the fuck's the matter? Is there something wrong?" In his anger and now worry DiBonio was spitting on every second word.

Wally figured he'd played his act out far enough.

"No, no, nothing's the matter. I was just checking my figures."

"And? And? What the fuck are they?" Spittle dripped down DiBonio's chin.

"About fifteen, maybe eighteen, percent better than the last time you asked me, Dickie. And every bet I got on the fifth race is for a number other than nine."

"That's great." DiBonio wiped his chin. Once he got in the mob, that prick Wally, and all the other pricks like him, always taunting him, would get their comeuppances. He turned and moved to the next ticket seller.

"What are your figures for the fifth at Fairplex tomorrow?"

***

Pap was just finishing his cold beef sandwich. Marie had half-heartedly complained that she was a cocktail waitress—and a top one at that, she said— and not a fast food server but she had taken Pap's order to the nearby kitchen. When the sandwich was ready she garnished it with some radishes, a stalk of celery, and a few mint leaves that she knew Pap liked to chew on.

"Look how pretty they fixed up your fast food order," she'd said, as she set the plate down before him.

"The jerks in that kitchen wouldn't know how to make a plate attractive," Pap laughed. "I know you did it. You're just trying to get back in my good graces so's you can get back in my pants."

She put a disgusted look on her face and stalked away. She smiled to herself, the old goat was still pretty sharp. They'd had a good thing together, maybe she should give him another shot.

"Eating again? Well, I guess you have to put something other than just booze in there occasionally."

"And a good afternoon to you too, Mr. Shant." Pap wiped his mouth daintily on his napkin and pushed back the chair he'd been resting his feet on. "Anything new since I last saw you?"

Shant sat down and smiled broadly.

"As a matter of fact, Pap, there is. How's the sandwich?"

"Just fine, thank you, and what the fuck is the news you're barely holding in? You won the pick 6 at Santa Anita?"

"You know that's worse than the lottery, Pap. No sane handicapper can pick the winners of six straight races. No, I have news of a non financial nature."

"DiBonio committed suicide?"

"Nope, but not too far off the mark." Shant reached into his inside jacket pocket and pulled out a folded piece of newsprint.

"Here, read it for yourself."

He offered it to Pap.

"I can't at the moment, my hands are all greasy and sticky from this sandwich. Read it out loud would you?"

"Okay." Shant spread out the paper, folded the creases backwards so the paper would lie flat.

"It's from the early edition of the Las Vegas Bulletin, Pap. It has an Associated Press byline. Here it is:

'Stuart Granger, Clark County Sheriff, has released details of a deadly gunfight which took place late last night and early this morning at a ranch two miles northwest of Beatty, Nevada.

'This gunfight evidently resulted when several people, reputed to be members of an organized crime ring from Chicago, invaded the camp of a biker group.

'Although no one at the camp would talk to the authorities, we have pieced together the sequence of events,' the sheriff said, 'mostly from nearby residents and several passersby. We cannot at this time identify any of these witnesses.

'The reputed crime family members attempted to enter the house on the camp property. Title to the land is registered to a Clarence Entwhistle of Los Angeles, California. Mr. Entwhistle, one of the dead, has a long police record of violent assaults and crimes and was a member of the motorcycle gang.

'Apparently the bikers resisted the incursion by the reputed crime family members and a fierce gunfight broke out.

'A total of seven men were killed,' the sheriff said, 'and another four men were wounded, two seriously.

'We have not been able to identify all the dead men, as few had any identification on them. However, two men have been positively identified as an Anthony or Tony Wagnessi and a Claude Pokcuk, although the latter had several different ID cards on his body. A third man was referred to as Ray by Wagnessi just before he died. All three men had airline ticket stubs showing they had left Chicago a some days ago.

'None of the four bikers killed in the shootout has been positively identified, the sheriff continued, as all of the bikers used pseudonyms and nicknames.

'We have no motive for the killings, aside from the attempted entry, probably forced, into the bikers' camp, the sheriff continued.

'Our investigation is continuing. Anyone with knowledge of this tragedy is asked to contact the Clark County Sheriff's office.'

Shant took a mouthful of the drink which Marie had placed before him halfway through his reading of the news item. He dropped the newspaper clip on the table, sat back, and looked at Pap.

"My god," Pap said. "Wishes do come true some times."

"Looks like they do, Pap. Our little morality play not only put the skids under Pedro's killers—and permanently at that—but also helped to reduce biker pollution in scenic Clark County."

Pap raised his glass. "We did our best for you, Pedro. We couldn't do anything about stopping those dirt bags in the first place, but I think you'd agree that we did a pretty fair job of getting you some justice, rough though it is.

"Here's looking at you, kid," he drawled in his best Bogart voice.

Shant raised his glass and drained it as well.

"You put it very well, Pap.

"We did our best, Pedro. Adios, amigo."

CHAPTER 19

"Today's your big day, Dickie. Excited about the fifth?"

DiBonio turned slowly to the speaker.

"That don't concern you, Wasko. Your job here at the Golden Future race book is to take orders—from me—and sell tickets on the races. You ain't employed to ask your superiors—that's me again, Wasko—no questions. Got that?"

DiBonio was nervous. Today *was* his big day. Either he'd make lots of bread for his mob bosses, and maybe even get a job promotion, or. He didn't really want to think about that or. And he sure didn't want to talk about it with jerkoffs like Ernie Wasko, a very junior ticket seller.

***

Solly looked no more pissed off than normal, so DiBonio felt relieved. His summons, as always, was peremptory: "Get up here now."

"Morning, Solly. How're things?"

Solly ignored the pleasantry. "Never mind things, DiBonio. How's that complicated deal of yours going?"

"Great. Just great, Solly. We got in more bread than I expected, and we been able to keep all the local bettors off the number nine, that's the horse we got set up for the win.

"So between our private pool, like all the bets we took on the fifth race but didn't push through the regular totes, plus all the money we got bet on number nine ourselves, at good odds because the local bets offset them, we figure to make well over a hundred thou, maybe as much as one twenty or even thirty."

DiBonio paused, expecting some small crumb of praise.

Solly didn't believe in praise, crumbs or otherwise.

"Like I told you a million times before, DiBonio, I don't understand all that racing shit, and I don't wanna. Can you get that through your fuckin' head? All I'm interested in is how much we put in our pockets at the end of the day."

He pulled out what looked like a dog turd, but lit it up.

Must be a cigar, DiBonio thought. The cheap prick smokes crap and here I'm making him a bundle.

"And what you're saying, Dickie, is that by the end of this day I'm gonna have a hundred and thirty grand more than I have right now. Do I understand the situation, Dickie?"

He should never have said one thirty, DiBonio realized. He should have said a hundred, then if he did hit thirty grand more he'd look like a real winner. Now he had to make about what he figured was the max. Any less, probably even just five or ten thou, and that asshole Solly would make him out to be a loser.

"Well, that's the top end, Solly. Actually, you know, we been aiming for an even hundred, so I think if we get that we've done pretty good." He nodded his head, hoping Solly would duplicate the move.

"We? We? What the fuck's all this we shit, DiBonio? From the start I said this was your deal. Not mine, not the organization's. You promised us a hundred and thirty in return for the pile we put up as front money.

"I'm expecting one thirty, minimum. By this afternoon, or whenever that fucking race is over."

"The fifth is scheduled to start at 4:03, Solly." Jesus H, he was right. By opening his big mouth about the max he expected, Solly now was mentally counting at least one thirty.

He'd have to goose those asshole ticket sellers to put on a last minute campaign, promoting any horse in the fifth. And he'd better get down there right now before the suckers wasted their money on other bets.

"4:03? A race takes what, a coupla minutes?" DiBonio nodded. "Then I'll see you up here at 4:15, DiBonio, with a hundred thirty thou. At least," Solly added.

What a prick he was! Now he was saying he wanted more than what DiBonio had promised as the very max.

"I'll do everything possible, Solly. Now I better get down to the race book and make sure those dummies ain't screwing up. See you later."

***

"Michael, my boy, the top of the morning to you." Pap affected the phony Irish brogue he used when pleased with things. "And can I buy you a wee dram of something golden?"

"Best offer I've had this morning," Shant grinned. He waved at Lucy who nodded and headed over.

"Where's Marie, sweetie?" Pap started to pat Lucy's behind, then thought better of it. She was sometimes less friendly than Marie.

"She doesn't come in today until noon, Pap. What'll you gents have?"

Pap placed the order.

"We're just about wrapped up, Mike. Any problems you can see?"

"Not a one, Pap. I checked with Jimmy Crandall about a half hour ago. He said everything at Fairplex was lined up as we wanted. He has three jocks in the fifth race who are going to do their damndest to make sure that DiBonio's horse, number nine, finishes at least third, probably outa the money completely. One jock owes Jimmy a favor big time, and if he has to, he told Jimmy he'd take a suspension if necessary to make sure nine finishes up the track.

"And Jimmy said he'd got all our money bet. Because all our local bets here weren't even booked by DiBonio, the odds on the longshots have stayed high, and with any luck we'll get one of them across the line first."

"So our return on investment should be substantial? That's exactly the news I, as your trusted financial advisor," Pap smiled at Shant, "like to hear."

"It's not a lock, Pap. You know nothing in horse racing ever is. But we have three competent jocks who are going to do their best to make sure number nine doesn't win. And because the field is loaded with longshots, we do have a pretty good chance of getting one to win.

"I can't see how our friend Dickie is not going to take a real hot bath on today's fifth at Fairplex."

"And that means, Mike, that he'll be in very hot water with Solly and his leg breakers from the east. Do you think there's any chance that DiBonio could weasel his way out of this situation?"

Shant took a long drink. "If I were a betting man, Pap, I'd lay 100 to one that Dickie will find himself in deep, really deep, shit."

***

DiBonio visited each of the seven ticket sellers working the race book that day. He stressed how important it was to push any horse in the fifth at Fairplex except number nine. He even upped his bonus offer to three percent of net bets. He figured if his plan worked smoothly he could afford to pay the extra cash himself from the promotion he was sure he'd get. If it didn't work out, well, a few bucks extra wouldn't make much of a difference.

Each ticket seller agreed to push a "hot tip" on the fifth race, giving any number as the supposed boat race winner except nine.

If they did even reasonably competent jobs, they should pull in another ten thou or so, and that would hit prick Solly's one thirty figure with some left over.

DiBonio checked a computer screen for Fairplex. The track conditions were fast for the dirt surface, and the first race was set for a 2:01 post time. There were as yet no scratches in the fifth race, although late scratches could be made on a vet's advice right up till post time.

DiBonio was now sweating so heavily that he went into his tiny office, pulled off his shirt, wiped a paper towel in his armpits, rolled on some fresh deodorant, and put on a laundered shirt he kept in a drawer for times he thought he had some broad lined up.

Out he went, again canvassing each ticket seller in turn, exhorting each to push the fifth race, anything but the nine horse.

The ticket sellers, all of whom thoroughly disliked DiBonio, also liked working at the Golden Future race book, and with the three percent bonus as an extra fillip, they all did load a lot of action on the Fairplex fifth.

Because all the Fairplex bets were privately booked, none of them showed up in the track live odds which were updated on computer screens every thirty seconds.

"Number nine is still showing at 22 to one," DiBonio muttered to no one. "If it holds somewhere around there I'll be well over the one thirty mark, and Solly will have to move me up in the organization. Even those old mob dinosaurs recognize money making talent, and they'll force Solly to take action."

Although he convinced himself, DiBonio was still sweating profusely, so he made another trip to his cubbyhole office. He didn't have another clean shirt, so he just opened the buttons and rolled the deodorant in his armpits, which now were soggy and smelly.

"Shit. Once I get this promotion I'll keep a couple, fuck, half a dozen, clean shirts in my new office. That way I'll always be ready when some broad gets the hots for me."

That happened very rarely, but DiBonio often recalled fondly the one time a partly drunk former pro had agreed to a fast half and half with him for half her regular rate, just fifty bucks, in the washroom behind the ticket cages. He'd got the first half of the transaction underway but then had climaxed prematurely and although he asked for half his fifty bucks back—"You only did the blow job part, not the actual screwing, so I should only pay half"—the pro had told him to go fuck himself, saying with a loud laugh that that would then complete her business deal with him.

"Anyway," he thought, "once I get this promotion the broads won't be charging me. They'll be lining up to get a little of the good stuff from this guy on his way up in the organization."

***

Pap had just completed a quick tour of the race book, nodding quickly to a couple of friends who were making last minute bets on the fifth at Fairplex. Each of them responded briefly, indicating that their part of the operation was moving smoothly.

When he got back to the bar Shant was absent from their table. Marie had just come on shift and she walked over, putting an empty chair between her behind and Pap's hands.

"Mike just left, said he was going up the street to make a phone call," she said. "He must be calling some chickie he wants to keep safe from your prying eyes, more likely your flying hands."

Pap made a halfhearted swipe at her behind and she stepped back laughing.

"You horny old goat, you can't even reach what you're looking at it. Appears you need an extension in several vital places."

"Don't you worry, sweetie, I can be just as large as it takes to get the job done." Pap grinned in what he thought was a wolfish way.

"Anyway, pop, sorry, Pap," she smiled, "Mike said he'd be right back. Want a drink?"

"A little later, Marie. Right now I'd love a hot cuppa coffee. With all your connections"—he leered at her very ample breasts—"could you find one?"

"For my second best tipper nothing is too difficult." Pap smiled at the double meaning, then sat down.

A minute later Marie brought a very hot cup of coffee, with a croissant next to it. "Just don't say I don't take of all my horny customers."

A couple of minutes later Shant entered, spotted Pap, and came over to his table.

"Just talked again to Cranston at Fairplex, Pap. He says everything is go. The race has no scratches, his three jocks are ready and willing to do their parts in this little play, and all our money has been put into action there."

Pap nodded. "I expected as much, Mike. Cranston is a fine friend, and when he gives his word you can take it to the bank. I've known him for a long time. He's never once failed to do for me what he said he would."

"You're a lucky man, Pap, to have as many friends like Cranston as you do. Many people go through life with none." He caught Marie's eye, and motioned to Pap's coffee cup and held up two fingers. Marie nodded and went over to the kitchen door.

Pap pushed his shirt sleeve up and looked at his watch. "Just after three, Mike. Our race should go off about an hour from now, providing the first four races run without any major accidents or steward problems. So we're all, you, me, and especially that prick DiBonio, going to know just what is hitting the fan within little more than an hour.

"For us let's hope it's money, enough to make DiBonio's payoff pure shit."

"Amen to that, partner. And Linda most of all will be rooting for that to happen."

"Yeah, I forgot there for a minute what this whole operation's about. What are we going to do about her if things work out as we hope?"

"I been thinking about that, Pap. You know Linda. She wouldn't take a dime no matter how much we cash in. She'd say it was our deal and she wasn't entitled to any share."

"That's for sure. I've never met a woman who was as independent as she is."

"I was thinking that maybe we could just give her a gift, maybe for her birthday that's coming up next month."

"That would work, but I hope you're not thinking of some chintzy present for her."

"Not exactly. You know how much she likes to travel, especially to the Latin countries. She works for herself, for me a lot of the time actually, but she's on her own and could take time off if she wanted. So I thought maybe something really nice. How about a six month, prepaid, all inclusive, trip to either Spain or Mexico, including a furnished apartment with a live in maid?"

Pap's face broke into a giant grin.

"That's great, Mike. Fantastic. She'd love it. But would she accept something like that? Must cost quite a few thou, and she might balk at it."

"Quite a few thou is right, Pap. Actually seventeen and a half, but that includes everything other than personal stuff. And I've sort of figured out a way to make sure she takes it.

"First, we'll say that I need a good researcher, and after her ordeal with DiBonio she needs time to get back to normal."

Pap nodded his agreement.

"Second, we arrange with the travel agent, I know a girl who will do exactly what we want, to say that the whole package is prepaid and non-refundable. If it isn't used, then it's wasted. It's stretching the truth just a pussy hair but I think Linda might buy it. I'll have the travel agent say that the whole thing was priced on a special, one time basis, and can't be cancelled or even moved in the dates."

"Fantastic, Mr. Shant, you've come up with exactly what Linda needs, and packaged it in such a way she won't be able to turn it down. Have you ever known any woman who could walk away from a one time, non–refundable deal? It's great!"

Shant smiled too. "Yeah, I think it'll help our Linda get over this messy situation here. And I'll even sugarcoat it a bit by saying I need her to do a little research while she's there, either Spain or Mexico, for a project I have in the works."

"Calls for a toast, Mike." Pap waved at Marie, who sauntered over, again putting a chair between her behind and Pap's hands.

"Marie, my pet, a bottle of your best bubbly. And preferably something bottled before last Friday."

***

DiBonio looked at his watch, then checked it against the giant wall clock shown next to the TV monitors in the race book.

"Almost three-thirty. The fourth is just about off," he muttered to no one. "Just a half hour more and I'll be the golden boy here at the Golden Future. First thing I'll do is start firing anyone who calls me Dickie." He smiled in anticipation of his forthcoming power trip.

"Hey, Dickie, Solly wants to see you upstairs."

Shit. The first to go would be that asshole Georgie who had just shouted at him.

"Okay, tell him I'm on my way."

Again to see Solly. What the fuck did he think he did here anyway? Didn't he know that he, Richard DiBonio, ran the entire race book operation? Fuck it. Before the day was out he'd have a lot more important job here, maybe even running the whole casino. Wouldn't that be great, being able to get all these morons to do exactly what he ordered, or else out the door, shitface.

The staff elevator was up on the seventh so DiBonio ran up the three flights. No point in pissing Solly off when he was so close to his goal of being accepted into the organization, and all the benefits that would confer on him.

Out of breath, he pushed open the door to the office Solly was using.

"You wanted to see me, Solly?"

Solly looked up, obviously irritated.

"I wanted to see you five minutes ago, DiBonio. And what the fuck you mean, barging in here without knocking? What if I had some broad in here blowing me, or even worse some important guy from back east? You think because you're out here

216

in the middle of the fucking desert that you don't got to knock on a man's door?"

Double shit. No matter what he did Solly found some excuse to complain. Well, even Solly would be outa the picture some day. Maybe even sooner than he thought, if my star keeps on rising.

"Sorry, Solly, I was busy in the race book. We're taking so much action on that Fairplex race, you know, the one I got set up in the fifth, that I hadda give the ticket sellers a hand."

"A lotta action? Is that good?"

"Oh yeah, Solly. The more bets we take on the other horses in that race, the more we get to keep. Our guys are making very sure, I gave them really firm instructions, Solly, that they take no bets on number nine, at least not to win."

DiBonio rubbed his hands together. "So all that bread is ours, Solly. We just have to pay out a small amount on any place and show bets, that's second or third horses, and they won't pay much at all because our longshot number nine will eat up most of the official betting pools."

"I told you a hundred times, DiBonio, I don't give a shit about all that race track crap. All I want to hear from you is how much we put in our pockets, and that figure better be over one hundred thirty thou. If you know what's good for you." On the last sentence Solly scowled so much his eyes disappeared completely and even his mouth was just a slit.

"Yeah, I remember you said you weren't too knowledgeable about the horse race business, Solly." There, that should put the asshole in his place, show him that I knew a lot more than he did.

As Solly started to angrily answer the implied slur, DiBonio hurriedly spoke up.

"We're getting real close to post time for the fifth race, Solly. I gotta be in the race book to take care of things."

217

"So go take care of them, Dickie. Just make sure you get back up here when that ship race or whatever it's called is over, with your hands holding big bucks."

"Boat race, Solly, it's called a boat race. Sure, I'll be here once the nine horse crosses the wire first and makes a potful of bread for us."

***

Some of the TV monitors were showing final results from eastern tracks. Several showed the third at Santa Anita; there had been a long delay in the second due to a multi horse accident. One of the horses had broken a front leg and was vanned off, probably to be put down by the vet, and two jockeys had suffered various broken bones but were able to walk off with assists from medics.

The remaining monitors, on DiBonio's orders, were turned to Fairplex, just outside Los Angeles. It was a bullring, just six furlongs around, and few of the major bettors followed it because normal handicapping techniques rarely held up at the smaller tracks. Also there were suspicions that boat races and other such shenanigans were not unheard of.

The fourth race had ended, and the payoff results were awaited. Once the stewards approved the filmed rerun the mutuel pools would be allocated to the first three winning horses, and the exotic pools, separate from the main pools, would be calculated for quinellas, exactas, and other non-traditional wagers. With computers the entire process took just a minute or two, then the results were posted on the track tote board and also on all the internet wagering web sites.

The results were posted. DiBonio noticed that a favorite had won the fourth. It had gone off at five to two odds, and would only pay about seven bucks to win. His horse in the fifth would do a helluva lot better than that.

At the track the betting windows usually closed about the time the horses were loading into the gate. On the internet betting sites the betting normally was closed about two minutes before the race started. That was to prevent any possibility of past post betting, which in the old days let some sharp crooks actually slip in bets after the race was started. A couple of times, using an electronic bypass to delay the race's apparent timing, memorialized in a popular movie of the era, sharpies had been able to place their bets after the race was actually over.

"Talk about a boat race," DiBonio muttered to himself. "Those guys didn't even bother to use a boat. They just drove up to the payout windows in a yacht and loaded up. I hope my boat race is as successful."

In the bar Shant and Pap finished their celebratory bottle, told Marie to keep their table and tab open, and headed to the race book.

"Win or lose, Pap, let's be where the action is."

Pap nodded.

The fourth race was history. The boards at the track, shown on the closed circuit monitors, now showed data for the fifth race at Fairplex. All nine horses were running, there were no scratches. Below each horse's number on the tote were its current odds, calculated on the track pools and also all the satellite pools from other internet sites.

"Look at number nine, Mike." Pap pointed to an individual television set screen, one of which was at each bettor's desk. "It's showing 12 to one. Dickie's bets placed at the track have brought it down from the morning line of 24, but the bets Jimmy and his boys placed on other long odds horses have kept it fairly high."

"Yeah, and look at that bunch of other dandies, all of which we have bundles on," Shant said. "Aside from the favorite at five to two, and Dickie's jocks will be gunning to keep it from winning, helping us although they don't know it, nearly every remaining horse is 16 or better to one. If Cranston's jockeys can do their jobs, one of those should win, and we'll clean up at the track."

"More important, Mike, all our bets made here at the Golden Future will have to be covered and paid by DiBonio personally, or at least from race book capital. He hasn't booked any of them through the regular mutuel pools, thinking he'd just pocket them when his boat race special number nine won."

Shant nodded. "And together we and our friends have put almost twenty-five, probably over thirty by race time, thousand on that race. A long odds horse wins, say at even 20 to one, and friend Dickie owes us over half a mill. Needless to say, Pap, boss Solly will not be pleased with that payout. In fact, I guess you could say that he'd be thoroughly pissed off at DiBonio."

"And remember, on top of that loss, you have to add in what DiBonio's bet through the regular pools on number nine. Let's see what has been bet on it."

Pap hit the button which showed the total win, place, and show dollar amounts bet on each horse.

"Right now there's about sixty grand in nine's win pool, another twenty odd in the place pool."

"And it's a safe bet, Pap, that most of that is from Dickie. Number nine is such a dog that few bettors at the track would even touch it, so probably a hefty share of those pools, maybe fifty thou or more, is Golden Future money. If Cranston's jockey friends can keep nine boxed in, while DiBonio's hired jocks do the same on the favorite, Dickie stands to take a bath of well over six hundred thousand." Shant smiled. "Do you think Solly thinks DiBonio is a high six figure employee?"

Pap laughed. "Not very likely."

***

DiBonio was pacing the floor behind the ticket seller's windows. He kept looking at his watch, then at the giant clock between the monitors to verify that it hadn't stopped.

"3:47. Sixteen minutes to post. The odds on nine are holding pretty firm, still at 11 to one. There must be a lotta local assholes backing those longshot horses. Fine, just more for us." DiBonio mentally clutched his hands around the giant payoff just minutes away. "I hope that prick Shant and his asshole buddy Pap have a lotta bucks on some of those dogs. It'll make my, our," he looked quickly around to make sure Solly hadn't heard his incorrect pronoun, "our win even sweeter."

***

Shant and Pap now took seats. Each turned his TV set to the Fairplex track where the "minutes to post" indicator now showed 14.

"I usually don't drink when I'm handicapping, Pap, but today is a little special. How about joining me in a little good bourbon salute to America's most thrilling sport, thoroughbred racing."

"Sounds like a commercial, Mike, but I agree wholeheartedly with the sentiment. Let me order, I know this waitress."

"I think you know them all, and probably all of them in the biblical sense," Shant smiled, "but go ahead. I'll have Jack D on the rocks."

Pap waved his arm and got the attention of the tall, well built waitress wearing the standard low cut blouse and very short skirt. The waitresses often complained that they almost froze in the air conditioned casino, but their requests for more sensible attire went unheeded by the male bosses.

"Hi, Pap. What can I do for you?" And immediately she corrected herself. "No, not that, it's a little public, don't you think? How's this," she grinned, "what can I get for you?"

"I liked the first offer better, Nancy, but maybe you're right, my friend Shant here might be embarrassed if we got it on. So I guess we'd better stick to two double Jacks, both on the rocks. Maybe a lime twist in mine, and," he looked at Shant who nodded, "make that in both."

"Ten minutes to post, Pap." Shant checked the odds line. "Not much change. The favorite's still bouncing between five to two and three to one, number nine's down to 10, and all the rest are in the high teens or higher."

Nancy returned with the drinks, and Pap tipped her a ten. He knew that, like several of the waitresses, she had a child she was raising by herself, after her unsuccessful gambler ex-husband had had to leave Vegas at the request of several casinos holding his unpaid markers.

The men leaned back in their armchairs; even the slightly seedy Golden Future race book had realized that race bettors stayed longer when furniture was comfortable. Shant stood up, shrugged his shoulders to relieve the kinks, and sat back down. Pap leaned forward and pressed the pools button.

"Just about the same as last time, Mike. I guess most of the bets are in. Some will still be coming in from satellites like the GF, and some from last minute track bettors, but the odds shouldn't change much now."

Shant checked the odds line. "The favorite's down to two to one, DiBonio's nine is back up slightly to 11, and the rest of the field are heavy longshots."

"I'm sure DiBonio's happy," Pap said. "He figures he'll pocket all that bread on the favorite and the longshots, pay out almost zilch on other bettors who have number nine, and collect a potful on nine himself."

***

DiBonio took a quick trip to the washroom, relieved himself, then almost jogged back to the race book. He looked at his watch, then checked it against the wall clock.

"Three fifty-seven. Just another six minutes to post, then a couple to get the results and payoffs posted," he muttered to himself, "then it's a golden day for yours truly here at the Golden Future." He giggled. "I'm even getting like a poet. I'll be a poet and head honcho at this casino once Solly and the other bosses see what I can do. How often do they make such a fast big payoff?" He looked around, but all the ticket sellers were busy punching up tickets, no one was paying any attention to his mumblings. "Well, whatever the figure is, it'll be a big one."

He pulled out a soiled handkerchief and mopped his forehead, then looked up at the clock.

"Three fifty-nine. Just a few minutes to go before Richard DiBonio gets the attention he deserves from Solly and the boys."

***

"Almost no change in the odds, Mike." Pap turned to look at Shant, who had stood up and was walking a short pattern behind the bettors' seats.

"Just getting a few kinks out, Pap. I'll be right back." He finished the circuit, then rejoined Pap and sat down. He leaned forward and checked the TV screen.

"One minute to post, Pap. What do you think?"

"About the world situation? Not much." He laughed. "About this fifth race at beautiful Fairplex Park? I think we, and our friends here, and Jimmy

223

Cranston and his friends at the track, have put a big one over on DiBonio and his mobster bosses."

"It's post time, Pap. We'll know soon if you're a good fortune teller."

Both men looked at their monitor screens. They showed the horses loading into the back of the gate, each horse and jock accompanied to the numbered slots by an outrider on a pony. These left once the gate handlers took the reins and steered, pushed, pulled, and did whatever was necessary to move the horse into its correct stall.

Horse number six was fractious, and its handlers backed it out of the gate, and took it for a short walk behind the gate, then tried again to get it in. It bucked slightly, and the jockey slid off. He got up on the gate structure and would remount once the horse was fully in the gate.

"I'll bet DiBonio is sweating bullets right now, Mike. He'll be worried that something, anything, might happen to upset his careful plans." Pap looked sidewise at Shant. "To be honest, of course, so are we."

***

"Jesus Christ, can't those fucking stupid handlers get that six horse in?" DiBonio wrapped his hands around one of the pencils given out to bettors and snapped it in two. "Cheap goddamned pencils! When I run this casino I'll give out ballpoint pens, not this cheap crap made in China."

He looked up at the big monitors. "Finally! Six is in. Now get the fucking race going!"

***

"They're away, Mike." He announced the obvious to Shant, who was also closely watching his monitor screen.

"A nice clean break, Pap. Look at three go, he's the favorite. His jock is trying to take him right to the inside. On a bullring track like Fairplex that's the best and shortest spot to be."

The three horse was sharply angling to the inside lane. He passed all but two of the other horses, and looked to have a clear shot at being the leading horse on the rail.

"Look at that!" Pap shouted. "The seven horse, that's got one of Cranston's jocks on it, just aced the six out, and he's ahead."

The seven horse had steamrolled right to the head of the pack and now led the three horse by several feet. The eight horse came up on the outside and ran just back of the seven horse.

"Beautiful! Did you see that, Mike?" Shant nodded, unnoticed by Pap, who continued to shout as though Shant was a block away. "They've boxed in the favorite. He can't go nowhere. Beautiful!"

Both Cranston's jockeys, on the seven and eight horses, now ran in almost synchronized rhythm, keeping their positions, and also keeping the favorite tightly boxed in.

***

"I don't know who those jocks are," DiBonio said, "but they're doing great, keeping that favorite boxed in tighter than a virgin's pussy. Now make your move, nine!"

Number nine was making his move. Although furthest out in the starting line, and in a normally disadvantageous position on the far outside of the track, the horse had fairly clear space in front of him because of the horses dueling on the rail.

"Way to go, nine! Keep it up and I'll buy you the best fucking bucket of oats you ever ate." DiBonio was now waving his hands wildly around—two of the ticket sellers had just moved out of his

225

range—and periodically slamming them on the counter. "C'mon nine!"

***

The horses had passed the two furlong mark. Four more to go to the six furlong finish line. And the track makeup was changing. Horse number four had now angled out from its mid-track starting position, and was now apparently aiming at the same portion of open outside track that number nine had designs on.

"Is four a Cranston jock?" Shant asked without looking up from his screen.

"I think so. Christ, I hope so," Pap answered, his eyes too glued to the screen in front of him.

***

DiBonio stopped waving his hands. They dropped to his side.

"What? What the fuck's that four horse doing? It can't go there, that's for my nine. Get outa there, you cocksucker! Move over, let nine through! Motherfucker, I'll kill you!"

Almost spitting saliva, DiBonio's outburst caused several of the ticket sellers to look warily at him, then move back even more.

***

The nine horse was now neck and neck with the four but the four seemed to be gaining slightly. The outside position was not bad if it was completely open, but because it was the longest distance to run, cheap horses—and the fifth race was full of nothing but—often tired there.

***

226

"Does nine look to you to be tiring?" Pap asked his television screen but neighbor Shant answered.

"I...I think so, Pap. Yes, four is now a neck ahead. Look at four's jock, he's really whipping his horse. Some of those cheapos really respond to a whip. Let's hope four is one of them."

***

"Goddamn it. Can't you see the fucking four, you asshole!" DiBonio was shouting, trying to get his number nine jockey four hundred miles away to pay attention. "Move your fucking horse! Put him in gear, you goddamned asshole!"

***

There was a horse in gear but it was not the nine, it was the four. It was now clearly pulling away, leading the nine by a neck, then a length of open air.

"Looks like the four is still gaining, Mike." Again Pap addressed his monitor.

"Yeah, but he's not picking up speed, those cheap horses rarely gain after half a mile. Number nine is fading, that run on the outside has tired him enough that four looks to be in command. And look at the inside of the track, Pap."

On the inside, both seven and eight were now almost a tandem team, with seven ahead just enough so that favorite three was still held tightly on the rail. The only way out for three was for his jock to pull him up enough to let eight move ahead and out of the way, then have three angle out into clear territory. But such a move was costly. It would cost three at least a couple, maybe as many as four, lengths, and few of these cheap horses had the stamina to make a comeback effort after they'd already run a tough half mile. But three's jock, a long time rider at Fairplex, knew he had no choice. He pulled back on the reins and forced his horse's head to the right, almost bumping into eight's tail. Both seven and eight continued on, picking up two, maybe three, lengths on number three. The horses were now just over a furlong from the finish line.

"Cranston's boys are going to take out the favorite," Shant said. "No way that cheap claimer can gain the three lengths it lost on moving outside of the eight and seven."

He looked up at the big odds board at the front of the book. "Eight's a 45 to one, Pap, and seven is at 30 to one. If either one can hold on the payoff will be great."

"Look at DiBonio's horse!" Pap pushed his chair back and stood up, bending over the computer screen.

Shant switched his attention back to the race.

"He's well back of number four. Almost a full length. But nine looks to be gaining a little."

***

DiBonio was jumping up and down, smashing his hands onto the ticket counter.

"Move it! Move it, you fucking asshole! Get past that goddamned number four! Stop waving your stick around, moron, and hit the fuckin' horse! There's only a furlong to go, what the fuck are you waiting for?"

***

The field had divided, with three horses on the rail, two on the outside, and the other four loosely bunched in mid-field far back of the leading five.

"It's going to be close, Mike." Pap had kicked his chair to the side and now straightened his back for a moment, then again bent over the screen. "I think the fav is too far back, he lost too much distance when his jock took him out and around. I don't think he has a chance."

"Looks that way, Pap, but the three is making a helluva game try. If he hadn't been boxed in there's no doubt he was the legitimate favorite. More importantly, though, DiBonio's nine horse is also putting up a real effort. Look, he's picked up half a length on the four, and they've only got a hundred yards or so to go."

"Close is putting it mildly, Mike. It's turned into a real horse race, even with all the fixes that have been put in."

***

DiBonio had exhausted himself. Now he slumped against the seller's counter, watching as his horse, the four, and two on the inside, looked like seven and eight, all blurred together as the finish line photoelectric beam recorded their crossings.

"Please, God, let number nine win. I won't ask nothing ever again. Just pull up that fucking number four in the photo. I'll even give ten, ah, a big gift to the church if you do this little thing for me."

***

The track announcer's voice appeared over the track picture, where the horses had all crossed the finish and their jockeys were slowing them down around the first turn.

"The stewards are now examining the photo of the finish and results will be announced soon."

On the track tote board the first four finish numbers were blank and blinking, indicating no winners had been announced.

***

"Any side bets, Pap?"

Pap groaned. "How can you think of more bets at a time like this, Mike? If seven or eight wins, we hit a giant jackpot. If four wins,"—he looked up at the tote board—"he'll pay about $20, and we still make a bundle. If that fucking nine managed to squeak through, we lose a lot. Worse, DiBonio wins big."

"Yeah. I didn't think it would be this close, Pap. Usually these cheap claiming races, especially at bullrings like Fairplex, have one clear winner, with the rest back several lengths. In this race, though, five of the bunch actually were racing over their heads." He took a long drink. "Just keep your fingers, toes too, crossed that nine didn't make it."

***

The minutes dragged on. The race had ended by Shant's watch at 4:05. It was now 4:09 and still no results.

***

DiBonio mentally checked his options. He though the race had been in the bag but those other horses, three of them, had somehow screwed his pat hand up.

He remembered now that during the race he had seen Pap and Shant at the rear of the race book, and Pap had been screaming as loud as he had. Could those pricks have had anything to do with how his boat race had been screwed up? Naw, no one knew anything about it, except the jocks fixed. And Solly, of course, and he wouldn't say nothing to nobody.

Solly! He had forgotten about him in the heat of the race but now his non-smiling, in fact frowning, face floated before him.

What if nine actually lost? How pissed off would Solly be?

DiBonio's face whitened. He knew the answer to that. Solly would be really, really, pissed off.

What would he do? Something, ah, extreme? Naw, he was too valuable to the organization, they wouldn't do that. Solly might kick him down in the casino, maybe put him in the food section or some thing for a while as a lesson, but surely he wouldn't....

The track announcer's voice!

"The stewards have carefully examined the photos of the fifth race, including tape reruns of the entire race.

"Number seven crossed the finish line first."

DiBonio staggered, then found an empty chair and collapsed into it.

"But the stewards have disqualified number seven and placed it fifth."

DiBonio surged to his feet, shouted "Yes!", and waved his hands above his head like a winning boxer. "Yes!"

"It was disqualified for cutting off and interfering with number three horse."

DiBonio was now grinning widely. He could already see Solly's now happy face.

***

"Could be bad news, Mike. If that means that three is the winner, it went off at low odds."

"But it would still screw DiBonio, it'd just lower our take, Pap."

***

The announcer continued.

"The number three horse was moved up from fourth position to third."

DiBonio and Shant and Pap now held their collective breaths. No bad news. So far.

***

231

"The stewards have ruled there is another disqualification."

Jesus H Christ, DiBonio thought. Would this fucking race never get official?

"The number four horse was found to have unfairly impeded both the number nine and number eight horses. It finished second but the stewards have ruled it impeded number eight the most, number nine less. Number four has been set down to an official finish position of fourth."

Everyone in the race book who had a bet on the fifth was now busily trying to keep track of all the stewards' changes.

DiBonio was scribbling on the back of a losing ticket someone had left on the counter.

"So seven is fifth, three—that's the favorite—ends up what, second? Or third?" He crossed out his earlier figures and started again.

***

"I know it's a little complicated," the track announcer, whose face now filled the screen, said with a lopsided grin, "but here is the official finish order."

He looked down at a slip in his hand and read from it.

"In fifth place is number seven. In fourth place is, I guess appropriately, number four." He laughed self-consciously.

"I can't remember a race where there were as many changes as this one."

"Never mind that fucking crap, asshole, just give us the results!" DiBonio was on his feet again, shouting at the announcer on screen.

"In third place, and in the last position for regular bets, is," he looked down at the paper, "number three. Three in third," he finished lamely.

"In the new, and official second place, is," he again looked down, then spoke to someone off camera. "I'm sorry, just a minute. I have what looks like incorrect information. I'll be right back." The camera caught him rushing off to the right before the director switched to a scene of the track, the fifth race horses still walking up and down as their jockeys waited to see who would get into the winner's circle.

***

DiBonio was now shouting at the TV monitor. "Goddamned assholes! What a fucking way to run a business! How can you have such morons...."

***

The camera caught the announcer taking his seat.

"Sorry, folks, I just wanted to make sure I had the changes in the right order. Okay, I do. Again, just to make it clear. Fifth position, horse number seven. Fourth spot, horse number four. In third finish position, horse number three. And in second, and first positions, the information I was checking..."

DiBonio threw a ballpoint pen at the screen. "Idiot!" he screamed.

"In second, number nine, and in first spot, number eight. Again, in order from first to fifth, horses eight, nine, three...."

***

DiBonio stood paralyzed, his right hand still raised from throwing the pen.

"Nine is second? No, no, that can't be. I bought a first for that cocksucker. There has to be a mistake, check it again...."

***

Shant pounded Pap on the back. "We did it, partner. We sunk DiBonio...."

"...and at the same time brought a 45 to one winner home!" Pap interrupted.

"45 to one? Each two buck ticket will pay over ninety dollars, Mike, and we have a bundle of those tickets."

"We sure do, Pap, and we're going to have a bundle of bucks for them. And Linda is going to get a really royal trip, something that will help her get over DiBonio's stupidity."

"Plus the fact that our plan has taken him down, Mike. To Linda that will probably be more important than the fancy trip."

***

"Hey, DiBonio, Solly wants to see you. Right now," he said. One of the boss's muscle thugs smiled broadly as he gave DiBonio the message.

Did he know something? Or did Solly just want to commiserate with him on his very narrow loss, which should have been a win anyway if those crooked stewards hadn't been paid off. Yeah, Solly would likely understand, he was a man of the world, and he knew how sometimes even the best plans didn't work out.

"He said now, DiBonio. Not when you get done thinking about the screw up you just made."

So this moron did know something, Solly must have told him something. That wasn't a good sign. But he could still explain it all to Solly, how just a goddamned foot or two, maybe even less, had cost him his great plan. And how next time he'd make sure that nothing happened to screw it up. After all, no one could predict perfectly. Not even Solly.

"Okay, DiBonio, I'll come with you, just to make sure you don't wander off. Like I said, Solly wants you up there now."

The thug pushed DiBonio towards the elevator.

CHAPTER 20

"So it was all just a accident?" Solly's eyes were not visible, and his mouth was definitely not smiling.

"Well, yeah, Solly, I mean, I had the goddamned race in the bag, but then a couple of asshole jockeys, you know those midgets have no brains, get carried away and screwed up my plan. So, yeah, it was just an accident."

Solly motioned to the muscle standing by the door. "Shut it."

He turned back to DiBonio. "Exactly how much did your accident cost us?"

DiBonio had hoped he could postpone this particular question until after he had properly explained how the race loss had happened. Maybe he could get Solly to laugh, at least see some of the humor in it. If there was any humor in it.

"Solly, it's just like a snafu. Remember in the war, all the guys talked about snafus all the time. Most guys didn't even know that snafu was just short for 'situation normal, all fucked up'." He waited for some appreciation from Solly.

"I ain't interested in any wartime bullshit, DiBonio. And I ain't gonna repeat the question. How much?"

DiBonio hesitated. Which was more dangerous, trying to stall Solly, or answering the question? He figured Solly wouldn't stand for any more stalling.

"Uh, I ain't got the final figures from the cashiers in the book, Solly, but, uh, it looks like there was a whole bunch a tickets we sold on that fifth race."

He paused to clear his throat. Solly looked at him, unblinking.

"But, ah, at the moment, Solly, it looks like we got about sixty-five thou in tickets total, but just a little over half, say about forty, on the actual fucking winner, but you know that asshole horse didn't even win, those fucking stewards just gave it to the eight, who really came in only fifth, so...." His voice trailed off as Solly continued to stare at him like a frog eyeing a fat fly.

"So, uh, on the race we got stuck for that forty-odd thou, Solly."

"How much we gotta pay out, DiBonio?"

He shifted his weight to the other leg, cleared his throat again. "Well, that fucking eight went off at 45 to one, but that wasn't fair, Solly, it... Well, we have to pay out 92 bucks on each ticket, because like you okayed, Solly, we booked all those bets ourselves, and that means we either welsh on them, and get the gaming commission on us, or pay them all off."

"I didn't okay nothing, DiBonio. This deal was yours. Period. What's the total we got to pay out?"

He figured it was time to get that goddamned number out, so Solly could get pissed off and get over it.

"With the mutuel odds at 45 to one, Solly, we sold just over forty grand of tickets. So we have to pay out, uh, not counting a few tickets where the guy had the eight horse to place or show, maybe just another 10 or 15 thou, nothing much," he summoned his courage, "about, uh, one point eight."

He tried to smile, gave up the attempt, and shifted his weight again.

Solly's eyes opened enough so that he could actually see them.

"One point eight? You mean one point eight million?"

"Uh, about that, yeah, Solly, maybe just another hundred or so to take care of those place and show tickets."

"Your deal which couldn't fail cost us about two mill? How much for the bets you made that lost?"

Jesus Christ, the guy said he didn't understand nothing about races, and now he's asking me all these technical questions.

"Ah, yeah, those bets, I sorta forgot them, Solly. Uh, they weren't that much, you remember I said we couldn't bet too much or we'd drive the odds down, so...."

"How much?"

Fuck. The guy was like a bulldozer which just kept on coming at you.

"Only a hundred, Solly. Maybe a little more, like I ain't got the numbers right here. But not more than two at the very outside."

For the first time in this meeting Solly actually moved. He sat back in his chair, reached over and picked up a pen and a telephone message pad. He tore off a sheet, turned it over, and scrawled some numbers on it. He frowned as he added them up, then carefully put the paper down, and placed the pen neatly beside it.

"Your foolproof deal, DiBonio, has cost us well over two mill, probably closer to two point five." He leaned forward again and looked at DiBonio. "Is my number work correct?"

Maybe he should just laugh and deny it. Or maybe he should say something like, 'It's just a couple mill or so, Solly. Chump change, ain't it?' But that probably wasn't too smart an approach.

"Uh, yeah, that's about it, Solly. But I mean, two mill or so ain't...."

"Shut up, you asshole." He signaled to the muscle by the door. "Joey, take Mr. DiBonio here somewhere quiet for about a hour, then phone me at this number. I gotta talk to some guys back east."

DiBonio was now sweating heavily and his shirt felt plastered to his body. This was worse than he thought it would be. Should he ask now for understanding, mercy even? Naw, that would have as much effect on Solly as a pinprick to a elephant. Maybe Solly would cool off when he had time to put the deal in some kinda perspective, like realizing a couple of mill or so wasn't that much.

The muscle grabbed and squeezed DiBonio by his upper right arm.

"I'll be with Mr."—like Solly he also emphasized the title—"DiBonio upstairs in the penthouse suite. That okay?"

On Solly's nod he steered DiBonio out the door and towards the staff-only elevator. As they left DiBonio saw Solly reaching for the phone which was swept for bugs twice a day.

***

Pap was weaving slightly on his feet.

"I've called you all here today to make an annunshment," he grinned and corrected himself, "announcement of vital importance. To no one except us three." He pointed to himself, then Shant and Linda, both of whom gave large mock bows.

"I come, like Caesar or whoever it was, bearing good tidings. Is a tiding like the tide, does it go in and out?" No one answered, so he plowed on. "Our little syndicate has accomplished its goals. And then some." He paused to take a healthy drink. "Notish that I didn't spill a drop? Okay, back to the tidings.

"Without a doubt Dickie DiBonio is now in hot water. Boiling water is likely more like it."

Both Shant and Linda clapped noisily.

"Please keep the applause till I'm finished. And that, my fellow Americans, is what we attempted to do from the start.

"So our mishhin, ah, mission, was totally successful. That's part one." He drank again, saw that his glass was empty, and refilled his glass from the bottle on ice. "Again not a drop of this lovely nectar wasted," he grinned.

"Now where was I? Oh yeah, on to part two. That's the money bit. As my good friend Michael Shant always says, 'To find out anything, just follow the money'. Now I never knew what the fuck that meant, but he's an intelligent guy so it must have great significance." Linda stood up, applauded, and sat down, barely hitting the chair seat.

"Thank you. Anyway, the money. I ain't got the exact figures in fronta me, but on good authority I unnerstand that our group did well, very, very well, on this undertaking. That's got nothing to do with undertakers, incidentally. So well, in fact, that Mr. Shant, sitting right over there," he pointed first to Linda, then corrected, "has an envelope in his left breast, oops, no disrespect to the females present, who may have thought I was talking about titties but I wasn't, just about Mr. Shant's inside pocket which happens to be on topa his breast, well, anyway, he has this envelope with some goodies inside it. I now relingsh.., reling, ah, fuck, give up the floor to Michael."

Linda and Shant both stood up and applauded, Linda adding "Bravo".

Shant remained standing, Linda sat down, again just getting half her behind on the chair seat, and she started to slide off but Shant reached over and pulled her back.

"Thank you, Papsy. You are right, as always. I do have an envelope here"—he reached in and pulled it out—"which you all can now see." He turned slowly around so both Linda and Pap got a good look.

"And what's inside, you ask? Well, Pap and I just wanted to show our appreciation to sweet Linda—she really does taste good," he grinned with what he thought was a lecherous grin—"and so we, Papsy and me, got her a little present from part of the ill-gotten gains we made on this DiBonio boat race. Which, however, was a pretty leaky boat as far as he was concerned." He took a drink.

"Anyways, Linda, we figured you like traveling, so we got you a ticket to Spain. And back, cause we don't want you to find some Spanish smooth talker and stay over there. And to give you enough time to get a sun tan, the ticket, which is non-refundable, non-cancelable, non-anything except to use, sweetie, the ticket thing also includes an all-inclusive stay deal at a pretty good resort on the south coast." He finished his drink, passed his glass to Linda for a refill.

She filled his glass, passed it back, and stood up obviously to express her thanks.

Pap got to his feet before she did.

"As always I agree with what Mike said, whatever it was," he laughed. "But my good, my best, friend forgot one thing, Linda dear.

"The ticket deal, as he so creatively called it, he is after all a writer, and everyone knows they're creative, is like he said, but he forgot to mention, sweet Linda—I can't vouch for the taste but I'm sure it is as my friend stated—that the ticket thing is for six months, and not one day less."

He sat down. Linda, who had remained standing, also sat down but this time she missed the seat completely, and fell giggling to the floor.

***

Joey nodded, said "Right away," and hung up the phone.

"Solly wants you. In his office. I'll go down with you."

Well, this was it, DiBonio thought. He hoped that Solly had cooled off in the two hours since their meeting had ended. Taking so long was a good thing, wasn't it, just like the longer juries were out the better the chances of an acquittal or at least a hung jury?

He thought that was how it went, so maybe this wouldn't be too bad after all. Solly and the other bosses would want some kind of penalty, just to make a point, but probably they'd thought over how important DiBonio was to the casino, and not just the race book either. They probably realized that he was a real important guy, a man maybe even critical to the long term success of the Golden Future casino.

"Siddown, DiBonio."

That was a good thing, he thought. Solly had never told him to sit down before. Maybe he was right about what they had decided!

"I been talking with the boys back east, DiBonio. They ain't too happy with that stunt of yours. Costing us over two mill is no joke."

Solly was smiling. Or was that a beginning frown? Or even a heart attack underway? With his jowls and rolls of fat almost completely obscuring his eyes it was hard to tell.

"But I put ina good word for you, so don't fuck up no more."

"I won't, Solly, that was just a bad break, you know, like it wouldn't happen again in a million"— poor choice of words, idiot!—"ina hundred years, Solly, so...."

"Shuddup."

Solly leaned back in his chair, then sat forward, putting his hands on the desk.

"Here's what we decided, DiBonio. We make you acting manager of the entire casino."

"Jesus Christ, Solly, that's great! Really great. I promise I'll do a great job for you, I mean I know all about the whole casino...."

Solly held up a fat left hand like a traffic cop. He didn't say a word but DiBonio braked to an immediate halt.

"You're making 65 grand a year now, right? We're putting you on the payroll in your new job at 325 thou a year."

DiBonio was speechless. He had hoped he might get out of this mess in one piece, but to have the organization not only forgive his slight error, but reward him with a juicy new job, that was incredible. What a tremendous job he'd do in his new position, it was that, not just a job, and how he'd repay the organization for their trust in him. He'd make the Golden Future the best casino in the whole downtown area.

"You'll get that like any other worker in paychecks."

DiBonio nodded quickly. Why was Solly belaboring the obvious, how else would he get paid?

"And each month you'll pay me, or whoever I say, 20 grand in cash."

DiBonio froze. "But, Solly, that'd mean I'd be paying back 240 thousand in cash a year. After paying taxes, probably 60 or 70 thou on my salary, I'd end up with, uh, about 25 thousand as salary. That's far less than I'm making now."

"Whatever. That's the deal, DiBonio. It starts now, today. You get paid on the thirtieth of the month, and I'll expect the 20 thou in cash the same day."

DiBonio was mentally figuring the numbers. Pay 20 thousand a month, even if he could find it. Solly was obviously using that two million loss number as the principal he owed. At the usual mob interest of twenty percent a week, the annual interest would be, holy shit, the 20 grand a month wouldn't even cover it.

"But Solly, that 20 grand in cash a month, not showing up as income to the GF, I can see how that would be a tax saving to the casino, but you mean that would be applied to whatever amount you guys figured I owed, right? I mean, if I was able to come up with the 240 grand a year, that would go towards my debt, right?"

He paused, he'd better not commit to any specific amount, maybe Solly had a smaller figure in mind.

"Like, uh, what's the total amount you have me on the hook for?"

"We're going easy on you, DiBonio, even though you're costing us more, we're putting your tab at just two point five. Partly that's because we will save on the phony payroll expense thing, partly because we think you do have some potential here in the organization."

It looked like Solly was smiling, even laughing maybe, when he said the last sentence but DiBonio couldn't be sure.

"Two point five? Two million five hundred thou? Jesus, Solly, that seems to me to be really a high number, I don't think the whole deal cost more than two point one or two."

"Maybe you think this meeting is for negotiating? It ain't, DiBonio. We put the number at two point five. Period."

DiBonio was rapidly calculating the ridiculously high numbers involved. Ease with numbers had been his key to success as a street bookie.

Okay, so say I agree—hell, I don't have a choice—to the two mill five, he thought. I know the vigorish is twenty percent, no negotiating on that. So I pay 240 big ones a year, going on to the debt amount of two five, less the, what, twenty percent of two million five, that's 50 grand, no, fuck, it's 500 grand a week, that means for each month I gotta pay two point something interest, less the 20 cash I pay Solly, so at the enda the first year I now owe....Holy shit, it was a bottomless pit. He'd be paying the 20 grand a month, trying to live on a gross of 25 grand

244

or so a year, far less than he was clearing now, and never get even. Actually each year he'd owe another coupla million or so.

"Solly, I been doing some figs in my head. Using the numbers you gave me, I'll never get even, never get close to even. I'll be earning 325 thou gross, paying you 240 cash, and after taxes I'll be lucky to end up with 20 or 25 grand, far less than I'm getting now."

Solly looked at him, his eyes completely invisible.

"So?"

DiBonio understood and a wave of nausea washed over him, leaving him drained. These guys didn't like him, they weren't grooming him for any executive type job in the organization, they were shitting on him. Solly and the thugs back east saw a way to save a few thousand on taxes a year, making him the patsy just because one deal of his had misfired slightly.

He saw his dreams of mob acceptance disappear. He had no future here, none, absolutely sweet fuck all. These guys weren't friends or buddies, they were just street thugs who had managed to use their leg-breaking techniques to pile up potfulls of cash.

He didn't owe them a thing.

"Solly, you know this deal is ridiculous." Solly started to get up from his chair. That wasn't good.

"I mean, there's no way I could ever pay off what you guys say I owe. I'd be working here until I was 90, and even then I'd still owe you guys millions."

"So?"

Jesus Christ, he was an absolute moron. Either he didn't understand the deal he had given, or he just didn't give a fuck. Likely the latter, DiBonio thought. If that's the case, fuck him. I got nothing to lose by playing the same kinda hardball.

"I thought my loyalty here in the GF casino would be worth something, Solly. But based on this deal it ain't. I can't do it, no way can I start living ina cheapo furnished room just so's I can pay you guys millions in interest."

He swallowed. Could he do it? What choice did he have? None.

"Solly, the only way I could get even with you guys is by coming into a big buncha cash quickly then I could pay off the two mill five and we'd all be square, right?"

Solly didn't move.

"And short a winning the fucking lottery, and we both know the chances of that"—he gave Solly his best man-of-the-world smile. Solly didn't move. Was he still breathing? Maybe he'd died?—"the only way I could get a quick bundle would be to, uh, well, you know, like those celebrities do, write a kiss and tell book."

There. He'd done it. He could feel the sweat literally pouring down from his armpits, he probably smelled terrible. But smelling bad was the absolute least of his problems.

Solly moved. Then his eyes opened, at least DiBonio could see something that looked like pupils.

"Whadda saying, DiBonio? You saying you'd try to sell some secrets you think you know? To who?"

"Anybody who'd pay me, Solly. I ain't got nothing else to cash in. The GF don't have no rich pension plan I can tap, no plan at all as a matter of fact. And my old man ain't rich like the Kennedy bootleggers. So all I could do, to get rid a that fuckin debt to you guys, would be to sell a story about, uh, like my experiences here in Vegas."

Solly's eyes were definitely open now. DiBonio could even see a trace of color, it looked like Solly's eyes were the same color as day old puke.

"And this story, DiBonio. What would it be about?"

"Like my, uh, experiences in a casino, Solly. I wouldn't hafta name specific names, you know, just give enough real info to make it sellable."

Solly crossed his hands on the desk, sort of in a praying position, DiBonio thought. A good sign? Or a forecast of someone's passing?

"If I understand you correctly, DiBonio, you are saying, if this deal goes through, that you'd turn on us and sell some schlock story about this here casino, maybe even getting the organization involved?"

He had Solly on the run. Didn't he? It looked like he might buckle, if just a bit more force was applied.

"I don't want to do nothing to hurt you boys, Solly, you know that. All I'm saying is, if you guys try to set me up in some deal where for the resta my life I'm gonna be in hock, and where there ain't even a candle at the end of the tunnel, I'd hafta do something to get out, wouldn't I? I mean, I wouldn't want to, you understand, Solly, but what choice would I have?"

He thought he'd done a good job, putting his case in a favorable light. And maybe Solly was sold, or at least partly convinced, because now he definitely was smiling. Well, his lips were visible, and they might actually be turned up a little.

"No choice, DiBonio. Tell you what. Your story, not the one you'd sell, but what you just told me, is interesting and I wanna check it out with the boys back east. So Joey here"—the muscle at the door stepped forward—"will take you upstairs to the suite and buy you a drink. And I'll call back east and see what the boys think of your, uh, story."

Solly did have a sense of humor, a good sign, DiBonio thought, because his mouth had definitely curled up on that last sentence.

Joey again took DiBonio's right arm, and herded him out and towards the staff elevator. As the door closed DiBonio saw Solly as before reaching for the bug-swept phone.

***

"Yeah, it looks like he's willing to turn rat," Solly said into the phone. "I was real surprised when he threatened to tell all, never thought he had the balls."

From Chicago a muffled voice, due to the debugging electronics, answered.

"So you think he'd really fink out? Is he really needed?"

Solly paused. DiBonio was a useful cog in the Golden Future casino. But certainly not a vital one. When the race book had first opened his street smarts had been necessary because none of the eastern boys understood odds and mutuel pools and all that crap.

But the race book was running pretty smoothly now, and a couple of the more experienced ticket sellers could probably handle the whole operation.

The race book didn't throw off as much net as the sports book, anyway, and any sports nut off the street could run that, just take bets and pay out less than you took in, no brains required, and most of the sports bettors, Solly knew, bet on the basis of team loyalties, not on the logical winner, so slanting the odds in the house's favor was not hard.

"I guess not, Tommy. No, he ain't. He has been a help in the past but he's just a guy now."

"Well, Solly, if he ain't needed, and if he could be a liability, I guess the answer to this here little problem is clear. Right?"

"Yeah. That's prob'ly the best thing to do."

"Okay, Solly, nice talking with you. Steve will be sorry he missed you. One more thing. No point in taking any chances, right? The early bird and all that shit?"

"You got it, Tommy. Consider it done."

***

"I talked with some a the boys back east. They think you got some reasonable points here in your plan, or whatever it is, and they figure it's worth talking about."

"That's good, Solly, I'm glad. Because I didn't want to leave the organization. I mean, I been with it for a lotta years now, and I figure I still got a future here."

Solly twitched his mouth. A smile?

"Okay. Now the guy you gotta talk to, he works outa a office in Pahrump, you know that little hick town just north a here?"

"Sure I know where it is. Why would a mo...an organization guy be out there?"

"We like to, ah, diversify like, not have all the guys here too conveniently in just Vegas. Anyway, why he's there ain't important, that's where he is. And he's agreed to see you right away, the sooner we get this thing cleared up the better."

"I agree, Solly. So how do I find this guy, does he have an office or what?"

"Don't worry, we'll take you right to him, the eastern boys said spare no expense in getting this matter finished. Joey here and his buddy Sam will give you a ride right to this guy. And the sooner you leave the sooner it's done. So like take off now, Joey."

***

"This guy has an office in the desert, Joey? Why ain't he in town at least?"

Joey shrugged and steered the Lincoln down what looked like an old mining trail. He had turned off about a mile south of Pahrump on a dirt road which soon fizzled out to this barely visible track.

249

Joey's buddy Sam was in the back seat with DiBonio. He hadn't said a word the entire trip. Now he turned his head to the right, nodded, and said to Joey, "Right here where it's at, Joey. Pull in just ahead by that fucking cactus."

Joey stopped the car, got out and opened the rear door. "Let's go, DiBonio. This is the spot."

DiBonio felt fear like he'd never felt it before.

"Hey, Joey, there ain't any office here. Anything, as a matter of fact. Why you stopping here?"

Sam laughed, an ugly sound. "No office maybe, DiBonio, but a home, sort of." He laughed again. "Yours. A permanent one."

DiBonio's knees buckled and he fell to the ground.

"Laying down or standing up, all the same to me," Sam said, as he pulled out a large pistol and aimed it at DiBonio. "Adios, asshole."

"You don't threaten the mob, DiBonio," said Joey, his words lost to DiBonio as Sam's gun seemed to explode in his face.

CHAPTER 21

"He's apparently missing." Pap said. "Nobody's seen him since Sunday afternoon, when George, the front door valet, saw him getting into a mob car with Joey and Sam."

"Sam? That would be gravedigger Sam?"

"The same, Mike. The only time he gets into a car is when it's a one-way ride for somebody. It looks very much like DiBonio tried to screw with the mob and lost."

"Likely over that boat race fiasco, Pap." Shant signaled to Marie and held up two fingers.

"We know he gave the casino a helluva bath, probably well over a couple million dollars lost, and for that kind of money the mob doesn't fuck around."

"He'll probably never be found, Mike. Joey and Sam are experienced mob guys, they'll bury him deep enough so he won't turn up like Pedro did."

"We didn't really want to get DiBonio killed," Shant said, "but after the bullshit way he treated Linda I can't honestly say I'm too sorry to see him go."

"Me neither. And remember our original plan was to get even for Pedro, who definitely was killed because of DiBonio, either directly or indirectly."

"Speaking of Pedro, look who just came into the bar." Shant pointed.

"Hey, it's Lennie. We haven't seen much of him since Pedro was killed. Let's buy him a drink."

"Good idea, Pap."

Marie came over with the drinks. "Marie, when Lennie is through talking to that guy at the bar, ask him to come over for a drink, would you?"

"Sure, Mike." And she inhaled just enough to put her behind out of Pap's outstretched hand.

"I talked with Linda a little while ago," Shant said. "She's all packed and ready for her Spain trip starting tomorrow. She was as excited as a little kid. We did the right thing in getting her away from Vegas for awhile, letting the memory of DiBonio's attack fade."

"We did, and I'll bet she was happy to learn that DiBonio undoubtedly won't be on the Vegas scene any more."

"Linda's soft hearted, Pap, she actually sniffled when I told her about what probably happened to DiBonio. But I got her talking about her trip plans and she cheered up quickly."

***

"Hey, did I hear something about free booze at this table?" Lennie grinned and took the chair Pap pushed out for him.

"You did, amigo. Good to see you. We haven't seen you around for awhile. Been shacked up with some floozies?"

"Not this time, Pap. I was a little under the weather about Pedro, I really liked that guy."

Shant nodded. "And I guess you heard about how DiBonio, probably the man responsible for Pedro's death, ended up?"

"Just now, from Joe Kilby there at the bar. He always has the latest gossip. Evidently DiBonio was the passenger in a one-way-ride car?"

"Looks like it," Shant said. "And I think Pedro might appreciate the irony of his killer, or at least

252

the man responsible, getting the same treatment he got."

"Better believe it, Mike. Pedro would bust a gut laughing."

The men sipped their drinks and were silent.

After a few minutes, Shant said, "So what's on your agenda now, Lennie?"

"Funny you should ask, Mike. I've just come across a deal which is guaranteed to pay off in six, maybe seven, figs. It's all about becoming a publisher on the internet. You know how popular it is, and how many people out there want to have their own business. Well, I got this writer guy, he's not very good but he can put stuff on paper, and we're going to start a business showing other people how to get into this booming, money-making industry."

Both Shant and Pap laughed. "Sounds like a real winner, Lennie," Shant said. "What're you going to call it?"

"I already got a name." Lennie reached into his jacket pocket and pulled out a card case. "Here, you get the first one." He handed one to Shant, another to Pap.

"Northwest Internet Research Associates." Shant looked at Lennie. "Isn't that pretty close to your last name, what was it, Northwest something?"

"It was Northwest Research Institute, Mike. My policy is to stick with winners, and that name was a winner." Lennie finished his drink and leaned forward.

"Now both you guys are buddies, so I'll give you a chance to get in on the ground floor. I have everything in place, just need a few thousand to cover starting ads in a couple of national mags. Once the first ads hit, I know the revenue will be more than enough to finance the rest.

"I figure we could run the scam, er, business, for about six months, cream off the easy sells, then unload the whole operation on somebody who wanted to carry it on.

"You guys put up say five grand each, a drop from what I hear you creamed off in that race deal, and I can almost guarantee that you'll triple your money, tax free at that, this is a cash business, within six months."

Both Shant and Pap again burst out laughing.

"Lennie, you are a super salesman. Let's have another round and we can discuss this legitimate business opportunity at greater length."

Still laughing, Shant stood up and waved at Marie.

"A round, Marie. And make them doubles. Hell, make them triples. Pap and I are going to get rich with Lennie!"

THE END

KEEP READING FOR A SNEAK PREVIEW OF "HAPPY ENDINGS OFF THE VEGAS STRIP" THE NEWEST NOVEL IN THE MIKE SHANT MYSTERY SERIES.

HAPPY ENDINGS OFF THE VEGAS STRIP

PROLOGUE

Her secretary smiled. "Go right in, Mr. Shant. She's expecting you."

"Thanks." He opened the large door with its impressive lion's-head knob, and walked in. The office was large and square, with windows on two sides showcasing Vancouver's lush green Stanley Park and the Inner Harbor, with the North Shore mountains gleaming with their white caps in the background. The harbor bustled with traffic: ferries arrived and quickly departed from their landing slips, open-sided launches gave tourists a watery tour of one of the world's most spectacular harbors, and work boats ignored all that to load and unload their goods from exotic ports.

"Hi, Mike. You look great." She moved out from behind her desk, long legs quickly taking her to him. She proffered her cheek. He gently turned her head and planted a firm and lengthy kiss on her sensuous lips.

"Do I look like your uncle? What's all this cheek kissing?"

She laughed. "Okay, I guess I wasn't thinking. It's been so long since I last saw you, I couldn't

256

remember whether we were friends, relations, or...." Her voice trailed off.

"We sure aren't kissing cousins. And it hasn't been all that long. We met in, what, October? Your memory doesn't go back that far?"

She laughed again, a tinkly sound that seemed to cover about three octaves. "You're right. It just seems longer."

She disengaged from his embrace and returned to her chair and sat down. She gestured at the comfortable leather chair off to her left side. "Plant it, bud."

Shant sat down, crossed his legs. "What's new, kiddo?"

Patricia Morgan reached down to her right, slid open the bottom desk drawer, and withdrew a bright red file folder. She placed it on her desk, then sat back in her high back swivel chair which looked like hand rubbed leather.

"A couple of things, Mike. First, we've had very good reactions to your series on Las Vegas shakers and movers."

[Reported on in Mike Shant #3, The "Lose Weight" Scam.]

"Glad to hear it, Pat. No bomb threats? While it wasn't an expose series I did probably piss off a few Vegas fakers."

"Not even an irate letter." She smiled. "You're settling down in your old age."

"What do you mean old age? I still have a few good years left, and given the opportunity"—he affected a Groucho Marx leer—"I may be able to show you a couple of new moves."

"Promises, promises, that's all I get." She turned serious. "Anyway, the series was good, and I hear from the sales people that both our circulation and big display ads in Vegas have zoomed since it was published. The results were so good, Mike, that the publisher of Your Money Magazine wants you to go back into that den of iniquity for another story."

"Not another 'Gee whiz, look how successful I am now' article? I can only stand so much of that syrupy stuff before I clog up."

She opened the folder and took out a handful of printed sheets.

"No, not another gee whiz story, Mike. In fact, quite a bit different. In your Vegas travels did you ever come across a guy named Gilbert Rheambault?"

Shant thought for a moment. "That name rings a very faint bell. There was somebody something like that name who seemed to be on all the radio stations nearly all the time, selling, if I remember correctly, heaven and other paradise real estate. It was pronounced sorta like you did, but I saw it once or ten times in ads, and it was spelled more like..."

"Rambow?"

"Exactly."

"Same guy, Mike. He was a Frenchie from Quebec, his parents never even learned English, and after he moved to Toronto he got tired of the anti-French feeling almost everywhere, so he bastardized the spelling of his surname to what he thought was a more English name."

"And you know all this lovely detail about our Frenchie preacher how?"

"Because my illustrious boss, god, better known as the publisher, has already had our researchers working on this story. Apparently one of his aunts was literally cleaned out by one of these phony radio or TV preachers, and ever since he's had an urge to expose one or more of them."

"So how did he hit on Senor Rambow?"

"One of his kids got a freebie Vegas trip as a college grad present. One night after he got back, and he and his old man were sharing a glass or two, he let slip that while in Sin City he'd had an especially satisfactory 'massage' in Vegas."

"So what? Nothing illegal about that. Or he got one of the good massages, and had either a hand or blow job?"

"He claimed both. But that's not the angle."

Shant got up and went over to the north facing windows. "You sure have a great view of the mountains. Ever go snow skiing up there?"

"Quite often," Patricia said. "There's quite a bit of development up there now, lifts, cozy bars, cabins, all that stuff. Do you ever ski?"

"I grew up in Winnipeg. I had enough snow and cold by the time I was 10 to never again voluntarily get close to either one." He turned back to face her. "So what's the hook, the angle, with Rambow?"

"Well, according to his son, the publisher learned that the massage clinic was actually owned by the preacher man himself."

"You mean Rambow?"

"None other. And so the publisher felt we could do a sort of expose article on this 'servant of god' who also ministers to somewhat baser needs. As you so succinctly put it, hand and blow jobs."

"You don't expect me to roll into Vegas and tell Rambow I want to do an article for a national magazine on how he successfully combines the good book and the good mouth. Or hands, if that's your preference."

"Fortunately neither are in my list of preferences, Mike. And no, that's not what we want. We figured you could get to Rambow, with a straight magazine article. Based on all we know about him, he'd bite on that offer immediately. Then you could do some investigative type sleuthing and end up with the real story. In short, use your renowned imagination to create a bell ringer story."

Shant grinned. "By imagination you mean deception? Lying? Bullshitting?"

"There. See how quickly that imaginative mind of yours is able to cut right to the heart of the matter?"

"How long would you want it?"

"Basically as long as necessary. When we have a publisher's pet underway length is no object."

"That's what all the girls say. How about pix?"

"Again, as many as required."

"Can I use Pap again, and pay his healthy rates?"

"Absolutely, we were very pleased with the bunch he did for the Vegas series."

"And my minuscule remuneration?"

She smiled. "That comes in two parts. The first, you get your top rate, all expenses, even for massages if essential, and if delivered on time I'm authorized to promise you a $5,000 bonus."

Mentally adding up these various dollar items, Shant hesitated, then grinned.

"Sounds barely reasonable, but okay. What's the second part?"

"That will be delivered to you this evening, at about 9 p.m., at 357 Broughton Crescent, Suite 1108."

Shant looked puzzled. "Wait a minute, I think I know that address...that's your apartment."

Patricia Morgan, the very successful and highly paid editor of Your Money Magazine, stretched, putting almost unfair pressure on the long sleeved sweater she was wearing, and smiled.

"Yes, it is. Will you be wanting bacon and eggs or cereal for breakfast?"

CHAPTER 1

"Don't tell me. That four-legged prick went to sleep again?"

"Okay, so I won't tell you." Big Bobby—BB to his many enemies and very few friends—swiveled around on his bar stool, along with a great deal of creaking as the ancient seat struggled to stay the course, and waved his empty glass at Joe the bartender to signal another vodka.

"Don't get cute, BB. Who the fuck won?"

"Let's just say you don't have to worry about cashing a ticket. Your selection-that-couldn't-lose managed to do just that. By 11 lengths. In short, dead ass last."

"Jesus H Christ! I had it right from a jock's lips that SatinSheets was primed and his connections were going to let him go. Those bastards." The last was said in resignation; he'd had a lot of experience with races going sideways. And backwards, for that matter.

BB slid off his stool, standing very erect to maximize all of his 62 inches. "Do you want anything on today's card? Hollywood goes at one."

"Yeah, put 50 on Mongooser in the third. That mother is due. He hasn't crossed the line first since Noah."

"Doesn't seem like too great a reason but it's your money. Incidentally, you owe me 150 from yesterday, plus 50 today, so cross my palm with two C's, amigo."

Rambow reached in his side pocket, pulled out a healthy fold of creased bills, and peeled off two hundreds. "Here, shove them where the sun don't shine. And I expect you to pay me just as fast when Mongooser strolls home first."

"I always do, amigo. Couldn't stay long in the sportsbet receiving and distributing business if I didn't. Don't worry. You'll get any payoff so fast the ink will still be wet on the bills."

Rambow frowned, then turned away just as somebody said, "Hey, you old fart. Where's all the pussy?"

"Where it usually is, asshole. Stuck to the top of all the broads' legs. Haven't you ever looked up there?"

"Not for at least ten minutes. When was the last time you looked, Rambow? Or are you still having one of your choir girls jerk you off to 'Nearer my God to Thee' ?"

Rambow grimaced, then stuck out his hand. "Well, it is true. Bad pennies do keep coming back. How you been, Georgie? Out on a day pass?"

"Naw, I ain't been in the can for a long time, at least a month or so." He laughed, exposing a mouthful of chipped and misshapen teeth. "You still trying to beat the ponies?"

"I do very well at handicapping," Rambow said, his mouth tightening like a virgin schoolteacher's vagina. "I am way ahead of the game, something that few players can say."

"Yeah, well, it seems every time I see you you're tearing up losing tickets. But maybe I just see you on those rare"—he laughed—"losing days. Just how do you pick your winners anyway, Rambow? Some kind of system, or just the ones with cute jockeys?"

Rambow frowned. "I use a scientific method, Georgie, to pick the most logical contenders in the race. Then I narrow those two or three horses down, based on past performances on today's track, the distance of the race, and how the horse performed in its last race. When I have considered all those factors, and factored in the trainer and the jockey, then I make my choice."

"Seems like a hell of a lot of work just to pick a loser, Rambow."

"I'm afraid people like you will never understand the intricacies of thoroughbred race handicapping. You're so used to making choices because some great white father on TV or even the radio tells you what to do, that when you're faced with a problem not resolved by some advertising huckster you're screwed."

Georgie burst out laughing. "That's rich, Rambow. Here you are, the biggest TV faker in Vegas, running down other fakers. If you didn't have an endless supply of rubes looking for some kind of salvation easily handed out by somebody like you with an impressive voice, with nothing behind it, you'd have to get an honest job. Maybe slinging burgers in some greasy spoon."

"Each of us is entitled to his own opinion, Georgie. Even when it's completely fucking stupid. And on the subject of salvation, why don't you...."

Now get your own copy of "Happy Endings Off The Vegas Strip" to continue reading about Mike Shant's adventures in Sin City.